Christmas at Terminal One

KC McCormick Çiftçi

If you can never have enough Christmas spirit, this one's for you.

One

If only the loose wheel on her suitcase would just give up the ghost and fall *off* already, then this trip would be complete. Claire dragged the offending piece of luggage through the terminal, fighting against the one wonky wheel that kept trying to pull her in the opposite direction.

It was as if the wheel were a symbol of everything that had gone wrong in the last six weeks. The European tour that Claire's publishers had arranged for her hadn't been anything like the book tours she was accustomed to in the United States. And it wasn't just about the fact that so much of the communication was done through translators—that part, at least, she could get used to. It was more the fact that she had been so utterly alone throughout it that was starting to sting now.

In the interest of Velvet Leaf Publishing's budget, presumably, Claire had been traveling alone, without a familiar, friendly face joining her from start to finish. The English publisher of her books had arranged the tour stops in London and Edinburgh, and the company that owned her German translations had covered Berlin, Frankfurt, and Munich. At the other stops, she had more or less been on her own.

And, apart from the days she had spent in Ireland with her best friend Emma and Emma's new husband Connor, Claire had gotten...lonely. She wouldn't have admitted it out loud to anyone who had asked—and her parents and her brother *had* asked, almost as if they (or really just Jeremy) were teasing her. She had laughed it off—"Can you imagine? Me, get lonely?"—but it hadn't stopped her from testing the waters with Bianca, her agent, to see if there was any chance of cutting the tour a bit short.

"I promise we'll have you home in time for Christmas," Bianca had said, "But I can't do any better than that."

"Really?" Claire had asked, trying to keep the disappointment from her voice. "Don't these kinds of things get canceled all the time? I'm sure they'd understand at the Munich Book Fair. Who's coming there to see *me*, anyway?"

"You'd be surprised. Your books, especially *Moonlit Melodies*, have really been taking off in Germany. And even if we wanted to bring you home early, the travel arrangements are already made and paid for."

Claire scoffed at the memory. "As if Velvet Leaf doesn't have the money to pay for a flight change." But as she approached the counter to check in for the flight, something in that statement hit her in a different light. "Wait. *Does* Velvet Leaf not have the money for a flight change?" As she looked back, the notable lack of Bianca joining her on the tour stuck out, as did the fact that the hotel rooms she'd stayed in hadn't exactly been the peak of luxury. And what about the fact that she'd been sitting in coach on the flight over? That didn't seem like the kind of thing an international bestselling author should be doing.

She handed over her passport to the woman on the other side of the check-in counter. If Velvet Leaf was in a financial crisis, they'd tell her, right? Did authors usually know before their publishing companies folded, or did they find out at the same time as the general public? And if Velvet Leaf was about to go the way of the dinosaurs, what did that mean for Claire? Sure, she'd built up a good career for herself as a writer of romance, but none of it would have been possible without Bianca and Velvet Leaf Publishing.

Claire was so lost in her thoughts, so consumed by catastrophizing what now seemed to be the inevitable end of her career and sole source of income, that she stepped away from the check-in counter with her brand new boarding pass in hand and no memory of the interaction with the friendly employee who had sent her suitcase on its merry way.

It would be so incredibly inconvenient if Velvet Leaf was about to go belly up. She shook her head at the thought. And here it was, just a few days before Christmas, which was notoriously the worst time to receive that kind of news.

And also the time companies were the least likely to want to deliver that kind of news, which might explain why no one has even dropped a hint that something like this might be about to happen, warned the part of her brain that loved to give her additional reasons to feel anxious.

"Awesome," she said out loud to herself as she bumbled around in search of the security entrance that would take her towards her gate. "Nothing like the Christmas miracle of wondering if you're about to be out of a job. Or the

New Year miracle of finding yourself jobless right in time to mess up all your New Year's resolutions. Seems like I should maybe be resolving right now to, oh...I don't know, manage my finances a little better?" While the future of Velvet Leaf Publishing was out of her control, the thought that had Claire in abject terror now was the fact that her checking account currently had $25.17 in it, thanks in no small part to some financial decisions that had seemed responsible only when her future career prospects looked a little more certain.

The world of publishing hadn't turned out to be quite as glamorous as Claire had imagined back when she was a middle school student writing fan fiction about all of her favorite characters. It wasn't as if, up until this point, her advances had been six-figure ones, and it hadn't turned out that all she had to do was write the book and everything else was taken care of. Case in point, she was currently schlepping her over-packed carry-on luggage through the Munich airport after spending the last six weeks doing anything and everything Bianca and Velvet Leaf told her to do.

No, there was no assistant running ahead of her to the private jet to put the champagne on ice before she got there, never mind the fact that there wasn't even a business class ticket with her name on it. She'd be in coach, and if the accommodations from the rest of her travel were any indication, she'd be sitting in a middle seat between two armrest hogs, within smelling distance of the bathroom. If any of those components of her flight weren't there, there was a very good chance it would upset the delicate balance of the universe, or at least that was what Claire would tell herself when she was sandwiched between two immovable and unconscious passengers, counting down the minutes until her feet touched firm ground again and she could use the bathroom without having to ask anyone's permission.

The line for security stretched nearly to the check-in counters, and Claire groaned as it came into sight. This was what she got for traveling so close to Christmas, not that it was her decision to do so. She dropped her bag onto the floor as she found her place at the end of the line, welcoming the break for her shoulder, which she massaged. Her bag hadn't been this heavy when she had left New York six weeks ago, but there wasn't any way she could have avoided it. After all, what was she supposed to do while touring so many fine European bookstores...*not* pick up a book or two at every single one? *Blasphemy.*

She had stocked up on English books with different covers than she'd seen back in the States, as well as German, Spanish, and Dutch editions of some of her favorite books. Even if she couldn't read them—though she would give the Spanish one the old college try and see how her high school studies still held up—she couldn't resist them. There were books in her suitcase, and once it had approached its weight limit, the spillover had found its way into her duffel bag, and now her arm was protesting.

She nudged the bag forward with her toe as the line moved slowly. Looking around, she let herself wonder what stories were unfolding around her at that very moment. Who was flying across the country or across the world to make a grand gesture? Who was heading home to see their family for the first time since a big, dramatic blowout had torn them apart? Who was anxious about flying, but was about to be comforted by the friendly and attractive passenger seated next to them? That was the thing about writing—and about writing romance, in particular. Once you started looking for stories around you, you realized they were everywhere. There were more stories begging to be written by her than Claire could possibly write in her lifetime, and there was something about that thought that was comforting, even if at the same time she felt the sweet frustration of never being "done." She could never use up all the stories, all the inspiration that came her way.

❤ • ❤ • ❤ • ❤ • ❤

The first time the announcement came, Claire thought nothing of it. *"Attention passengers. Our flight today is overbooked. We are looking for two passengers to take the same flight tomorrow. You will be put up in a hotel overnight, and you will receive meal vouchers, as well as a payment of 500 euros. Please come see me at the counter if you are interested."*

Claire gave a mild "hmm" and looked around to see who was going to take the flight crew up on the offer. It sounded great...for someone else. Maybe someone had been feeling disappointed that their time in Munich had been so short and would love the chance to spend another day in the city. Or maybe an anxious traveler would be eager to delay the inevitable. Or maybe that extra cash would be just what someone needed...

"Hmm indeed," Claire murmured again. Extra cash. Did *she* need extra cash? If her fears were accurate and she was, in fact, about to be left high and dry, then wouldn't any extra cash in her pocket be the sort of blessing she shouldn't dare turn down?

But she didn't budge from where she stood. No, more than she needed a little extra money, she needed to be home. Sleeping in her own bed, and not in yet another unfamiliar hotel room. Eating a proper breakfast—a bagel sandwich, thank you very much—instead of whatever the aforementioned hotel room had offered. Besides, there were only a couple days left before Christmas. If she didn't leave now, she might not be home in time.

She craned her neck as she surveyed the crowd to see who would approach the counter. But while she saw other rubberneckers doing the same, she didn't see anyone take a step towards the uniformed woman at the counter.

Finally, she saw a man approach the counter, and she felt simultaneous relief and disappointment. Someone else was taking the offer, which meant she didn't *have* to. But it also meant she didn't *get* to. That she wasn't going to be thrust into an adventure.

But when, after the conversation was finished, the man returned to his seat, took out his phone, and began tapping on the screen, any hint of disappointment Claire had been feeling was gone. The man wasn't taking the deal from the airline, depriving her of a potential adventure. He had simply been speaking with the flight crew about...well, any of the other reasons a person would approach that counter. Maybe he was looking for an upgrade—*good luck, the flight is full, buddy*, she thought—or maybe he wanted to check his carry-on luggage through to his final destination. Or an update on their departure time. Or...or...or...

Claire shook herself. Now wasn't the time to make up stories about strangers, even if airports were prime story harvesting grounds. The point was, she wasn't going to get the satisfaction of knowing what the man had been speaking to the uniformed woman about, and did it really matter? It was probably something mundane, ultimately a letdown. She doubted he was an air marshal, checking in to see if there were any suspicious passengers on that day's flight. She doubted he was arranging an elaborate in-air proposal for his partner, who would be arriving any moment from his connecting flight and...

These were all great beginnings of a story Claire might want to write someday. That was, of course, *if* she was in a position to keep writing. Between the uncertain future of Velvet Leaf Publishing and the fact that she'd spent so much time recently in promotion mode rather than in drafting mode that she wasn't sure she even remembered how to write a sentence or a paragraph, let alone a novel...

Well. The odds of Claire Davis writing an airport meet cute or a proposal at 30,000 feet anytime soon were slim.

The woman at the counter spoke into her microphone again, repeating her earlier announcement. This time, the amount of euros offered had increased to 800 per person.

Claire's pulse picked up, the beat echoing in her ears even though that seemed physically impossible. That money would make a big dent in her rent, and she could use the help after straying out of her budget (and not just a little) to buy Christmas gifts for her nieces.

She found herself once again searching the crowd, both curious to see who would approach the counter and anxious that someone else would claim the prize before she had a chance to do so.

Wait. Do I want this? Is that what this feeling is? she wondered to herself. *More than that, am I going to act on it?*

And without fully realizing what she was doing, she was taking her carry-on bag in hand, and walking towards the counter.

Two

Claire's pulse hadn't calmed down until she was in the hotel room the airline had provided her for the next 24 hours. During the long walk to the counter, her senses had been tuned in like a prey animal on the savannah, seeking out potential threats. Was a lion about to appear out of nowhere and claim her delicious prize for itself? Did she need to walk a little faster—or run, even—to get to the counter before all the other people about to offer to take the next flight home?

But in the end it was only Claire—and the same man she had seen speaking with the airline staff earlier—standing in front of the counter. Her heart was still racing as he stepped up and had a conversation she couldn't hear. Maybe he wasn't traveling alone after all, and he and his companion were happy to stay in a hotel until the same time the next day. Maybe Claire was just standing there like a fool, about to be sent back to her seat, denied the adventure that she suddenly felt sure she *needed* in her life.

A second airline employee stepped up to the counter, beckoning Claire forward with a smile and a nod of her head. As she slid into place next to the man, he turned in her direction, a frown on his face as he gave her a quick once-over and then resumed his conversation with the woman behind the counter.

Claire scoffed at the man's rudeness, pointedly ignoring him as she put on a smile and stepped forward, greeting the counter agent who was waiting for her with a smile of her own.

"Hi," Claire said with a small nod. "I'd like to take the offer to fly tomorrow, if it's still available."

The agent's smile got even wider. "That's wonderful." She turned to her colleague, who was still helping the man. "Charlotte, we have a second volunteer. Let's get these two rebooked for tomorrow and then on a shuttle to Holiday Hotel as soon as possible."

While the two women behind the counter tapped away at their keyboards, Claire chanced a glance at the man next to her. He was looking at his phone, a frown on his face, as his fingers flew over its screen. His body language, combined with the way he had looked her over—had that been *disdain* on his face?—were enough for her to size him up, assign him an archetype as if he were a character in one of her books. He was clearly the self-important, work obsessed businessman. He was dressed casually enough to almost make her doubt herself, but the way he was glued to his phone practically *screamed* "circle back touch base follow up leverage the synergy" Bro-speak. Claire barely suppressed a shiver. This was the last person she wanted to be stranded with for the next 24 hours—or not the *last* maybe, since dictators and serial killers existed. If fate or the hotel staff tried to play matchmaker and she heard the words "only one bed," she'd be out on the street, thumb in the air, hitchhiking her way back to New Jersey.

"Alright then, here you are." The smiling woman behind the counter handed Claire one paper after the other as she continued speaking. "Here is your boarding pass for tomorrow's flight. Here are meal vouchers that work at any restaurant in the airport. We will take both of you to the hotel in a shuttle to get you checked in. You also have the option of eating your meals at the hotel in their restaurant, which is complimentary as well. And here is a form for you to fill out to get your 800 euro payment. We'll just need your bank details and then the money will be wired to you." She gave a rueful smile. "On behalf of the airline, we are truly sorry for the inconvenience, and we greatly appreciate your willingness to accommodate us today."

"Of course," said Claire. "It's an adventure, isn't it?" She held up the papers in her hand. "And it's not as if I'm suffering. You've certainly made up for any inconvenience."

The friendly women behind the counter directed Claire and the man to a bank of empty seats at the next gate over, with instructions to wait there for their shuttle to the Holiday Hotel. When they were seated, the man still tapping away on his phone's screen, Claire pulled out her own phone to send a few messages as well, letting her family and Bianca know that her plans had changed. She texted Emma, too, the only person likely to respond this early in the day given that she was in Ireland and not on the east coast of the United States.

"So, the airline just did one of those 'we need two people to take the next flight out tomorrow in exchange for a hotel room and some cash' and...guess who's spending the day in Munich?"

Emma sent back three dots and an unimpressed emoji. Then: "You didn't. Of course, if you didn't, then I don't care who did. Was it seriously you? And what are you going to do with the extra time? I thought you were dying to get home? It's too early for you to confuse me this much, Claire."

Claire glanced at the time at the top of her phone. It wasn't *that* early in Ireland, but if Emma and Connor had been up late making googly eyes at each other like they always did when she was around, she supposed her friend might have preferred sleeping in.

"Sorry for the wake-up text, then." She hesitated, not wanting to unleash her financial concerns on her best friend. After all, it wasn't Emma's problem to solve, so why should she be bothered by it at all?

"The adventure of it all was a little bit exciting, I guess. And there's nothing wrong with a little extra cash."

"Who's the other person?" Emma asked.

Claire rolled her eyes, glancing again at the man who was still glued to his phone. "Some dude. Tech Bro, if I had to guess, considering that he hasn't taken his eyes off his phone once."

"You have my sincere condolences." Emma knew all too well what people in the tech industry were like, having been the founder of a social media app herself before trading in that lifestyle and relocating to the western coast of Ireland. That was the kind of crazy thing that people did for love, Emma and Connor acting like two characters in one of Claire's stories.

Not that Claire's stories were inspired by her own experience. Since her last relationship ended, she'd been insisting to herself, her mother, and anyone who asked about her "ticking biological clock" that she was more than content focusing on her career. And it was actually the truth. Claire didn't feel her ovaries twinge at the sight of a cute baby, didn't wipe a tear from her eyes over tiny baby shoes. And she did feel genuine joy and pride at seeing her books stocked on shelves the world over, at picking up a translation in a language she couldn't speak. And even though every time she started a new writing project, she had to go (again) through the journey of convincing herself that she *did* in fact know how to write, that her first draft was allowed to be terrible, and that she hadn't forgotten everything she ever knew about the craft of telling a story...she loved what she did.

The only problem, the only tiny hiccup in all of it, was that she did miss having *someone*. A special someone who was there when she came home, who was a warmer and chattier companion than her laptop and her notebooks and her own imagination.

Not that Eric, her ex, had been better company than being alone. *All men are not created equal*, Claire thought to herself. *A warm body is not the only requirement, even if it is cuffing season.* Maybe she should adopt a cat.

From the seat next to her, a voice cleared. She set her phone in her lap as she turned, surprised to find the man—her companion on this 24-hour adventure—looking at her with a rueful smile on his face.

"I'm sorry for the interruption," he said, having the decency to actually look apologetic, even a bit humbled. "It's just...I was so distracted while all this was happening that I think I zoned out and missed the plan. We're waiting here for...?"

Claire shook her head, scoffing softly. "It's okay. I'm sure you were busy with something really important, right?" She nodded towards his phone. "Let me guess, you're performing surgery right now. It's some new technology that you can control remotely from anywhere in the world." Now her imagination was getting away from her, imagining a device and wishing she wrote futuristic or dystopian fiction. "But what happens if there's a smudge on your screen and you go to wipe it off and end up severing a major artery..." She shook her head. "Sorry, train of thought got away from me there." She tipped her head in the direction of the counter, where the flight crew were now beginning to board the plane. "They told us to wait here for the shuttle. Though I can't imagine an actual shuttle is going to drive right through the terminal." She shrugged. "I'm sure they won't forget about us." She looked meaningfully at his phone, still clutched in his hand. "You can get back to your surgery. I won't let the shuttle leave without you."

The man was blushing now. "It's not...I'm not..."

"Not really doing surgery on your phone? It was a joke, but not a very good one. Don't worry about it. As you were, soldier."

Claire turned her attention back to her phone, aware that in her peripheral vision, the man was still looking at her, his mouth still agape.

It was a short drive to the hotel, but Claire was pleasantly surprised not to be staying at a true airport hotel, just walking distance from the terminal. Instead, Holiday Hotel was nestled right in the city center, walking distance from plenty of places to explore if she kept feeling adventurous.

Her companion had finally tucked his phone away in his bag and was looking out the window, showing interest in his surroundings for the first time since Claire had laid eyes on him. The way his gaze was trained out the window, the way he shifted in his seat to get a clearer view...there was something almost childlike about his curiosity. And if he hadn't spent the last 40 minutes glued to his phone like he was remotely diffusing a nuclear bomb, then she might be charmed enough by his behavior to at least initiate a conversation.

As focused as he was on the journey, she took a moment to study him. If she didn't know that he was the worst variety of bros, the Tech Bro, then she could appreciate that he was a handsome man. He was tall, and he had the kind of confidence and comfort in his own skin that might come from the ego of knowing that his latest app update was "going to change the world," but it still suited him. His dark jeans, button-down shirt, and even his shoes and his bag fit him—and fit with each other—as perfectly as a well-tailored suit might on a different man.

So, Claire thought, making a snap judgment, *either someone else is dressing him or he's an egomaniac. Either way, good for him.*

He turned to her then, as if he had felt her gaze on his back, smiling as their eyes met. It was a good smile, too, the first genuine one she had seen on his face.

"I'm Jack Holloway," he said. "Probably should have introduced myself by now, but I've been a little distracted, I guess. What's your name?"

"It's okay," she replied, her own smile surprising herself with how natural, how genuine it felt. "I'm Claire. I hope you've put out whatever fires were keeping you so busy and you're ready to enjoy an extra day in Munich."

"I've never actually been here," said Jack. "I was just flying through from Krakow. It'll be nice to explore a new city though, I suppose. Any recommendations?"

Claire shook her head. "Oh, I barely know anything about Munich. I've seen the inside of a hotel room, a bookstore or two, and that's about it."

The corners of Jack's lips dipped in an upside down smile. "That is..." He shook his head. "No, I can't figure it out. It doesn't sound like how anyone would spend a vacation, but it doesn't sound like a work trip, either..."

Claire raised her eyebrows.

"So it *is* a work trip?" Jack asked. "You do something with books, then. And it probably isn't international quality control, where you travel from city to city making sure everyone's got their genres straight and hasn't messed up alphabetical order."

That got a laugh out of Claire. "Believe it or not, I don't think that's anyone's job description."

He studied her a moment longer, his eyes traveling over her face until he lifted a finger, an expression of success flashing across his face. "Are you Claire Davis?"

Claire's jaw dropped open. "How in the world would you know that? You aren't exactly the target audience for my books."

Jack smiled. "That doesn't mean I haven't seen probably every single paperback you've ever written." He glanced at his phone and shrugged. "And I've picked a few up, read the blurb on the back, glanced at the author photo—that's why you looked familiar."

"But you've never read one?"

Jack gave a firm shake of his head. "Under pain of death, no."

Claire laughed again. "Jack, is someone threatening you? You can tell me. I'll get you help."

He smiled. "It's just a difference in reading styles. The copies of your books, they're all in Hazel's—that's my sister—library."

Claire gave an encouraging nod. "Go on..."

Jack gulped. "Well, you know...Hazel loves her books. Keeps them pristine. Uses those little tab thingies to mark the passages she really likes. Posts everything all over Instagram."

"I know the type." Claire smiled. She loved to see reader annotations of her words, had a feeling she would really like Hazel. "Does she not want you to read them because you'll mess up the tabs? Or because it's just too personal to see what she has highlighted?"

Jack rubbed his neck, his eyes not meeting hers. "It's worse than that, I'm afraid." He gulped once, then looked up. "I break the spines."

Claire recoiled in mock horror. "Of humans? Or of books?"

Jack chuckled softly. "Only of books. But the way Hazel reacted the last time she saw me do it, you'd think it was the equivalent of murder."

"I see," said Claire, a finger rising to stroke her chin in exaggerated thoughtfulness. "I suppose you dog ear the pages, too?"

Jack gave a guilty shrug. "I'm not often carrying a bookmark with me, so…"

She held up a hand to stop him from speaking further. "I'm afraid I'm going to have to side with Hazel on this one, Jack. I don't think you should be sentenced to lifelong deprivation from reading my books, but I do think you should keep your hands off Hazel's copies. If she took revenge on you for damaging her collection, there's not a court in all of Bookstagram that would find her guilty."

Jack closed his eyes for just a moment, shaking his head as he chuckled softly. When he opened his eyes again, he lifted his phone, tipping his head towards it. "I should tell Hazel about this conversation. It will make her day, be just what she needs to turn it all around." He looked hesitant as he met Claire's eyes. "Would you mind taking a selfie with me? I just don't think she'd ever believe I met you without some evidence."

"Pics or it didn't happen," Claire said with a nod. She patted the seat next to her. "No problem, let's take one."

Jack slipped across the shuttle's aisle and into the seat next to her before the driver could notice anything amiss.

Claire leaned into his side to fit both of their faces into the small screen of his phone, aware at once of how sturdy he felt, how good he smelled, and how piercing his green eyes were on the phone screen that was facing her. They both smiled, but while Jack was aiming his smile at the camera at the top of the screen, she was studying him. What kind of man was familiar enough with the world of romance novels to even recognize her face? What kind of man went out of his way to send a selfie with a stranger to his sister?

She blinked once, slowly, hearing the thoughts that were cycling through her mind. Were her expectations of men so low that anything Jack had done in the last 10 minutes qualified him to win some kind of award?

Still, though, she had a better impression of him now than she had had back at the airport. Maybe it wouldn't be so bad—and might even be fun—to be stuck as him with her companion for the next 24 hours.

He thanked her for the selfie, slipped back to his original seat, and began typing on his phone again, his expression the same as it had been when she had first seen him.

When he finally dropped his phone to his lap again, the darker expression that had crossed his face while typing evaporating, Claire spoke. "I have to say, it's rare that I meet a fan—or I should say, the sibling of a fan—out and about in the real world. I don't exactly get recognized a lot."

Jack was looking at her in disbelief. "First of all, even if I haven't read your work yet—through no fault of my own, I might add—"

Claire interrupted him. "I'm sure your sister would disagree. Spine breaking is a serious offense to her people."

"You're right." Jack nodded, a small smile appearing on his face. "And I know what I have to do. Get my own copies. Don't leave such an important thing up to the whims of Hazel."

"Break the spines to your heart's content. Dog ear a few pages." Claire shrugged. "Maybe spill a whole cup of coffee on it."

"Now you're talking." Jack's smile shrank. "But in all seriousness, even without reading a word yet, I'm a fan. Have been for quite some time, actually."

Claire knew her face betrayed her confusion. How could it not? What he was saying didn't make any sense.

"It's about my sister," Jack explained. "And what your books have done for her."

Three

Claire waited for him to continue speaking. She must have misheard him; it wasn't as if the little old love stories she wrote were doing much more for her fans than providing a nice little bit of escapism from the realities of day-to-day life.

"They helped her realize how she deserved to be treated. That her ex was far from the kind of guy you would write a book about. That the way he spoke to her, the way he treated her...that wasn't love." He met Claire's eyes then. "And as a brother who'd been watching all of this unfold, who'd been trying to tell her that she needed to leave him..." He shook his head. "I'm so grateful to you for helping her get to that realization on her own."

The concern and care he so clearly felt for his sister made Claire pause, thinking of her own relationship with Alison, her older sister. She missed caring about her like that—and being cared for, too—but that ship had long since set sail. Claire swallowed, not quite trusting herself to speak. She cleared her throat. "How is she now?"

Jack's smile had a hint of sadness to it. "Well, let's just say I hope that selfie reminds her of what your books taught her..." He trailed off, the concern he felt for his sister written all over his face.

Something occurred to Claire then, and shame washed over her. "Is...was it your sister you were texting at the airport?" She bit her lip. "When I was giving you shit about performing remote surgery on your phone?"

Jack nodded. "It's okay, Claire. I can appreciate some comic relief in the middle of a fairly tense scene."

"I'm so sorry." She shook her head. "If I'd had any idea..."

Jack shook his head back at her. "If you'd had any idea, you'd have been either a mind reader or a hacker, reading my messages before I even sent them."

"Fair enough." Claire nodded back. "That's the kind of thing you should disclose, anyway, isn't it?"

The shuttle pulled to a stop in front of the hotel then, the driver turning back to them once they were parked. "We are here," he announced. "I'll help you with your luggage."

"Oh, shit," Claire breathed. "Luggage. I didn't...did you?"

Jack was already shaking his head. Neither one of them had picked up a suitcase at the airport, and the other would obviously have noticed. "I totally forgot," he said. He patted the side of his carry-on bag. "This will have to do for the next 24 hours."

Claire bit her lip. There were things she needed in that suitcase. She hadn't exactly packed her carry-on with living out of it in mind. Her toothbrush, glasses, pajamas... "This is less than ideal," she said with a sigh.

"I'm sure the airline would bring us our bags if we asked," Jack offered. "It seems like they'd want to do anything possible to make our stay more comfortable and all."

She nodded. "That's true..." But there was something about the idea of waiting in a hotel room for her bag to arrive, waiting while there was a whole new city out there to explore, waiting while she could be having a conversation with Jack—assuming that was how he wanted to spend his afternoon anyway—that had her waving a dismissive hand. "I'll figure it out. As long as the airline doesn't wrongly assume that our bags are unattended and need to be destroyed, then there's no problem, really."

"As long as you're sure. We can always stop by a pharmacy later, if you realize there's something you need that you forgot." Jack's ears were turning pink before he'd finished his sentence. If he, like Claire, was surprised to find his plans for the rest of the day automatically adjusting to include her, he was doing a terrible job of hiding it.

"Thanks," was all she managed to say. Should she suggest doing some sight-seeing together? Was that a normal thing people did in this scenario? It wasn't as if it were a particularly common scenario, she had to admit. The majority of the time that two people took an airline up on an offer like this, they were probably a couple traveling together. That had the added bonus of only costing the airline one hotel room and the two passengers having a built-in companion for the duration of the delay.

It would be a perfect opportunity for a couple on their honeymoon. That thought entered Claire's mind unbidden, and she barely stopped herself from cringing at the absurdity of it. While it was no doubt true that a pair of newlyweds would have plenty of use for a free hotel room, it was not the scene she needed to be setting in her mind. She, after all, was in this situation with a nice enough man, but one that she had only met a few minutes before. She knew nothing about him beyond the fact that his sister had great taste in books, he cared about his sister a lot, and he was traveling from Krakow to New York via Munich. Not exactly the firmest foundation on which to base a relationship of any kind, and she was *only* in the market for a friendship.

Still, it would be nice to have someone to wander through Munich with. It would be a waste of this beautiful day to spend it cooped up in a hotel room.

By the time they were inside, waiting to check in at the desk, Claire had worked up the courage to take the first step. "So," she began. "What are you going to do with an extra day in Munich? Explore the city a little bit?" Before he could respond to either of her questions, she lobbed another one at him. "Want some company?"

Jack's eyes were wide as they met hers. "I...yeah. That would be great." He rubbed the back of his neck. "I hadn't actually thought about it at all. I've been so focused on Hazel that I took the deal from the airline without even thinking through the ramifications of it."

"So you would have just spent the whole day in your room texting your sister?"

"Of course not. At some point, she has to sleep." He shook his head at himself. "But you're right. I've heard too many good things about Germany...the food and the beer in particular, and I don't want to waste the chance."

Claire smiled. His words were music to her ears. She'd been on her own for long enough on this book tour that she was more than ready for some company. There was nothing wrong with sitting alone in a restaurant or a cafe...in fact, she considered it a great exercise of self-love and self-confidence to do just that. But she'd frankly had more than enough of it and would *relish* having someone to talk to. And as far as seeing the sights, wandering around and playing tourist, well, that was something she'd done surprisingly little of over the last few weeks.

It wasn't just that she didn't especially enjoy walking around with her eyes glued to her phone or a map, trying with no success not to look like a tourist while she looked for a museum or an old building. It was the lack of someone to share it with, the lack of someone to take photos with and of—she had taken her last awkward selfie in front of a historical site during this trip, she was sure of it—and all the other lacks. No, it was going to be a nice change of pace having Jack around, she was sure of it.

A smiling young man had stepped up to the counter now, greeting them with a friendly, *"Servus,"* and immediately switching to English at their awkward attempts to respond. "How can I help you?" he asked, making eye contact with Jack first and then Claire. "Checking in?"

"The airline sent us," said Jack. "We are taking the next flight tomorrow, so they put us up for tonight here."

"Yes, that's right." The man was looking at the computer screen. "You are...let's see. Jack Holloway and Claire Davis, yes?" His eyes searched between them again. "But

I have you down here for two separate rooms. Is this a mistake?"

"No." Claire hurried to explain, as if she were afraid the oldest trope in the book was about to materialize right in front of her. "There's no mistake. We need separate rooms, please." She looked at Jack then, before directing her gaze back at the young man, smiling to soften the intensity of her response. "We just met," she explained. "Just a few minutes ago, actually. Staying in the same room would be very awkward, I'm sure."

The young man's eyes widened as he resumed his typing. "Of course. I apologize for the mistake. You shouldn't assume that just because people are being friendly to each other that they are sleeping together." He looked up then, directly into her eyes. "They might just be American!"

That got a laugh out of Claire. "I...guess?" She looked at Jack, shaking her head, while their new friend continued to chuckle to himself, fingers flying on his keyboard. Jack was looking back at her with a puzzled expression on his face, as if he were solving an equation written there, one he couldn't quite remember from his high school pre-calculus days. "You okay?" she asked in a lowered voice.

He nodded. "I am. Why don't we get checked in, get settled, and then meet down here in...say, half an hour?" Claire was already nodding back. "We can find our way around the city and just see where the day takes us?"

"That sounds like a perfect plan." Claire stopped holding back her smile, letting it spread as far as it wanted to across her face. "You'll have some time to chat with Hazel. Make sure everything is okay there, and I can check in with my people, too."

A throat cleared behind the counter, and Claire looked over it to see the clerk there with a smug expression on his face.

"I have given you adjoining rooms," he said, handing them their keys. "Not that you *need* to open the doors between them, but...well, certainly if you want to, then that's what they're there for." He lowered his voice to a whisper, leaning closer. "And I won't tell Hazel if you don't."

A laugh barked out between her lips before Claire could stop it. "First of all, Hazel is his sister. But second of all, do people really conduct their affairs that openly, making plans right in front of you?" She leveled a glare at the clerk. "And do you really enable it like that?"

The clerk's expression was impassive as he crossed his arms over his chest. "I work in the hotel industry, ma'am...I've seen it all. Things that you wouldn't believe. Things you would want to unsee." He shrugged. "But alas, I cannot unsee them, no matter how hard I try." He fixed his lips in a straight line. "But it is not in my job description to tell anyone how to live their lives or to judge them for the decisions they make. I do what I can to keep them from destroying hotel property or making the other guests uncomfortable, but whatever they decide beyond that is up to them."

Jack chimed in then with a firm nod. "Isn't that just life, then? Even if you're sure someone is making a mistake, it's theirs to make."

"I guess that's true," Claire agreed, looking at him before looking back at the clerk. "For what it's worth, though, we aren't having an affair. We just met, for one thing, and for another thing, I don't even know if Jack here is married."

She pointed at her chest with her thumb. "I don't have anyone back home to cheat on, not that I would if I did." She felt her cheeks heating. Why was she even explaining this? The clerk certainly didn't need to know her relationship status. Unless she was sharing it for Jack's benefit...

"Not married," offered Jack, saving her by making it seem as if this were a perfectly normal conversation to be having in a hotel lobby.

"Good to know," said the clerk, who was clearly not playing along with their little charade. "I, too, am single. Though as a rule, I do not date hotel guests."

Claire and Jack both nodded, not making eye contact with each other. This conversation had reached the point of such ridiculousness—and strayed so far from the bounds of normal human business interactions—that it wouldn't take much to have her slapping her knees and laughing until she couldn't see straight.

Once their keys were in hand, Jack and Claire made their way to the elevator. As soon as the doors closed behind them, the laughter that had been barely suppressed burst forth with a vengeance.

"That...was..." She could barely get the words out.

"Awkward?" Jack offered, chuckling softly himself as he watched her. "Abnormal? Unprofessional? Inappropriate?" He shook his head. "There are so many words, but none of them quite do the situation justice, do they?"

Claire wiped her eyes at the sound of a ding and the opening of the elevator doors. "It was instantly one of my favorite memories from this trip, that's for sure. I haven't laughed like that in a long time."

Jack nodded. "And it was a nice reminder not to try to change or control others. Maybe a timely reminder while I'm trying to help my sister."

Claire's mood sobered at his words. "Is everything okay there? I'm sorry, I know it's not my business—"

"No, it's fine," said Jack. "And it's...she's fine. That's the important thing. It's just protective brother stuff. Not wanting to see her make a mistake that's going to get her hurt."

"Of course not," said Claire. She studied his face, the haunted look in his eyes. This was a man who cared deeply about his sister, who had seen her have her heart broken or worse and was perhaps afraid to see it happen again. It wasn't quite the same as Klaus the clerk telling them they could sneak back and forth between their rooms to their heart's content.

Not that it was any of her business. She put on a bright smile, touching Jack's elbow to get his attention. "Adjoining rooms, huh? We can slip notes under the door! *Do you want to go to dinner? Meet me in the lobby in 5 minutes. Turn on Channel 3 if you like rom coms.*"

Jack smiled back at her. "Ah yes, the oldest form of communication, notes slid under the door. Certainly beats face-to-face communication."

"Indeed," said Claire, playing along. "We wouldn't want any of that, now would we?"

They arrived in front of their rooms then, the doors just next to each other. Jack huffed out a laugh. "I guess Klaus really wasn't kidding about the adjoining rooms, was he?" He paused with his keycard just above the lock, looking at Claire with a slight grimace and an apologetic expression in his eyes. "In advance, I am deeply sorry if my snoring tonight keeps you from sleeping." He tapped on the wall between their doors. "I'm guessing these babies aren't exactly soundproof."

Claire chuckled, shaking her head. "There is a very good chance you're right about that." She shuddered in horror. "You wouldn't believe the things I've heard these last few weeks, sleeping in a different hotel room each night. Oh, there were the standard loud movies, phone calls with hard-of-hearing grandparents, amorous couples..."

She trailed off, but Jack's interest was piqued. "What else? All of those things are bad enough, but..."

She held up a hand to stop him. "Oh, you don't want to know." Then her face split into a grin. "Who am I kidding? Of course you want to know!" She held up her fingers as she counted off some of the more egregious displays of poor neighborliness. "There was a guy who was clearly rehearsing lines for an audition of some sort. The middle of the night furniture rearrangers. The farting contest..."

"Farting contest? Really?"

"I assume so." Claire shrugged. "Judging by the giggles, they were all winners, though. And I couldn't tell you how many contenders there were."

Jack was shaking his head. "I wouldn't have guessed any of those. And I can promise you not to disrupt your sleep any more than the world farting championships already have."

"Oh, gee, thanks." Claire wiped her brow with exaggerated relief. "I'll sleep well tonight, then." She slipped her key into the door with one last smile at Jack. "I'll see you in a bit, Jack. Get ready for an adventure!"

He smiled back at her and then they were both in their rooms. Claire flopped onto the bed and was almost sure she heard the telltale groan of springs from next door to suggest Jack had done the same.

Four

Claire and Jack met as planned, half an hour later in the lobby. She had heard him puttering around in his room, even heard the door close behind him as he entered the hallway.

But she hadn't gone out to meet him then, and hadn't gone to the door of his room earlier, lifting her hand to knock.

She hadn't opened the adjoining door, either. Suddenly, it had all felt too intimate. The proximity made it feel like they were practically sleeping on top of each other—*poor choice of words, brain*, she chided herself—and the lack of soundproof walls had her tiptoeing, practically walking on eggshells.

She had never cared this much who was staying in the room next to hers. Of course, she couldn't remember a time when she even *knew* who was staying in the room next to hers.

And it's not as if you really know Jack, her brain reminded her. *Meeting him less than an hour ago doesn't exactly make the two of you old friends.*

She let the door close behind her as she stepped out into the hallway, testing the handle to ensure it was locked. She had spent the last half hour unpacking her meager belongings—she had far more paperbacks than she would need for the next 24 hours, nothing in the way of clothing if she needed to add a layer or wear a different outfit the next day, and all the jewelry she had packed for the trip. The last thing this already-inconvenienced trip needed was something going missing from her hotel room.

She had also, during the time she had been in her room, sent a few more texts and emails to update all interested parties about her travel plans. Bianca would be unavailable, both because of the time difference and possibly also because of how close the holidays were and the fact that she needed some well-deserved time off, so Claire had simply emailed her. She hoped her willingness to be flexible would work in her favor the next time she was negotiating a contract—and she couldn't shake the feeling that something was coming down the pike.

Emma had been surprised at the turn of events with Jack—"So he's not actually a Tech Bro? Huh. Didn't see that plot twist coming," had been her first message—but had embraced it annoyingly quickly. At the news that Jack seemed actually to be a much more solid example of humanity than their initial impressions had allowed for, Emma had changed her tone completely. Now it was all, "Be open to possibilities, Claire. You never know what might happen..." and Claire had to put an abrupt end to the conversation before her best friend once again regaled her with the tale of how she had met Connor.

It was a cute story, Claire could admit. But just because Emma's travel mishaps had ended with her meeting the man she would marry didn't mean Claire's had to. She was prepared to spend the day enjoying a friendly outing around an unfamiliar city with a new acquaintance...and then probably never see or speak to him again, unless he wanted to get a book signed for his sister's birthday. She highly doubted they would be the type of friends to wish each other a happy birthday or even to catch up once they were out of sight, but that didn't mean they couldn't enjoy the day.

As the elevator arrived at the lobby and the doors opened, Claire's eyes landed on Jack's and there was a lurching sensation. She thought briefly that it must have been the elevator, its brakes coming on too hard, but as the expression of concern wrinkled Jack's eyebrows and she saw his mouth forming the words "Are you feeling okay?" she realized it had only been her who had felt it, whatever it was. Something had rocked her world, and she wasn't sure she cared for that particular sensation.

Claire gulped, nodding as she stepped forward into the lobby. Her cheeks were heating, she knew, and her heart had picked up its rhythm. It was the strangest thing—if it hadn't been a malfunction of the elevator, then what? Her heart had skipped a beat at the sight of Jack? Please. This wasn't one of her novels.

Even if it was possible to develop a crush on someone that quickly—and of course she knew it was, she'd been a human for nearly thirty years by now and experienced every variety of crush possible in that time—there was still no reason for her to have one on Jack.

Sure, he was handsome. And the way he looked out for his sister was heart-stoppingly sweet. And he had quickly become the most fun part of this whole misadventure of hers. And he was looking at her like she was the only other person in the room, much to Klaus's dismay. And...

Shit, thought Claire. *These are definitely the makings of a crush. How inconvenient.*

She smiled and gave Jack a reassuring nod. He was still looking at her as if she were about to swoon and need to be caught and placed on a fainting couch until her delicate constitution could recover. The concern in his eyes faded as he smiled back at her, placing a reassuring—and warm—hand just above her elbow as he fell into step with her, guiding her back to the desk where Klaus was waiting.

Or...and hear me out, please, Claire's brain was chiming in again. *What if having a crush on this man isn't an inconvenience or a source of embarrassment but...it's actually just a bit of fun? A pleasant change from all the stress? A shot of dopamine? Maybe even a wee ego boost? A little crush, maybe even some light flirting, never hurt anyone.*

Claire held that thought close, a hand of cards she didn't want anyone else to see, a secret just for her. At surface level, it might be the worst cliche imaginable—a romance writer, a hopeless romantic imagining a love story with the first man who spoke to her that day. But it wasn't as if this sort of thing was the norm for Claire, either. Since Eric had left the picture, she'd been much more inclined to be wary and suspicious of men than to see them as potential love interests. It had made writing her romantic heroes more than a little challenging. And if for no other reason than that the heroine of her next novel deserved it, she could nurture this little crush on Jack for the next 23 hours.

The reminder that their time together was finite, that an entire hour had already ticked away, vanishing into the void, stirred an unfamiliar sensation in Claire's stomach. It was an aching, bordering on nostalgia, a longing for something she couldn't name.

She shook it off, bringing herself back into the room. It wasn't the time to do a deep dive on her feelings about the situation. It was time to figure out their next steps and—first and foremost—lunch.

It was a short walk before they found themselves surrounded by options to explore. Though they had meal vouchers for the hotel restaurant, how could they pass up the opportunity to seek out the best Munich had to offer?

Claire shielded her eyes from the midday sun as she took in a beautiful building with a large clock, where a crowd was gathering seemingly in clock-related anticipation. "Uh," she began with hesitation. "I have an embarrassing lack of knowledge about German cuisine. All I really know about is the beer, and that's not exactly a meal, now is it?"

Jack nodded. "I wouldn't be opposed to having a beer *with* lunch, but beer *for* lunch sounds like a recipe for disaster. I'd prefer not to party so hard today that I end up hungover on the flight tomorrow."

Right. Because they were flying tomorrow. Claire couldn't let herself forget that fact, not even when it felt like a totally new vacation was just beginning.

The last six weeks haven't been vacation, either. Don't forget that particular fact.

And that was the truth. There had been a lot of bookstore visits and signing events scheduled for this particular tour. Looking back, that's probably the first observation that had clued Claire in to the potential financial struggles of Velvet Leaf Publishing. After all, if everything was fine and dandy and there was plenty of money left in the budget, then why else would this trip have been scheduled like this? No, they had to be thinking about saving money. One or two nights, three at an absolute maximum in any city, and then on to the next one.

And she'd been traveling from city to city by train, not that she minded. Claire loved seeing the countryside, the places she perhaps could have visited had there been a little more time to do so. But it did seem odd that Velvet Leaf hadn't even asked if she preferred to fly or take the train. Yet another indicator that the writing was likely already on the wall and she would be unemployed by the new year.

Back to happier thoughts, then. With worries like that swirling through her mind, she at least deserved a good meal.

"I totally agree," she told Jack with a smile. "So what should the meal be, then?"

He tilted his head in thought. "I'm pretty sure German cuisine is fairly heavy on pork. As in, I think that's their specialty. Does that sound appealing to you, or...?

Claire nodded. "Oh, I could definitely eat. This morning I was in such a rush to get to the airport on time that I'm ready for, like, a *meal*. You know? Not a snack, not *something light to tide me over until dinner*." Her hand flew to her stomach, as a sensation there agreed with whatever she was saying. "It's time to eat."

"Alright then. Follow me." He held out a hand for her as he started to cross the street, but she didn't take it. It wasn't that the offer didn't appeal, it was that it probably appealed *too* much. Instead, she picked up her pace to fall into step next to him as the two of them jogged across the street and into a wooden building with script on the front that she couldn't read.

Claire looked at Jack with a quizzical expression on her face. "I thought you'd never been here before?"

"Oh, I haven't. I just figured we couldn't go wrong wandering into a strange building in a country where we don't speak the language and expecting to find a gourmet meal inside." His face was deadpan. "I mean, seriously. What other possible outcome is there in that scenario?"

"Um...well, I can think of a few. Do you want to hear the regular, everyday, more likely ones? Or the unhinged ones?"

"One of each, please."

"Okay, then. Well, it could either *not* be a restaurant or not be a very good restaurant. *Or* it could be the headquarters of a local chapter of angry extraterrestrials who are planning to take over the earth and they'll wear our bodies like suits after they vaporize us and use them to infiltrate the human population."

Jack's eyes were wide. "Are you sure it's just romance that you write? Because I have a feeling that brain could do just fine with some science fiction if you gave it a crack at it."

Claire stopped in her tracks and crossed her arms over her chest. "I think that's supposed to be a compliment, but yes, it is *just* romance that I write."

Jack was back at her side in a flash. "I didn't mean it that way, please don't take any offense."

She let her serious expression fall away, replaced by a grin. "Oh, I didn't. But I did want to make you sweat. And perhaps also tell me the truth about why you are steering us so confidently towards this mysterious building."

"You really want to know?"

She nodded. "I really want to know."

"I looked it up on my phone. *Best restaurants in central Munich.* Scoped out a lunch menu or two. Picked the one closest to our hotel, the easiest one to find." He gave her a tentative smile then. "Were you impressed until I revealed my tricks?"

"Even after you revealed them, I was impressed." At the puzzled expression on his face, she continued. "I can't say I've ever traveled with a man who bothered to do any research. Who wasn't happy to just leave every decision to me. 'Whatever you want is fine with me' and all that."

"Yeesh." Jack grimaced. "I guess that's supposed to sound easygoing and fun but it just means—"

"That everything is left to me to figure out?" She nodded. "Ding ding ding, you are correct!" She sighed. "But I should be fair and say that I know not all men are like that and yada yada yada. That was just my ex, and there is a reason he is an ex and not my lifelong travel companion."

Jack nodded. "Well, after what you have shared, I am truly shocked. I would have expected that breakup conversation to go something like, 'It's not you, it's me, but I hope we can still travel the world together.'" He gave her a warm smile then, pausing before opening the door of the restaurant. "I'm sorry that happened to you, though. And I hope that in the rest of our time traveling together, I can give you a little taste of a different way of doing things."

Claire felt her cheeks heat as she stepped inside the door Jack was holding open. "I appreciate that. And so far, you do seem like an absolutely ideal travel companion." She glanced over her shoulder to purse her lips at him, studying him with suspicion. "I just wonder what you're hiding. What it is that I won't find out about you until it's too late to change my mind and get a new travel companion."

"I might be a bit of a blanket hog, but I don't expect that to be a problem for you." His cheeks were red now, burning brighter than hers already had been. "I didn't mean...I just meant..."

She stopped him with a raised hand, putting him out of his misery. "It's okay, Jack. Slip of the tongue, I'm sure." She forced a laugh. "It's not as if you were suggesting the two of us should share a bed this evening. No matter what Klaus thinks."

Jack laughed, too. "Oh, Klaus. I'm glad you spoke up, or I think that little matchmaker might have just told us there was only one bed at the inn and the heat was broken."

"Ah, so you *have* read some romance novels." She shook her head with mirth. "I admit, 'only one bed' isn't my favorite trope to write, but it *is* one of my favorites to read. All that delightful tension and awkwardness right up until...well, you know." She couldn't quite meet his eyes. What was she doing keeping this conversation going?

"And as much fun as it is—or so I hear—to read, living it would only be awkward, I'm pretty sure. Good thing, then, that we have two beds between us."

"Four, actually," said Claire. "Or at least my room had two queens in it. I assumed yours did, too?"

Jack shook his head. "Just the one. Still, though, I think we've got an abundance of beds between us."

"That we do." Claire looked around, anywhere but Jack's face to break the tension she was feeling. They were inside the restaurant now, a dimly lit space with large wooden tables and exposed beams on the ceiling. They had been standing just inside the door as they continued their conversation, but Claire lifted her hand towards an empty table. "Should we sit?"

"I guess?" Jack was hesitant. "I didn't know if this was one of those 'wait to be seated' situations, but there was no sign by the door like in an American diner."

"Believe it or not, American diner rules do not seem to be ubiquitous. I know! I was shocked to learn that, too!" Claire teased. She started walking towards the table, aware of Jack's presence behind her.

As they took their seats on opposite sides of the table, she continued. "Imagine my surprise on this trip when I learned you have to get your server's attention to get the bill." She shook her head, exhaling with amusement. "The first restaurant I went to, I think it was in Amsterdam...I sat there and waited, polite smile on my face and not even one single bite of food left on the plate in front of me. I kept waiting for someone to come over and say, 'Can I get you anything else?' so I could say, 'No, just the check, please.' But finally I clocked on to the fact that everyone around me was just asking for what they wanted. Raising a hand, making eye contact, a gesture in the air...and there I was, like I was trying to win a contest. Be rewarded for sitting silently and politely long enough that someone would just come give me exactly what I wanted." She sighed. "I'm pretty sure there's a metaphor for life in that, but I don't care to figure out what it is."

Jack raised an eyebrow. "No? It seems pretty straightforward from where I'm sitting. Just, uh...ask for what you want instead of waiting for someone to read your mind and give it to you."

Claire shrugged. "Who can say? It's a great mystery."

Jack shook his head. "Well, I do think that at least in the context of this restaurant, we should ask for what we want. None of that, 'Oh, just surprise me! What's your favorite thing on the menu?'"

Studying the menu, Claire nodded. "That's a fair request. Although..." She flipped the menu over, but the other side was blank. "Well, I'm sorry to tell you that my German comprehension skills are non-existent and I have *no* idea what to order on this menu. Do you?"

"Yeah, it's awfully hard to ask for what you want if you don't even know what you options are." He lifted his gaze, searching the restaurant until they landed on a server, who started heading in their direction. "Let's get some help then."

Five

Thanks to the help of Michael, their server, Jack and Claire were soon tucking into a feast. They had ordered a few different sausages and pork dishes to share, along with all the potatoes and dumplings Michael had suggested, topping it all off with a weissbier for each of them.

By the time Claire leaned back from the table, slouching in her chair with the sheer effort of all the digestion her body was beginning to undertake, she was full, tired, and peaceful. It was possibly the most peaceful she had felt after a meal since taking off from Newark three weeks prior, thanks in no small part to Jack's company. Even an experience that could have been embarrassing on her own—stumbling over an unfamiliar menu, butchering any attempts to pronounce the names of the foods they were ordering correctly, the introvert's hell that was trying to track down a busy server...even all of that was somehow fun and not embarrassing with him along for the ride.

The two of them had laughed at themselves and at each other practically non-stop since taking their seats.

Throughout the entire lunch, the flow of conversation and laughter and even silence had felt so natural, so comfortable, that Claire had to remind herself that Jack was still practically a stranger.

As he continued to pick over the last of the spätzle, Claire decided it was time to dive a little deeper. "So, Jack," she began. "Considering that I misjudged you as a Tech Bro at the airport, what is it that you actually do when you aren't busy texting your sister?"

Jack smiled. "Believe it or not, she isn't always having a crisis. Sometimes we go for days at a stretch with no communication at all."

"I'm glad to hear it. And I'm curious about her, so if you don't think she'd mind you sharing..."

"Not at all." He shook his head, then scratched his neck, looking slightly sheepish. "Actually, when I was chatting with her at the hotel, she suggested getting your perspective on everything." His eyes met Claire's then. "'As long as she promises not to write me into one of her books,'" were her exact words, if I remember correctly."

Claire nodded solemnly. "Of course not. But you and your sister should both consider yourselves warned: while I may write relationships like I know what I'm talking about, the evidence from my personal life might suggest differently."

Jack frowned. "Really? I just assumed..."

She raised an eyebrow at him. "You assumed that, traveling alone just a few days before Christmas, no mention of a partner, boyfriend, husband..." She exhaled a laugh. "And let's be honest, through those paper-thin walls? You would have heard if I made a phone call." She shrugged then. "What can I say? Plenty of men, as it turns out, are intimidated by the idea of being with a woman who writes romance novels. Afraid of ending up the villain, I guess. No one thinks they can behave themselves long enough to be written as a hero."

Jack recoiled. "Seriously? Is that a thing that's been said to you, or is that your interpretation of events?" He held up a hand before she could speak. "I'm not saying I don't believe you. I just want to know if I need to be angry at a specific man for talking shit or at my entire species for causing you to lose that much faith in us."

"Can it be a little bit of both? My ex definitely had issues with the books, not that he read them. He would just look at the cover art—which I have no control over, anyway—or read the blurb or skim a few pages and then jump to wild conclusions, either about how I felt about him or about whatever other men there must be in my life who were providing inspiration." She shrugged. "I'm surprised we lasted as long as we did. But after him, I went on a few dates, and the books always came up. I guess people just can't resist googling each other anymore." She shook her head. "But it was always something. Either it was, 'You're not going to use this date for inspiration in a book, are you?' or offers to help me spice up my sex scenes, which I don't even write. One guy brought an NDA to the date to guarantee that he wouldn't end up in a book. I guess I'm not supposed to be telling you that, but it's not like I told you his name. He wasn't even that interesting, to be honest. Would have made for a very boring hero. Not even a terribly compelling side character, either."

Jack was shaking his head as he listened to her speech. "I have to say, I'm not exactly impressed by the men you've encountered lately. On behalf of the rest of us, I feel like I should apologize."

"You really don't. I know you're not supposed to dismiss an entire population based on a small sample size like that, so I'll probably keep giving men a try here and there. I just know now to keep my expectations reasonably low." She smiled at him. "So you're telling me that if you were the one I was on a date with, you wouldn't have pulled any of that crap?"

Jack held out his hands, gesturing to the table between them. "You tell me. What you see is what you get, so if this had been a date, I don't think much of it would have been different. I would have flirted a bit more, but everything else would have been the same."

"Good to know," said Claire, feeling her cheeks heat slightly. If Date Jack would have flirted *a bit more*, did that mean that Regular Jack had been flirting a standard amount? And if so, what did that mean? Because she wasn't *not* interested in him...

"So," she said, interrupting her own thoughts. "You dodged my question. What do you do?"

"Well..." Jack looked sheepish. "You weren't totally wrong about the Tech Bro thing."

Claire grimaced. "Ah. Sorry about all the jokes then. How bad is it, anyway?"

"What do you mean?"

"Well, are you a 'circle back leverage the synergy vertical integration touch base' kind of Tech Bro or...the other kind? I assume there *is* another kind..."

Jack was laughing and shaking his head. "Well, you've definitely got the type down. But no, I haven't founded my own app that's 'going to change the way humans interface with technology' or anything like that." He shrugged. "I'm an engineer. Computer engineer, so I work on the code for those kinds of things. But in my own life, I'm generally not that glued to my phone."

"So today was the exception?" She raised an eyebrow at him, and he nodded.

"Definitely. It's just...I don't know, Hazel is going through some stuff. Rethinking some decisions that I don't think are in her best interest to rethink." He lifted his shoulders. "I was just trying to be supportive. Remind her why she did the things she did."

Claire nodded, digesting his words as, once again, her own sister came to mind unbidden. "And yet you still decided to delay your travel plans? Make it make sense, Jack. It's not like you couldn't have texted her on the plane, swooped right in there to save the day tomorrow."

"It doesn't work that way, though. While I can give her advice, remind her of how strong she is...it's still her life. She's still the one who has to decide what's right for her."

"Huh." Claire was stunned into silence for a moment. "That surprises me."

Jack shook his head. "Don't let it. It's only partly the selfless older sibling passing the baton to the rest of the family to figure it out. I also thought it sounded like a bit of an adventure. And then I saw you heading towards the counter, and well...my feet started moving before I even knew what I was doing."

"You...what? Me?" Well, *that* was certainly a surprise. She remembered the way he had looked her over at the airport, which had felt like the furthest thing from *noticing* her, but now he was suggesting she was the reason he had been standing at that counter in the first place?

She shook her head as if to clear her ears, sure she would hear something different the next time he spoke. "Really?" she asked. "Or is that just a line?"

"That depends," he said. "If you think it's creepy, then it's just a line. But if you think it's charming, then it's real." He smiled, leaning back in his chair. "What do you make of it?"

"I don't think it's creepy," she said, surprising herself to find those were her true feelings. "But I do think it's surprising. You must have great peripheral vision, then, because you certainly seemed to be glued to your phone any time I glanced your way."

The look he gave her then had her cheeks heating in a millisecond. "So you were checking me out too, then?"

"I noticed you," she admitted. "It would be hard not to, though, the way you were staring at that phone so intently that someone easily could have stolen your bag while you were sitting...or you could have run right into a pillar when you were walking."

"Ah, so you weren't watching me *that* closely if you think those things are only remote possibilities." He gave her a sheepish smile. "I actually did bump into one of the pillars. Glad to hear you somehow missed that."

She smiled at him, then directed her attention back to the condensation on the bottom of her glass, where just an inch of beer remained. It was time for a subject change.

Jack was either just teasing her about noticing her—and why would he do that?—or things were about to get uncomfortable. "So, given that you have her permission, want to tell me about your sister?"

He gave a knowing smile, then nodded. "Sure. Settle in and get comfortable, because it's quite a story."

"I'm ready," she said with a nod, "as long as it doesn't begin in a galaxy far, far away."

"It does not. It actually begins at our middle school, about fifteen years ago."

"Oh." Claire felt her eyes widen in surprise. "Did not expect that. A bit of backstory?"

Jack nodded. "Yes. That's when she met Daniel, her best friend. The two of them were inseparable. Of course, everyone was always teasing them about being a couple, or about how they were going to get married some day. But they were just kids, you know? Didn't care about any of that stuff." Jack sighed. "Anyway, they stayed friends. Hazel started dating this guy, her first real boyfriend, her senior year of high school. It made things weird with her and Daniel, but that wasn't the thing that concerned me. She just..." He shook his head, his emotions evident on his face. "She lost herself in that relationship. And he wasn't a good guy. He made her feel insecure about...well, everything. It was like we were losing her. Anything that made Hazel *Hazel* was just gone, replaced by whoever she thought this guy wanted her to be."

"Wow." Claire's voice came out hushed. "That must have been awful for her. And for you, too."

Jack nodded. "That's where the books came in." He lifted his eyes then to find hers, a smile appearing for the first time since his story began. "She started reading romance novels…I don't know which one she picked up first, but I'm pretty sure she has read every book you've ever written so many times the covers are falling off. Somewhere along the line, she started to have second thoughts about the relationship." He shrugged. "It was like…she knew the books were fiction, you know? But she couldn't believe—couldn't let herself believe—that they were total fantasy, either."

Claire gave a knowing nod. "That there had to be a kernel of truth there. That good guys had to exist—which I would think she would already know, considering that you're her brother—and that she deserved to be treated like the heroine in a romance novel."

"I agree with most of that." Jack looked uncomfortable. "Not sure little sisters like to think of their brothers in terms of being romantic heroes, though."

"That's fair." Claire chuckled. "It must have been hard for you and the rest of your family to watch her go through all of this."

"That's the thing," said Jack. "We didn't know most of what was going on until after it was already over. Hazel keeps her cards close to the vest and isn't too inclined to ask for help." There was a pained expression on his face. "If she had…if she had told me what was going on, I would have wanted to have a word with her ex, that's for sure."

Claire reached over, placing a reassuring hand on top of his and giving a light squeeze. "It's always better if the heroine saves herself, Jack." She gave him a small smile. "I know it makes for a great story when someone else swoops in and rescues her. So dramatic, such a thrill. But it doesn't always stick. She had to see for herself how bad things were with this guy, and then she had to remove herself from that environment."

A thought occurred to Claire then, concern rippling through her as she gripped Jack's hand more tightly. "Is that what you're talking her through now? Is this scummy ex-boyfriend back in the picture? Do we need to go put the fear of God in him? Run him out of town?"

Jack smiled and shook his head softly. "No, thank goodness. He is well and truly old news now, and the whole Holloway clan is grateful for it."

He flipped his hand over, giving her palm a soft squeeze. "I appreciate your willingness to form a posse with me and ride him out of town. Maybe you should write westerns."

That got a chuckle out of Claire. "I'll consider it next time I'm suffering from writer's block. The thought of starting over again in a whole new genre that I don't even read should work a charm at scaring me back onto the straight and narrow path." She removed her hand from Jack's, reaching for her water glass. As nice as it had been having that contact with him, the two of them didn't need to be sitting there holding hands and making googly eyes like they were on their honeymoon.

"So what is it, then? What's going on with your sister?"

Jack sighed. "It's a new problem, that's for sure. And perhaps the opposite of the last one."

"How do you mean?"

"Well, while the last problem was solved by romance novels, this one seems to have been caused by them."

Six

Jack explained his sister's dilemma, and Claire listened, rapt. It seemed from his telling that Hazel had read a few too many friends to lovers stories and had gotten it into her head that Daniel, her childhood friend and constant companion, was also destined to be the love of her life.

The only problem? It was unrequited love in its highest form. Not only had Daniel never expressed an interest in anything more than friendship with Hazel, but the night before the two of them had gone out for a pre-Christmas drink and Hazel had spilled the depths of her feelings for him...to him. She had gotten sympathy and compassion in response, but not even the faintest glimmer of reciprocation.

"Ouch," Claire said, taking a drink of her second beer. They had ordered refills of their drinks when it had become clear that story time in the cozy restaurant was preferable to getting back on their feet and braving the December weather. "How did she take it?"

Jack shook his head. "She was crushed. I mean, right after it happened, at least, she was crushed. But by this morning, she was already sure that he was just too scared of his feelings for her and that's why he said he wasn't interested. I think she believes if she just holds on longer, he's going to be able to admit that he loved her all along."

"See, this is why I don't write friends to lovers," said Claire. "Because, sure. There might be individual cases where that's true, where someone is afraid of their feelings and lies about them and just needs time to admit them." She shook her head. "But that doesn't mean it's a universal law. Sometimes people really do know themselves, know what they do and don't want. And there's nothing you can do to contort yourself into being their ideal partner. I'm sorry for your sister. It can't be easy."

"It isn't. I was talking her down from going over to Daniel's house in the morning to make a grand gesture—"

"Oh God, no!" Claire interrupted. "A grand gesture is only a good idea if you're confident of how it's going to be received. And I mean confident in a positive way, because I'm pretty confident of how this one would be received and it would *not* be a nice experience for sweet Miss Hazel." She gave Jack a warm smile, touched by the kindness and concern he had for his sister. "I'm glad she has you."

"Thanks. I wish there was something I could do besides just talk to her." He shrugged. "I mean, I wish I could change things, you know? Make the person she loves love her back, if only it were that easy."

"I'm afraid this is a rite of passage that many of us have to go through. Most of us don't get lucky the first time around, and we need to get our hearts broken in order to learn some of the more valuable lessons love has to teach us. If only we could just read them in a book and absorb them that way..." She lifted her eyebrows and shoulders in tandem, thinking of her own heartbreaks, including the most recent one. Eric had left a mark on her psyche, but it was fading. "Doesn't usually work that way, though."

The look on Jack's face was knowing. He was no stranger to heartbreak himself, then. Claire wished there were a book about his life, a novel she could devour instead of sleeping. She would stay up all night just to read one more page, one more chapter.

But that wasn't how real life worked. You couldn't just meet someone and a couple of hours later ask them to share their core wounds with you. Well, some people could. That was pretty much what happened when two introverts met for the first time, after all. But a blossoming friendship was a different situation entirely than whatever was developing between her and Jack...

Or was it, really? Hadn't she decided to have fun and see where this could go? If they only had 24 hours to share their lives, what was the use of playing games, of hiding any parts of themselves under the illusion of disclosing them later? There *was* no "later" where the two of them were concerned. Tomorrow they would get on a plane and go back to their real lives and these 24 hours in Munich would soon become the kind of memory that you weren't sure was a dream or reality.

With that thought in mind, she delved right in.

"So, Jack," Claire began. "I realize this isn't really how people normally get to know each other, but"—she gestured around them—"these aren't exactly normal circumstances, now are they?"

His interest was piqued, and he nodded. "They are certainly a bit unusual. I can't say I've ever had an experience like this before."

She cocked her head to the side, studying him. "No? Never had someone come into your life and you knew it was only going to be for 24 hours?"

Something flashed on his face that she couldn't read. "Can't say I have. It's unusual to know when things are going to end before they've really even begun." He hesitated for a second before plowing ahead. "You might say that's the case for us, too. Just because we're flying out in 24 hours doesn't mean we have to never see each other again."

Claire's pulse picked up speed at his words. Did he *want* to see her again? And if so, why? They barely knew each other, and an extended layover did *not* lifelong bosom buddies make. She took a sip of her drink, forcing the pause that was necessary if she was going to manage to play it cool with her response.

"I mean, I guess we might meet again," she admitted. "Seems like we both do a fair bit of traveling, and we're both heading to Newark." She shrugged. "It's a small world, as they say. Never know where you might run into that new friend you made at the airport."

"I don't think anyone does say that," said Jack with a smile. "But there is always the possibility—if we enjoy ourselves in the time we have together, that is—that we could meet up on purpose, even." A look of mock surprise lifted his eyebrows high on his forehead. "We wouldn't even have to do it by accident. Unless you're envisioning the kind of scenario where we can only meet up again 'if fate decides to intervene' and you're going to write your number on a piece of toilet paper and flush it or something like that." He put his hands up in protest. "If that's your thing, then I'm not participating."

"Not a fan of digging through sewage to try to find a cute girl's phone number?" Claire stacked her hands under her chin, batting her eyes at him.

Jack leveled a look at her that had her heart racing again. "First of all, 'cute' is an understatement. Let's be clear here. But my objection is actually not just about the sewage, believe it or not."

"What else could it possibly be?"

Jack leaned forward. "If you want something, why leave it to chance? Why waste the time you could have shared on trying to read the signs to find your way back to it?" He shook his head. "No, if I like something—some*one*, I should say, let's be clear here—then I don't want or need to take chances."

Claire's mouth was dry as she swallowed. "That's good to know, then."

His smile was patient as he waited for her to move the conversation along. "So, what were you going to ask me?"

"Well, uh..." She cleared her throat. "I was think-ing...you know, we've talked about your sister's romantic history, which is certainly an unusual topic for the first meeting. But considering that this is, in theory, our first and last day together, then why don't we just skip the social norms altogether and just ask each other whatever we want to know?"

Jack crossed his arms over his chest, a pleased look on his face. "I'm impressed. That sounds…"

"Unhinged?"

"No, it sounds like a lot of fun. A breath of fresh air. Potentially like a free therapy session for one or both of us, which could be a good or bad thing, depending on what it uncovers."

Claire pursed her lips in thought. "That's true." She shrugged. "Whatever, though. I'm game if you are."

"Oh, I'm definitely game." He gestured magnanimously towards her. "And considering that the idea was yours, why don't you ask the first question?"

"Well, I suppose we should stay on the topic of relationships. Considering, I mean, that we're already there and things have already gotten…well, a little bit personal." She blushed at the memory of his intensity when he had referred to her as "more than cute," had spoken of going after what he wanted. "You're single, right?"

He nodded, confirming her suspicions.

"That's good then," she said. As he raised an eyebrow, she rushed to explain. "I just mean…if you weren't, well, I'd feel pretty awkward about some of the conversation so far."

"You mean some of the flirting?"

"If that's what you want to call it, then yes."

"I certainly do want to call it that. If my intentions were unclear, I apologize." His smile was devastating. "But from the first moment—or at least the first moment, after I unglued my eyeballs from my phone and actually took you in—that was precisely my intention."

"Why?" she blurted. "And to what end? Is this...what, are you like a cool guy with a girl in every city and this is a conquest? A fun challenge for you to pass the time before your flight tomorrow?" She folded her arms over her chest, studying him. "I'm not saying it *couldn't* be a fun way to pass the time, but if you don't own up to it upfront, it's going to be trouble for you, mister."

But Jack was already shaking his head. "I'm not trying to seduce you, Claire, if that's what you're asking. Just want to get to know you better." He shrugged. "And if that leads to both of us wanting to get to know each other better, maybe even exchanging phone numbers to meet up again when we're Stateside...well then, so be it."

"That's another question I have. Where—?"

Jack interrupted her with a raised hand. "You already asked your first question, which I believe means it's my turn now. May I?"

She nodded.

"Why did your last relationship end?"

Claire exhaled like she had received a gut punch. *Oof.* "Going right for the big guns, are we?" She grimaced slightly and then plowed ahead. "I guess the easiest way to say it is that we were never quite right for each other, and it just became more obvious the longer we spent together."

"How long was that?"

"Long enough. Four years. I think he would have kept me around longer, but at some point I just couldn't take it anymore." Now that the words were flowing, she wanted to keep going. Get all of it off her chest. "Even if it never seemed like he cared that much about me as a person, I think he liked the way I looked on his arm. What having me as his girlfriend said about him."

Jack's forehead wrinkled with confusion. "Huh?"

Claire sighed. "Eric was a regular guy, you know? A guy's guy, as they say. Works in finance, loves fantasy football, more than a little pretentious...I was like his own personal Manic Pixie Dream Girl. You know the trope, right? The quirky, unique girl who saves the boring guy from his boring life, from himself." She gestured to herself. "Only I'm not anyone's Manic Pixie Dream Girl. For starters, my hair is way too boring for that. I don't even dye it to match my mood." She picked up a lock of blonde strands from the collarbone of her sweater before tossing it over her shoulder. "Anyway, for Eric, for his friends, it was like having a girlfriend—or even just a girl they were stringing along but would never actually commit to—who was artistic or creative, as long as she looked good in a cocktail dress...that made them look good. The girlfriend was there to look pretty and on the off chance that she ever dared open her mouth and express an opinion, the men would just all exchange glances among themselves and laugh it off. He might pat my hand in one of those infuriatingly awful 'bless your heart' moves."

"And you had enough?"

She nodded. "I did. I'm embarrassed that it didn't happen sooner. That I stuck around for as long as I did, but..." She shrugged. "Even those of us who write the love stories, who should know better than most how a main character deserves to be treated...even we can forget about it when it comes to our own lives. You can tell Hazel that, if she's ever feeling embarrassed." She pulled her mouth to the side, rethinking her words. "Or don't if you think it means she won't want to listen to my advice anymore."

"I appreciate your humanity," said Jack with a smile, "but I doubt there's anything you could do that would knock you down a peg in Hazel's eyes." He shifted in his seat. "Now, surely you have another question for me. You've been in the hot seat long enough."

"I sure have. Whose idea was this game, anyway?" She chuckled before taking another sip of her beer. "Well, I was going to ask you where you lived, but that seems like a waste of a perfectly good turn." She tapped her chin. "So I'll turn your own question back around to you. Why did *your* last relationship end?"

"I'll give you a freebie and tell you I live in New York. You?" Claire nodded, and Jack smiled. "Good. I'd hate it if we got too excited about spending more time together only to realize one of us lived on the West Coast." They both shuddered at the thought. "Give me snow for Christmas, thank you very much. Even if it's followed by months of cold and a blizzard or two."

"Amen," said Claire, lifting her glass to clink with his. She loved the beach—or at least a *vacation* at the beach—as much as anyone else, but the magic of December and especially the week between Christmas and New Year didn't feel right without a scarf wrapped around her neck and her cheeks and the tip of her nose blushing crimson in the cold.

"Anyway, to answer the other, more important question..." Jack sighed, nodding once. "Not my finest hour, I'm afraid. I mean, I thought we were happy...or at least happy enough. We got along well, arguments were rare, and..." He shrugged. "I don't know, it was comfortable. We fit. Or at least I thought we did. But as it turned out, it was too boring. Or at least that's what my ex told me." He shook his head, a soft laugh escaping his lips. "Not arguing meant there wasn't enough drama, and that in turn made her doubt the depth of our passion. If we weren't smashing dishes on the floor and slamming doors, then that apparently meant that the 'spark' wasn't there. She left to look for it with someone else."

Claire grimaced. "Is this another area where authors like me are to blame? Making everyone think that dramatics and grand gestures and third act breakups are all the norm, that a life without them is only half a life?"

"Beats me," said Jack. "There's more to the story, though, unfortunately. In order to try to convince her to stay, I did break a dish. I suppose that's a natural side effect when someone broaches a topic like this while you're washing them after a meal. She said she wanted passion and explosions and excitement, and in a moment that truly felt like an out-of-body experience, I just picked up the cup that I was washing at that moment and dropped it right on the kitchen floor. Told her if that was what she wanted, I'd be happy to give it a try. I wasn't trying to call her bluff or anything." He shook his head, mouth open. "I was desperate. Didn't want her to go, still can't believe she's gone. And I thought—I guess this is where Hazel gets it—that if I could just become what she wanted, then she wouldn't leave."

Claire was quiet, chewing on her lower lip. A few words slipped past her lips, almost too quiet for him to hear. "Didn't work?"

Jack sighed, shaking his head. "It never works, trying to be someone else. You and I both know that." He met her eyes then, for the first time since he'd started telling his story. "Of course, it would have helped if I'd paid attention to which dish I was dropping on the floor." He looked sheepish then, reaching up to scratch the back of his neck. "Turns out it was a mug I had given her for Valentine's Day the year before. Rather than taking it as a sign that I was going to change for her, she took it as an omen. Packed up her things and was gone that same night."

Seven

Jack and Claire were outside the restaurant now, blinking into the winter sun. After finishing their stories, they'd asked for the check and split the bill in relative silence. Claire was second guessing their decision to divulge so much, feeling vulnerable and exposed for all that she had shared and sure that Jack was feeling the same way.

"So..." she began, the toe of her boot tracing a crack on the sidewalk.

When she looked up, Jack was looking at her with a smile on his face, warmth in his eyes. "So," he said with a nod. "Feeling a little sheepish, are we?"

"Perhaps," Claire admitted, though she couldn't suppress her smile any longer. "That wasn't exactly a normal first meal."

"No, it certainly wasn't." Jack looked around then, taking a deep breath and sighing it out. "But isn't that a good thing? Sure, we could have kept our deep dark secrets to ourselves and pretended to be normal, been on our best behavior to impress each other. 'Ooh, look how witty I am, how good I am at eating a meal.'" He blew a raspberry in the air then, making Claire laugh. "What kind of bizarre mating dance ritual is that? No, I think we've made it very clear that relationships built on trying to become what the other person wants are doomed for failure, either in the immediate future or in the long-term. And I don't know about you, but I don't want to waste any more time on that way of thinking."

"No." Claire's voice was soft as she shook her head, eyes still searching his. "I don't either. I'd rather be courageous and honest. Though I have to admit, it does feel vaguely terrifying."

"Nothing vague about it." Jack's eyes were bright, like his smile. "Everything I just said to you, I was saying it for my benefit, too. As soon as we left that dim restaurant for the bright of day, my first thought was, 'Oh my God, what have I done? Now she knows you aren't a cool guy!'"

Claire threaded her arm through his, tugging him gently along the sidewalk. "For what it's worth, I think you're a very cool guy. Anyone who shares like you did…" She nodded in thought. "Well, it's very impressive. Attractive, too."

He stopped then, looking at her with a quizzical expression on his face. "So…if we can see that it's an attractive quality in someone else, is it so farfetched to believe that it could be an attractive quality in ourselves, too?"

She laughed then. "It's a huge leap of logic, of course, but…" She held up her thumb and first finger, a small space between them. "There's a tiny chance that's true."

He put his hand over hers and steered them back to the sidewalk. "So you're telling me there's a chance?" Looking back down at her, he smiled. "So where to, then?"

Claire looked around them then, shrugging. "For the first time in weeks, I don't have any plans, and I think I love it. Is there anywhere you want to go?"

Jack matched her raised eyebrow with one of his own. "I don't know enough about Munich to even name one place, especially now that we've eaten great food and had a couple of beers. Want to just walk around and see if we either stumble onto something cool or get ourselves lost?"

"That sounds like a perfect plan," said Claire.

They continued walking, the conversation flowing so naturally between them that Claire couldn't keep the grin from her face. How was it possible that she hadn't known Jack a few hours ago and yet he already felt like the most important part of her entire trip?

"Ooh, let's go in here," Jack said, tugging on her elbow to direct her into a shop.

Claire blew out the cold in her lungs as the door closed behind them, only then looking around to see where they were. "A bookstore? Haven't seen many of these on my trip," she teased him, rolling her eyes.

"Yes, but have you seen this one?"

She shook her head. "I have not. What's special about this one?"

Jack gestured around them, as if the answer was self-explanatory. "Books, Claire. Does it need more than that?"

"You're right, that was a silly question. All bookstores are special, just like all books are special." She traced her fingers over the covers in front of her, displayed on the bestseller table. She paused over a political biography, rolling her eyes. "Okay, maybe not *all* books."

Jack was making a beeline towards a sign on the back wall that read "English books" and Claire followed after him. She had already filled her bags with enough books she couldn't read, even if they were her own words, translated into other languages. In fact, she shouldn't be buying any more books today, not as far as her luggage or her budget were concerned, but why should that stop her from looking?

"Here they are," Jack said as he came to a stop, his head tipped to the side to read the spines of the books. His fingers traced along until he lifted one...two...three books from the shelf and held them out to her.

Claire redirected her attention from the shelf full of classics, looking down at the books she had taken from Jack without even being fully aware of it. It was only then that she realized what they were...they were *her* books. Three of her favorites, in fact: *Eternal Embrace, Sapphire Serenade,* and *Moonlit Melodies.*

Her forehead wrinkled as she looked at him. "I...uh. What? I'm not going to buy these. I mean, they *are* great books, if I do say so myself, but why buy the cow when you can get the milk for free?"

Jack chuckled. "Believe it or not, I wasn't suggesting that you should buy them. Or even that you should be surprised to see them, since apparently they have a healthy collection of Claire Davis books here." He gestured back to the shelves behind him, and Claire nodded at the familiar spines. There would be more in the larger German section of the store too, if her climbing translation sales numbers were to be believed.

"Are you buying them? Christmas present for Hazel?" she offered, transferring the stack of books from one hand to the other.

Jack shook his head. "She's already got quite a collection. As well as something called a TBR that is apparently a mile long. No, these are for me. I'm just handing them to you so you can tell me if I'm on the right track for an introduction to your work."

"Ah." Claire's cheeks were heating, and she was grateful for the distraction as she studied the books in her hands. "While I do love all of these, perhaps a little more variety in your tropes. Do you have a favorite trope?"

She looked up as the silence stretched, smiling when she found only confusion in Jack's expression. "I'm not even sure what a trope *is*, sorry."

"That's okay. They're like the themes of books, reliable ones that readers like to read and writers like to write. That way, we aren't reinventing the wheel every time we sit down to write, and readers know what to expect. So we've got, like, enemies to lovers, friends to lovers, forced proximity, fake dating..." She trailed off, studying his face. "Any of those sound interesting to you?"

"Well...after everything we've talked about with Hazel, I think I'll steer clear of friends to lovers."

Claire nodded. "There aren't any of those in the stack, so you're safe so far."

"How about the others, then? Enemies to lovers, forced proximity, and...what was the last one?"

"Fake dating." Claire leaned forward and picked up another of her titles, *Serendipity Springs,* from the shelf, swapping it for *Eternal Embrace.* "This should be a great introduction, then. Claire Davis 101." She tipped her head to the side. "Or at least an introduction to my work, since there aren't as many personal details in those books as some people might like to think."

Jack held up *Sapphire Serenade,* with its cover illustration that featured a cartoon hero, as the name suggested, serenading the heroine with an acoustic guitar in front of the deep blue sea. "You mean this isn't autobiographical? I want my money back."

Claire shook her head, thrusting the remaining books into his arms and pushing him towards the cashier. "You haven't even paid yet. Speaking of which, are we done here? Time to move on?"

"That depends on you." He held up the books. "I've got what I came for, but if you want to browse some more or...I don't know, tell the employees who you are and see if they want you to sign their stock of books?"

Claire grimaced. "It feels so weird to do that. Like I think I'm some kind of celebrity or something."

"To some people you are. How about if I just mention when I'm buying the books that you wrote them? Leave the ball in their court?"

She chewed on her lower lip. "That's fine, I guess. I'm just going to hang back here while you do that, if you don't mind." Claire walked slowly around the German new releases table while Jack made his way to the cash register. She enjoyed signing events when they were organized, even enjoyed doing the occasional sneak signing in an airport or her local Target. But it was easy to feel like her enthusiasm might be unwelcome, like a bookseller with discerning taste might look at her illustrated covers, knowing the books contained nothing but happily ever afters, and turn her down in favor of the next literary fiction all star writing the next great American novel.

"Or probably the next great German novel here, duh." She was grumbling to herself as her fingers traced the raised letters on what looked like a domestic thriller. She glanced up in time to see Jack gesturing back to her, a broad grin on his face and a puzzled expression coming from the man who was helping him at the register.

She redirected her attention back to the table. Moments later, Jack approached with a shopping bag in one hand and brandishing a black pen for her in the other. "Come on," he crowed, "you've got some signing to do!"

The bookseller was following close behind him, his confusion replaced with a warm smile. "Welcome, Ms. Davis," he said, reaching out to take her hand. "It's an honor to have you here in our store. Please, follow me." He directed her to a table, where two of his colleagues were arranging piles of Claire's books. Judging by the smiles on everyone's faces and the general lack of animosity, all of Claire's concerns about being judged inferior simply because she wrote romance were sorely unfounded.

She took a seat and was just about to open the first book at the top of the pile when Jack's shopping bag appeared on the table in front of her.

"Will you sign these for me?" he asked, looking just the tiniest bit sheepish as he ducked his head at the booksellers around her. "I know I could wait, but well, you've got one of those good author pens now and it'll probably be better than having you sign it with a crappy hotel pen or an eyeliner pencil later."

"Of course," Claire said, sliding his books out of the bag. "Anything in particular you want inscribed?"

He shook his head. "Surprise me. And Jack is spelled J-A-C-K, just in case you weren't sure." He winked at her then.

"Not J-A-C-Q-U-E-S? Wow. You really do learn something new every day."

She scribbled in the front of the books, a different line in each one, followed by her practiced author signature. It was bigger and loopier than the one she used to sign checks—when was the last time she'd signed a check?—but it looked great on a title page. As soon as she slid Jack's books back into his bag and handed it to him, she felt a moment of stomach-turning anxiety. She hadn't put *too* much thought into the messages she'd written into Jack's books, but...well, should she have maybe put just a *little* more thought into play? What if he misread her words, interpreted them the way she *definitely* didn't mean...

But she just smiled at him and slid the first copy of *Sapphire Serenade* off the stack. It was too late to overthink it now, and, thankfully, Jack had left the books in the bag and was simply watching her. He would read them later, and she wouldn't have to be there witnessing it, wondering what he was thinking at every turn of the page. It was better that way.

She was aware of him studying her as she got into the flow, signing one book after the other. Then he did something that no one other than Bianca had ever done for her before. He put down his bag, took a stack of unsigned books and began opening them to the correct page and stacking them on top of each other. That simple gesture brought a squeezing sensation to her chest. It was silly, she knew. It wasn't as if he was doing this just to be helpful to her or because he had anticipated her needs. No, surely he was just doing it because this was going to take *forever* otherwise and no one in their right mind would want to spend the whole afternoon watching someone write the same two words over and over again, no matter how pretty and loopy their handwriting was while they were doing it.

She put her head back down and got back to work

·❤·❤·❤·❤·❤·

By the time they left the bookstore, Claire was shaking a cramp out of her right hand and Jack was promising two of the booksellers that they would meet up with them later at the Christmas market. Hendrik, the first person who had helped them, was describing the various glüh-wein booths, making it clear where he would be waiting for them. Jana, a quiet young woman who had been by Claire's side throughout the entire process, had squeezed her hand and whispered that she would be there too. And the third bookseller looked truly remorseful to have a family dinner that she couldn't get out of to join in on the fun. It seemed Claire's momentary bookseller-related insecurity had been completely unfounded, something she should have known from the very beginning. *Imposter syndrome can strike at any moment, it seems, and make you believe some really wacky stuff.* Handshakes were exchanged all around, and then she and Jack were out on the sidewalk.

When the door was closed behind them, she spoke to Jack out of the corner of her mouth. "Are we really meeting them at the Christmas market, or is that like when two Americans say they should definitely meet up later on and they both know it isn't going to happen, but they still have to say it anyway?"

Jack shrugged, clearly amused. "Your guess is as good as mine. I say, we go to the Christmas market, regardless. If our new friends are there, the more the merrier. And if they aren't, well...would it really be so bad to be stuck with me?"

She laced her arm through his and grinned up at him. "Not at all. I might even prefer it, no offense to our new friends." Was it her imagination, or was he blushing?

They continued along on the sidewalk, making a few more stops along the way. There were photos to snap, bars of German chocolate to purchase to be tucked into every spare inch of her carry-on, and a toothbrush to secure to make up for the one currently enjoying its stay at the airport in Claire's suitcase.

By the time all of those errands had been run, the two of them were in need of a break...and a seat. "Should we go back to the hotel?" Claire asked, her voice betraying the hesitation she felt. She knew herself well enough after six weeks of traveling to know that retreating to the hotel room for a short nap was likely to end with her falling asleep for the night and missing the Christmas market entirely. And if there was one perk to being in Europe—in Germany, no less, and specifically in Munich, where the massive Christkindlmarkt was—it was Christmas markets. She had heard about them for years from her friends and colleagues who traveled more than she did, had even seen the lights of a few out the windows of trams and taxis over the past weeks, but she had yet to actually step foot in one. It was by far the biggest perk of this extra 24 hours in Munich, and she couldn't—*wouldn't*—let herself miss it.

She looked at Jack then, trying to gauge his thoughts on what the two of them should do next. But he was already shaking his head as he studied her. "I need a break, too," he said, "but we can't go back to the hotel or we'll never leave." He looked down at the bags they were both carrying. "It would be nice to go back and at least drop off this stuff, but I think we have to soldier on. We can sleep on the plane tomorrow."

Something about that "we" tugged at Claire's heart. She had the briefest flash of the two of them sitting side by side on the plane, in their own little worlds with headphones on and movies playing on their screens, yet together at the same time. Sharing a meal together, drifting off to sleep, waking up with her head on his shoulder and his easy, warm affection in his eyes when she looked up at him. She liked that image more than she cared to admit. If she were a little smarter, a little better at protecting her heart, she would extract herself from every single "we" right now and retire back to her room to be alone.

But instead she swallowed, smiled, and nodded. "Sounds like a perfect plan."

Eight

The day flew by in a way that was entirely incongruous given the amount of time spent on increasingly tired and achy feet, the crisp, cold air, and the exhaustion of the previous weeks rapidly catching up to Claire. Because despite all of it, she was having fun with Jack—how could she not? The two of them hadn't stopped talking and laughing since they had stepped foot in the city, apart from a few comfortable silences.

How is it possible to have inside jokes with someone you just met? she wondered, as Jack pointed to a Santa figurine in a souvenir store and mouthed, "I think he *knows*," in her direction. She shook her head at him and chuckled, going back to rifling through the postcards.

This day had been so much more fun than it would have been if she'd spent it in 29D, falling asleep with a crick in her neck and waking up to a seat companion who needed her to move in order to get to the restroom.

And what was waiting for her on the other side, even after that interminable flight was over? She would be spending the holidays at her parents' home in Hoboken, drinking too much wine as she tried to avoid finding herself alone with her sister, who seemed to have nothing but contempt for Claire's "career." If anyone asked what was new in her life, this was what she wanted to share with them. *I was adventurous. I met someone special. It was pure magic.*

I wish I'd never left.

That last thought surprised her, and she shook it off. It wasn't true—couldn't be, actually. Because Munich was a beautiful city, and she could certainly see its charm while she was surrounded by Christmas decorations and holiday spirit.

But she knew full well that the most magical element of this day wasn't the location. It was the company.

And it was special in a way that she made her want to protect it. Didn't want to hear her relatives poke holes in a relationship they couldn't possibly understand. Claire wasn't even sure *she* entirely understood her relationship with Jack. Trying to explain or understand what it was might scare the magic away, and so instead she just kept browsing through the postcards. You could never have too many postcards.

"Hey, do you mind if we stop in here?" she asked, when they were back out on the street, just about to pass a pharmacy. "I should pick up a toothbrush, toothpaste, things like that."

Jack nodded. "I should get some toothpaste, too."

Claire waved a small tube at him. "We can share mine. I don't mind."

Jack pursed his lips in thought, then nodded. "I was about to suggest you provide the toothpaste and I provide the toothbrush, but I have to draw the line at sharing a toothbrush with you."

She widened her eyes at him. "Ew. I mean, thanks. I like you, Jack, but mingling our dental plaque is, like, way too intimate." She shuddered as she pushed the door of the pharmacy open.

"It's really not the same as kissing, is it?" he asked as he followed along behind her. "I mean, the thought of kissing someone you like is...well, hopefully, it doesn't make you shudder in horror." He exhaled a laugh. "It definitely doesn't elicit that reaction in me." He stopped then, turning to look at her with new interest. "Have you ever shared a toothbrush with someone?"

Claire's lips curled down as she nodded. "I didn't know it at the time, but yes."

"How do you unknowingly share a toothbrush? Let me guess...you were sleepwalking. Hypnotized. Under a wizard's spell."

She pursed her lips to keep from smiling at his increasingly ridiculous suggestions. "You gonna keep guessing, or do you want me to give away the ending? The plot twist?"

Jack shook his head. "I'm never good at figuring out plot twists." He gestured for her to continue. "Please, put me out of my misery."

"The answer, then...the way you share a toothbrush without being fully aware that you are doing so...is when someone else accidentally or intentionally uses your toothbrush and doesn't tell you until it's too late. I was on vacation with my friend Emma, sharing a bathroom with her." Claire shrugged. "I was getting ready for bed, put my toothbrush in my mouth, and something just felt...wrong.

Like, even though I had put water on the brush, there was *too* much water there. And then I saw that Emma's toothbrush was the same color as mine and..." She trailed off.

"...bone dry?" Jack offered, an apologetic glint in his eyes.

"Bone dry," said Claire with a nod. "We laughed about it eventually, but that certainly wasn't my initial reaction."

Jack raised an eyebrow. They were in front of the toothbrushes now, Claire perusing her options before making her selection.

"Oh, it wasn't pretty," she offered. "There was some shouting, a bit of gagging. A pillow thrown at her face."

"Wow," said Jack, taking a new interest in the toothbrushes Claire was studying. "Let's make sure we get you one that doesn't look too much like mine, then. I'm not sure our new relationship could handle that level of drama."

She punched him lightly on the arm. "I was thirteen, jerk. I like to think I've dialed down the dramatics a bit since then."

"If you say so," he said, lifting his hands in surrender.

"Plus, we aren't sharing a bathroom. So as long as you don't come over to my room with the express purpose of using my toothbrush, I think we should be good."

"No promises." His smile was sheepish. "If I'm bored, it could happen."

"Let's just make sure you aren't bored, then."

"Good idea," said Jack with a nod. "Find one you like?" He nodded towards the toothbrushes.

"This will work," said Claire. She picked one up and headed for the checkout.

"Do you need anything else?" Jack asked as he looked around the pharmacy. "You can borrow anything of mine, but you might not want to use, like, my deodorant."

Claire wrinkled her nose. "I definitely don't. Not that you don't smell great, but..." She knew her cheeks were flushing again. He didn't need to know she thought he smelled great, so why had she told him? "I brought my own. Not a big fan of smelling like Icy Mountain Smash or Musk and Manliness or whatever scent they've cooked up for you this time."

"Leather and Cookies, actually."

She whirled to look at him. "Was that a joke? Because I'm pretty sure mine were."

But Jack just shrugged. "You'll have to sniff me to find out. I'll never tell."

She rolled her eyes and stalked away. There would be no sniffing.

They still had about an hour before it was time to meet the booksellers at the Christmas market, and Claire's energy was flagging. Nothing sounded better than a nap, but there was no chance of that.

"Come on," said Jack, grabbing her hand and tugging her across the street. "Let's go get warm and off our feet for a bit."

Claire didn't protest, just let him pull her along. The sun was sinking in the sky, and the cozy glow emanating from the cafe Jack was heading towards was calling her home like a beacon. She didn't drop his hand once they were across the street, either, though she covered it by nestling deeper into her scarf with her other hand. *No, I'm just too cold to realize what I'm doing. I'm not holding on to you on purpose.* She nearly laughed out loud at herself, so transparent were her actions.

At the realization, she clasped Jack's hand more tightly. With intent. Let him know that she was doing it on purpose, that she was enjoying it, and that she saw no need to let go. They weren't pretending to be a couple. They were simply two people who had met that same day, had spent almost every waking moment together since, and were currently holding hands. If anyone needed to define what was happening between them, then good luck to that person. Claire, for once, was going to enjoy the moment.

Jack moved to the side, letting go of her hand as he held the door open for her. If she felt the absence of his hand, it didn't last long. As soon as she was over the threshold, he stepped inside the cafe as well, placing that same hand on the small of her back. The gesture was somehow more intimate, even, than their fingers intertwining had been, and she simultaneously leaned back into his hand while also moving forward towards the counter.

The smile Jack gave her was uncharacteristically shy, tentative, but the one she returned to him was unabashed. "This was a good idea," she said to him, looking around the cozy cafe. "Want me to go claim those seats by the fireplace?" She gestured towards a small couch with a low table in front of it.

"That's perfect," said Jack. "What do you want me to order for you?"

"Surprise me," she said. "As long as it's some form of coffee and..." She craned her neck to catch a glimpse of the counter. "Something sweet would be good, too. Maybe we can share a piece of cake or something?"

Jack nodded, his expression serious. "I won't let you down."

Claire rolled her eyes. "I will be happy with whatever you bring back from your hunting and gathering, so...at ease, soldier."

That got a genuine smile out of him. "Well, that's a relief. So, you aren't allergic to carrot cake or anything like that?"

She shook her head and chuckled softly as she made her way to the couch.

Claire checked her phone while she waited for Jack to return. It was well into waking hours in New York by then, so there were messages waiting for her from Bianca.

"Sorry to hear about your travel delays," she had written. "Was hoping to schedule a meeting with you before the holidays, but that's unrealistic at this point. What about meeting for a quick coffee on the 27th?"

Claire's stomach gripped in discomfort. If Bianca had to talk to her about something that couldn't wait until after the start of the new year, that didn't bode well. But while it felt cruel to be delivered bad news just after Christmas, it wasn't as if waiting to hear it was going to make things any better.

With that thought in mind, Claire fired off a message.

"What if we just schedule a call later on today? When I'm back in the hotel for the night, we can talk. Whatever it is, I promise I'd rather know now than have it hanging over my head."

She tucked her phone back into her purse, resolving not to check for a text back from Bianca until they had at least left the cafe. Claire did *not* need to be glued to her phone, not now and not ever.

"Everything okay?" Jack asked as he took a seat next to her—close, she realized, noticing only then that the couch was much more of a loveseat than a sofa. He placed a tray on the table in front of them, but his eyes were on her face, taking in the frown there.

"Fine," she said with a smile. "Just taking care of some business. I need to speak with my agent tonight, so I probably shouldn't stay at the Christmas market too late—and being more sober than tipsy would probably be a good plan, too."

Jack nodded. "I wasn't planning on smashing shots of mulled wine, believe it or not. Let the youngsters do it if they want, but you and I have a plane to catch tomorrow."

"That we do," Claire agreed. "In general, though, I don't think people do shots of hot beverages." She nodded towards the mugs on the tray in front of them. "Speaking of hot beverages..."

"Ah yes," said Jack, picking up one mug and handing it to her, handle out. "This is their festive gingerbread latte. But I asked, and it's not like a typical seasonal beverage with eight different syrups and so much sugar you could push a steam engine...for ten minutes until you need to take a nap. It's basically a latte with some spices—ginger and nutmeg and cinnamon."

Claire lifted it to her nose and took a deep inhale. "Mmm," she breathed. It smelled heavenly, like her grandmother's Christmas cookies dipped in coffee. "What did you get?" she asked, tipping her head towards his mug.

"The same," said Jack. "It sounded good, and I always figure ordering two of the same thing stands a better chance of not having the order messed up."

"That's probably true. But only worth doing if the thing the other person wants isn't something vile and disgusting."

"Oh, trust me. If the person I was with wanted to order a mayonnaise sandwich, I would have no problem ordering the exact opposite."

"Ooh, same." Claire nodded. "I'm actually thrilled to find out we have the same feelings on mayo. Pretty sure that's the foundation of any lasting relationship."

Jack's expression was sincere as he nodded. "Things definitely wouldn't work out between us without that." He cleared his throat before turning his attention back to the remaining items on the tray—two plates, each with a different slice of cake on it. "I got us these to share, too. One is a Black Forest Cake and one is a cheesecake." He handed a fork to Claire before using the other one to take a bite from the end of the cheesecake.

Claire sunk her fork into the chocolate cake before bringing it to her mouth. She closed her eyes as the flavors danced on her tongue, at once rich and light. A groan escaped her lips, startling her eyes open to find Jack watching her with a bemused expression as he swallowed his own mouthful.

"Good?" he asked, gesturing towards the cheesecake with his fork. "Because this one is amazing."

Claire could only nod, eyes bugging out of her head. When she had finally swallowed, she spoke. "That vastly exceeded my expectations. What time does this place open? We *have* to come here again."

As soon as the words were out, she felt a pang of regret. Even if the two of them managed to return to the cafe in the morning for pre-flight caffeine and cake, that was the end of it all. Not only would there be no more sweet, sugary goodness, but there would be no more reason to continue referring to herself and Jack together as a "we."

Unless...

But she shook her head to the side quickly, just once, dismissing the thought. Let tomorrow worry about to-morrow. Let any potential future with Jack worry about itself in the future. If she knew anything about love—and she definitely *should*, after twelve books—the surest way to scare it away was to examine it too closely and put too much pressure on it. Ask Jack when he wanted to see her again and watch him squirm and make up an excuse to cut the evening short. Tell him that she liked him as more than just a 24-hour friend and see how quickly he could shake himself loose of anything even remotely resembling a commitment that lasted longer than the lifetime of a mayfly.

Jack was looking at her with a curious expression on his face, fork paused halfway to his mouth. He opened his mouth, no doubt about to ask her why she was shaking her head at herself, when a sound interrupted him. It was a phone, ringing, and judging by the way Jack snapped to attention, it belonged to him.

His fork clattered as he dropped it back onto the plate, bite forgotten, digging his phone out of his pocket. "Sorry," he said, tapping a button and lifting it to his ear. "I've got to take this."

Claire nodded, chastising herself for the gesture—what, did he need her permission to answer his own phone? And was he supposed to tell her who it was or what it was about or how long the call would take? Of course not, that was ridiculous.

But what should she do? Should she excuse herself? Give him some privacy? Pretend she couldn't hear anything he was saying even though she was sitting right next to him, so close that his knee had pressed into her thigh when he had twisted in his seat to retrieve his phone.

Jack was speaking now into the phone. "Hazel? Is everything okay? What's up?"

The worry creasing his face eased as he listened and then laughed. He looked up then, his eyes meeting Claire's, and she felt caught. Caught not only for paying far too much attention to his conversation, but caught *in* them, too. She was like a fish ensnared in a net, and she couldn't get away from him even if she wanted to.

"She's right here," he was saying. "Do you want to talk to her?"

And then he was holding the phone out to her. "It's my sister," he explained. "She wanted to talk *about* you, but when I offered the chance to talk *with* you..." He blanched then, his other hand coming to cover the mouthpiece of his phone as he pulled it back. "You don't have to, of course. Oh God. Don't feel any pressure. I'm sure it's so obnoxious to talk to fans. I'll tell her you're busy."

"Nonsense," said Claire, already reaching for the phone. "I feel like I know Hazel already, and the only thing missing is actually getting to hear her voice. Give that phone here."

Nine

Jack's shoulders dropped as he let her take the phone from his hand, their fingers brushing against each other's. His smile was warm and relaxed as Claire lifted the phone to her ear, making a shooing gesture at him. "It's girl talk time, Jack. Get out of here. Or at least pretend you aren't listening." She directed her attention to the phone then. "Hazel? It's so nice to get to talk with you."

"Oh my gosh, that's my line. I seriously can't wrap my head around the fact that you are *you* and that Jack has gotten to hang out with you all day. He isn't annoying you, is he? You can tell me if you need a break and I can make up a reason to get him out of your hair."

Claire laughed, her eyes finding Jack's. "No, your brother is a lot of fun, actually. I definitely don't need to be rescued from him." Jack was shaking his head. And was it her imagination, or were his cheeks turning pink?

"How's your heart?" she asked Hazel then. "Feeling alright today?"

There was a choking sound from the other end of the line. "Dang, you don't beat around the bush, do you? Jump right in to the deep end."

Claire shrugged even though Hazel couldn't see her. "The way I see it, if you've read my books, you've already been inside my psyche. What's the point of making small talk about the weather when we both know that's not the reason you called?" She bit her lip then, worrying it between her teeth. "I know it's probably weird that your brother talked to me about your relationship—"

"Are you kidding?" Hazel interrupted. "It's not even *close* to being weird, it's more like the coolest thing that's ever happened to me. I mean, if there was anyone I was going to ask for relationship advice, it'd be a tie between you and Esther Perel, but considering that you are the one stranded with Jack, that's just the universe deciding for me."

"So you don't want me to call Esther to get a second opinion?"

There was silence on the other end, as if Hazel had been stunned.

"I don't know her, Hazel, and I definitely don't have her phone number. I'm afraid you're stuck with me."

"Oh, good." Hazel sounded genuinely relieved. "I was not prepared to have the two of you talk about me. My head would have exploded."

"I'll remember that for the future, in case Esther and I ever become friends." Claire smiled. "So...what can I help you with?"

"Oh, you don't have to do that. It's silly." There was a self-deprecating chuckle in Hazel's voice. "I won't bore you with that. That's what brothers are for."

"I promise I don't mind," said Claire. "And if it helps at all to talk about it, then what have you got to lose?"

There was a pause. "Well..." Hazel began. "You're sure you don't mind?"

"Not at all. What's going on?"

Hazel groaned. "It's this whole mess with Daniel...you know, the part where I told him I liked him as more than a friend and then he had the nerve to comfort me and tell me it'll pass, rather than excitedly tell me he'd been feeling the same way all along."

"Right," said Claire. "I heard about that. Does not sound like a fun experience at all."

Hazel snorted. "Oh, it definitely was not. The problem is that Daniel and I have this standing Christmas date. We always meet up on Christmas Eve for breakfast and to exchange presents. And I'm honestly torn. I haven't spoken to him since that whole mess the other night, and it's not like he's been trying to call me, either. It feels on the one hand like I should cancel and probably avoid him for at least the next six months. Do you think that would be long enough for me to get over him?" She didn't wait for Claire to answer what had clearly been a rhetorical question. "But on the other hand, he's my best friend and I can't bear the thought of throwing our Christmas tradition right out the window. So what if one of us has some inconvenient little feelings? Can't we still be best friends and do best friend-y things?"

As Hazel paused to take a breath, Claire spoke up. "What feels more healing to your heart? The thought of sitting there across the table from him, knowing you can't have him? Or the thought of giving him—and yourself—some space?"

The silence stretched before Hazel responded. "I actually feel sick when I imagine not seeing him on Christmas Eve. Like it's the beginning of the end and I'll lose him for sure after that."

Claire sighed. "Ouch. That does sound painful. But does being physically close to him change anything? Either way, he isn't yours."

Hazel's sigh was deep. "I know. At least, on some level, I know. But I have to say something out loud even though it makes me feel like a total crazy person. Are you ready for this?"

Claire shot a glance at Jack, as if he could hear the conversation. His expression was puzzled, but there was amusement twinkling in his eyes. "I'm ready. Fire away."

"There's this part of me...and it's unfortunately not a small part of me, that thinks that things are going to change between us. That by keeping him close...I don't know. He's just eventually going to get it. Realize that what he's looking for is right under his nose and that he's been in love with me all along. And I don't know what it is that's going to make him realize that, so—"

"Hazel," Claire interrupted. "Sorry for cutting you off, but sometimes we need someone who cares about us to save us from our own brains." She sighed. "Do you think he's going to see you in a really gorgeous dress and things will move in slow motion as realization dawns on him? Or you'll get your hair cut and it'll be like the veil has been lifted and he can finally see clearly? On behalf of the romance industry, I think I owe you an apology. Those things that happen in books and in movies...it doesn't really work like that in real life."

"But sometimes it does." Hazel's voice was small. She sounded younger, more delicate than she had at any point prior. "You don't know that."

"You're right," said Claire, sending kindness and compassion through the line. "Friends *do* become lovers, it's true. But it doesn't happen because one of them talks the other one into it or is just always there..." She shrugged, sneaking a glance at Jack to find him watching her intently, something in his eyes that she couldn't quite read. "It's because there was something there all along. Or they both discovered it at the same time. Or they were separated and missed each other so much that they realized there was more at play." She pursed her lips. "I'm not trying to discourage you or be mean or give you some 'he's just not that into you' speech. I just don't want you to waste your life trying to talk someone into loving you when the right person will never need even the tiniest amount of convincing."

She looked up in the silence that followed to find Jack nodding along, a thoughtful, faraway look in his eyes.

"Hazel?" Claire asked. "You still there?"

"Yeah." The emotion was evident in Hazel's voice, and Claire wished she could reach through the line and hug her.

"I know I don't know you, so what I'm going to say might sound just like empty words." She looked up at Jack, her eyes meeting his. "But I've spent enough time with your brother to know that he's a good person. Got a good head on his shoulders and a good heart." She blew out a sigh. "And the fact that he cares about you so much...well, even if I didn't already believe in the inherent worth of every single woman all over the world, I would know that you are special, too. You and Jack both are." She smiled at him, at the confusion in his eyes. "And as much as I am confident that Jack deserves to be happy and loved and swept off his feet, I'm sure of the same thing for you, too. And I'm confident that the person who will jump at the chance to love you that way is out there. You just have to stop wasting time on lawyering your way into someone's heart."

Hazel sputtered. "*Lawyering*? What does that even mean?"

Claire blushed. She *may* have gotten carried away in her monologue about love worthiness. "You know...like, gathering evidence to make a convincing argument that will convince a jury of your peers that Daniel should find you guilty of deserving to be his girlfriend and then be sentenced to love you forever."

"Ah." Hazel was quiet, but Jack had a bemused look on his face.

Claire pressed on. "You know what to do about your Christmas tradition with Daniel. I don't have the answer, and I don't think Jack does either." One glance at him earned her a shrug in response, confirming her suspicion. "Relationships are more complicated than that. I could tell you not to see him, to take a break or cut him off completely..." She felt herself soften. "But he's not my best friend, so that's awfully easy for me to say. You have to do what's right for you. Though as someone who cares about you, I hope that whatever is right for you is *also* the option that will cause you the least pain."

"Thanks, Claire." Hazel's words came around a sniffle.

"You're welcome. I hope it helped." She shot a glance at Jack. "Did you want to talk to your brother again or...?"

Hazel let out a laugh that sounded wet. "No, that's okay. I don't think there's much that can be added to this conversation, but don't tell him I said that." She sighed. "He does usually give good advice, you know. I just think I'm all adviced out for right now."

Claire smiled. "Maybe a nap then. Be gentle with yourself."

"Thank you. Again. I would be embarrassed to be spilling all of this to you, except I really don't think I can help it right now."

Claire chuckled. "And we've already established that it comes with the territory. No need to feel embarrassed about anything at all. Unless you want to swap embarrassing stories just to lighten up the mood a bit?"

It sounded like Hazel was blowing her nose. "Maybe next time?" she asked with a soft laugh. "Give Jack my love. And have fun, you two."

When Claire had ended the call, she met Jack's inquisitive gaze with a tentative smile, feeling slightly shy, a little exposed. She had been aware of his presence there while she had shared with Hazel, and she found herself wondering now what he had thought about it all. Not that his opinion mattered more than whether or not the words had been helpful to Hazel.

But still, she couldn't help but wonder what her diatribe had looked like from the outside. Had it been too much? Too intense for her first real interaction with someone she didn't even know?

This was always the way, wasn't it? Even if conversation flowed in the moment and every word felt almost like she was channeling wisdom from a higher source, as soon as she had a moment to herself again, every word would be scrutinized. And if it was annoying in this moment, just think how much more obnoxious it would be when it was keeping her awake at 2am in an unfamiliar hotel room.

But Jack, apparently, didn't agree. "You," he said with a shake of his head, "In case you didn't already know it, you are like a wizard with words. I was watching you the whole time, as if I could take notes from your example and use them for the future when it's just little old me coaching Hazel through a moment like this." He shifted in his seat, leaning forward to straighten a spoon on the table. "But I couldn't come close to that, what you just did. I usually just suggest she get on a dating app or ask her if she wants me to have a word with Daniel."

Claire snorted, surprised by her own amusement. "And has she ever taken you up on that?"

Jack shook his head. "As much as she might struggle with the idea that 'someday' he's going to realize he loves her, even she knows that her big brother isn't going to talk him into it."

"That awareness makes my job a hell of a lot easier," said Claire with a smile. She leaned forward to take another bite of cake. "If Hazel needs a piece of cake chosen for her, you are definitely the man for that job." She licked the last traces of frosting from her lip, Jack's eyes tracking the movement. "You have great taste."

It was completely dark when they left the cafe for the Christmas market, though it was only five o'clock. Jack had suggested asking one of the friendly cafe workers for directions to the market, but Claire just shook her head as she tugged him out the door.

"We'll find it," she reassured Jack. "If we can't, then they've really failed at choosing a central location for it."

"A valid point," said Jack, tucking her hand into the crook of his elbow as he put his hands in his pockets.

They hadn't needed to worry, though. Between the bright lights and the steady stream of people heading in the direction of Marienplatz, it wasn't long before they found themselves gazing at the square covered in Christmas lights, the wooden stalls lit from within and selling a wide variety of goods, the crowd bustling around it all. And the smells...the sweet and savory smells, the spices...all of it beckoned Claire closer.

Taking it all in, Claire didn't realize she was frozen in place until Jack took her hand and started guiding her forward, towards the stalls.

"This is...lovely," she breathed, drinking it all in.

Jack was quiet as he nodded. "Your first one, too?"

"It is," said Claire, "But now I'm regretting all those evenings I ordered room service and crashed in my hotel room. If I'd known *this* was an option..."

Jack pointed in the direction of one of the more popular booths, judging by the line that had formed in front of it, and they started walking in that direction. "I imagine it would still be nice to come to one of these by yourself, but having someone to share it with seems like a vital part of the whole experience."

Claire was silent as her heart squeezed painfully. That was how it was supposed to be. If Bianca had been traveling with her, the two of them would have had so much fun. She would be coming away from this trip with more memories, more photos, inside jokes with one of her dearest friends...

Claire squeezed Jack's hand and gave him a smile. "I'm glad you're here with me." Now wasn't the time to dwell on the hurt of Bianca canceling her trip. That would only lead to frustration with her friend or fears about the future of Velvet Leaf, and that wasn't what tonight was about. She tried to push from her mind the reminder that Bianca would be calling her later, that even while this far away and this removed from the business of the day-to-day, the work side of writing could make itself known.

But even if today was going to end with bad news about the future of her career, that wasn't going to change anything right now. Claire could enjoy Jack's company and whatever came along with it at a German Christmas market.

"Oh, there they are!" Jack called over his shoulder as he tugged her towards a small table near the booth with the long line. He had spotted Hendrik and Jana, who were waving and gesturing the two of them over. Claire smiled and picked up her pace, eager to distract herself with some friendly faces and a festive mood.

Ten

"You made it!" said Hendrik with a broad grin. He elbowed Jana in the side and continued. "Jana said you were just being polite and there was no chance of the two of you actually coming tonight, and yet look at us." He gestured at the four of them. "I wouldn't have expected it either, and yet here we all are."

"I wouldn't let Hendrik get in the line for glühwein yet," said Jana, looking over at him with an almost boastful gaze. "I told him it wouldn't be good hosting behavior if we didn't at least wait for the two of you for some time." She rubbed her hands together. "Now that you're here, though...I see no reason not to join the line. You want glühwein, yes?"

"Is that mulled wine?" Claire asked, and when Jana nodded, Claire returned the gesture. "Then absolutely."

The two women fell into step as they approached the line, with Jack and Hendrik behind them. "Have you enjoyed Munich today?" Jana asked. "And how long are you staying? I don't think I asked you that."

"It's been lovely," said Claire, "though we are actually leaving tomorrow. It's sort of a mistake that Jack and I are even here. We were supposed to fly yesterday, but then the airline had oversold the flight and we both volunteered to take a later flight and spend 24 hours in the city."

"Wow," said Jana, who looked impressed. "That's quite the adventurous spirit. Where were you two coming from then?"

"I was here already, and Jack was coming from…Krakow, I believe?"

Jana looked puzzled. "You weren't traveling together? I think I missed something then."

"Oh, no." Claire was rushing to explain, already feeling her cheeks heat. "We just met this morning. After we separately volunteered to take the next flight. It's just dumb luck that the two of us actually get along and have been enjoying exploring Munich together."

"Right." The way Jana was eyeballing her now was pure skepticism. "But when the two of you came into the bookstore, it sure didn't seem like you were practically strangers. You were like…I don't know, like a couple who's been together for years and yet he's still so proud of her and the books she writes that he can't help stopping in every bookstore to buy a copy or get her to sign the stock." She pursed her lips. "On second thought, he probably wouldn't buy a copy in every bookstore. No one needs that many copies of the same book. Though he might buy a copy just to put it in one of those little free library things or hand it to a stranger who looks like they need to read a good old love story."

Claire laughed. "Well, believe it or not, Jack bought those books today because he's never actually read a word I've written before. And why would he, since we just met? But I appreciate what you're saying. It has been very...comfortable, the two of us spending time together. I think it's a very nice turn of events that the two of us ended up getting to spend this time together."

Jana shrugged. "Sure. I have to say, I read that book of yours, *Moonlit Melodies,* this afternoon after you left. I mean, I had to skim some parts of it because I was trying to finish it before I saw you here again today."

"Oh?" Claire felt that old familiar anxious feeling in her stomach that came when someone told her they'd read her work and didn't *immediately* offer their glowing opinion. Still, she asked the question she normally didn't dare ask. "What did you think?"

"Yeah, it was good. Not the kind of thing I normally read, but I liked it. It was cute." Jana smiled then. "Have you ever thought about writing, like, a true crime book? I would definitely read that."

Claire smiled back at her. "I...haven't. I think it would be kind of intense to be immersed in that world for the months that it takes to write a book, you know? At least with my little love stories, I'm surrounding myself with uplifting things. I think if I started looking at the darker side of humanity rather than the happily ever afters, I'd be sleeping with all my lights on."

"Oh, that's definitely true." Jana was nodding, her expression serious. "But even if it makes me a little...shall we say...*paranoid* when I'm home alone, at least it has taught me a lot about staying safe while I'm out in the city.

You know, not wearing headphones, paying attention to your surroundings, no ponytails, always carry your keys arranged between your fingers like this…" She pulled a hand out of her pocket to show Claire her keys poking out between her fingers like the world's worst Wolverine cosplay.

Claire asked Jana about her favorite true crime books, making mental notes of a few titles that she had little to no intention of ever reading. It wasn't that she didn't respect the genre, but the books she read had a way of working themselves into her writing style or works in progress, and the last thing one of her light-hearted women's fiction novels needed was a serial killer crouching behind the bumper of a parked car, knife at the ready.

When they had reached the front of the line, Jana turned to include Jack and Hendrik in their group. "What do you all want?" she asked. "This first round is on me. You can get glühwein or if you want something a little stronger you can get it with extra alcohol, or if you want just, like, some hot chocolate, I think they have that, too."

"Glühwein for me, please."

"Me, too."

"Make that three."

Jana nodded. "Hendrik, you can help me carry it back to the table. Claire and Jack, why don't you go find us a place?" She gestured towards the small tables nearby. There were tall tables interspersed with standalone heaters, and there was a vacant one that had their name on it.

Claire thanked Jana and set off, trusting that Jack was behind her. Something Jana had said, some observation she had made about Claire and Jack and whatever this thing between them was had made her almost painfully aware of herself, of him, and of their confusing unspoken dynamic. Having someone on the outside verbalize just how naturally they fit together, how easily they gave off the vibe of being an established couple rather than a couple of strangers...it was definitely troubling the water, making everything appear murky and uncertain.

There were two warring sensations at play. One reminded her that they were, in fact, nothing. They were strangers turned travel companions turned friends, and that was it. But the other side of her heart had loved the reality that Jana had seen, had hesitated to correct her. If, in the reality that existed only inside Jana's brain, Claire and Jack were a happy couple who visited bookstores and signed books and explored new cities and laughed and loved and drank cozy beverages...well, even if Claire couldn't actually live inside Jana's brain, couldn't she at least appreciate the iteration of herself that did? That version of Claire was loved and happy...and no longer existed, now that Claire had set the story straight.

"Everything okay?" Jack asked as Claire put her purse on the table next to her, claiming the whole surface, just in case any lone Christmas market connoisseurs wanted to join their little group.

She looked up, surprised, finding his gaze intent on hers. "Yeah, why wouldn't it be?" Had he been reading her thoughts? And if so, why? Was it because he was thinking the same thing? "What did you and Hendrik talk about?"

Jack smiled at the question, the corners of his eyes crinkling. "Oh man, Hendrik is great. He does all the tech support at the bookstore, and he's full of great stories. He's hilarious. We swapped numbers, and I think I actually want to keep in touch with him."

Claire felt her face drop just the slightest before she put her smile back in place. "That's nice," she said, and of course it was true. It *was* nice that Jack had enjoyed his brief chat with Hendrik enough to want to stay in touch with him. It was stupid of her to think that the fact that he had so easily befriended someone else, so naturally felt the desire to keep that person in his life, took anything away from the fact that the same thing had happened with her.

It did make her wonder, though, if they were on the same page. Claire had been traveling for weeks by herself and had met exactly one person she wanted to keep in her life. Sure, she had experienced plenty of hospitality and friendliness, but this thing with Jack wasn't like that.

Or at least it wasn't like that for her. Judging by how quickly he had decided he wanted Hendrik to be the best man at his wedding, she would guess his phone was full of contacts like "Cool Guy I Met At The Urinal" and "Police Officer Who Pulled Me Over For a Broken Tail Light." And she was destined just to be "Claire From The Munich Airport."

While she was still debating if she should say something to Jack—because did she *really* want to let him see the insecure side of herself that was desperate to know where she ranked in comparison to his new friend?—Hendrik and Jana were back with four steaming mugs, which they dispersed across the table.

"Okay, so, drink it while it's hot," said Hendrik, lifting his mug. "*Prost,*" he continued, bringing it towards their mugs so they could clink them together.

As they clinked their mugs together in turn, Jana suddenly interjected while placing a hand on Claire's arm. "Ah! No!" she exclaimed, shaking her head. "You have to make eye contact."

Claire and Jack had just clinked their glasses together, but Claire had been avoiding his gaze. She let out a nervous laugh then. "Okay..." she said with some confusion, repeating her attempt to tap their glasses together and achieving it that time.

"What's that about?" asked Jack, after taking a sip. "The eye contact, I mean."

Claire brought the mug to her lips and took a sip, immediately feeling the back of her throat tickle from the alcohol in the steam. The hot, spiced wine coated her tongue and warmed her all the way down to her toes. It tasted like a cozy winter day, right before Christmas, nestled in blankets in front of a roaring fire while something delicious baked in the oven and a blizzard came down outside.

"Seven years of bad sex," said Hendrik, interrupted her reverie.

"Sorry?" Claire sputtered, barely stopping herself from choking on her wine. "What did you say?"

"It's why you have to make eye contact when you cheers," said Jana. "If you don't, it's seven years of bad sex." She elbowed Claire in the side. "And I think for you, that might not be such a good thing for your job. How can you write love stories when you're stuck living seven years of bad sex?"

Claire exhaled an approximation of a laugh. *If Jana only knew.* She wasn't exactly writing sweeping love stories or steamy bedroom moments between her characters based on any kind of real-life inspiration. As a newly single lady—sure, it had been six months, so it was probably time to stop saying that—she hadn't necessarily been putting herself "out there" to give new romance any sort of chance to bloom.

And for the year that she had been with Eric, apart from the sparks-flying excitement at the very beginning of their time together, she had been finding her inspiration anywhere but her own life or her own bedroom. Perhaps that should have clued her in a little sooner to all that was broken between them.

Instead of saying any of that, Claire simply lifted her mug again, pointedly looking Jack in the eyes as she extended it towards him again, refusing even to blink until his mug met hers. She repeated the same thing with Jana and then with Hendrik before shrugging and taking another sip.

"You can't be too careful about these things, can you?" she said with a smile.

In the end, they stayed at the Christmas market for hours. However much Claire's energy had been waning while exploring the city, there was something about the market that had revived her.

They stayed at the table, sharing two mugs of glühwein before Hendrik suggested taking a turn around the stalls. Claire had purchased some handmade wooden ornaments to take home for her family, planning to tuck the carefully selected tiny works of art into each family member's stocking. They had also stopped in front of a few different booths that had pulled them in with the delicious smells that were wafting into the square. Jana bought a small bag of sweet, roasted almonds for them to share, and Jack purchased a large gingerbread heart that said "Meine Liebe" on it and they all broke off pieces to taste it.

Then, it had been time for some more mulled wine, then some German sausage, and one final round of wine—"We all have to treat the others to a round," Hendrik had insisted, while securing the final four mugs—and then Claire and Jack were making their way back to the hotel full, happy, and ever so slightly more tipsy than they had planned to be the night before their big journey.

"That was fun," said Jack, tucking Claire's arm into its rightful place in the crook of his elbow, probably hoping that the point of connection would help them both stay upright for the last few blocks of their journey. "More fun than I'm used to having outside on a December night, that's for sure."

"Ugh, you're so right." Claire groaned. "I don't even want to go back to New York now. Winter in my apartment is just prime time for all the loneliness and darkness. It's like, as soon as it's dark outside, I don't want to go out anymore. Which makes sense. I mean, did our ancestors leave their caves to go socialize when the sun was gone? Not likely!"

Jack sniffed. "It does make sense that so much more fun stuff happens in the summer because the sun's out longer. And it's warmer. Who wants to go to a barbecue when there's snow on the ground?"

"But they had the right idea at the Christmas market, didn't they? Outdoor heaters, hot wine, lots of festive lights...I think this was the most festive December evening I've ever had. Definitely since I was a kid." That thought made Claire smile. "I think this was the closest I've come to feeling the Christmas spirit since I was still a child who believed in Santa."

"If you're about to tell me that Santa isn't real, then don't. This was a nice evening, Claire, so just quit while you're ahead."

She shook her head as she bumped into him. "Don't you agree, though? I wish we had some more of this energy back in the US. I mean, it wouldn't help with the worst parts of winter, but at least it might help people get into the Christmas spirit more than all the hustle and bustle and time-sensitive sales and pressure to buy the right *stuff* for everyone on your list."

Jack was quick to nod in agreement. "No, it was definitely special. I'd like to come back here in December again. Maybe even for longer than 24 hours. What an idea!"

"I'd like to do that, too," said Claire, surprising herself. "And who knows, maybe we'll end up coming at the same time and having an airport reunion."

Jack looked at her, puzzled. "You don't think we would, I don't know, *tell* each other our plans? Are you planning to cut me loose as soon as we're back Stateside?"

Claire shrugged. "I don't know your life, Jack. I mean, look at Hendrik. It seems to me like you make friends so easily that you might not even notice if I did." She rushed to explain, to make it all seem better because she had clearly said more than she intended to. She could thank all the wine for her lack of filter. "I just mean that someone like you can definitely plan an impromptu trip to Germany and make enough friends and memories along the way that you don't need to coordinate plans with a travel buddy or anything like that. And you could bring Hazel! I bet she would love it."

"And you don't think my sister would love a trip to Munich even more if she could spend it hanging out with Claire Davis?" He shook his head, but his smile was playful. "It's not that I'm enjoying every part of this trip, every person I meet just as much as I've enjoyed getting to know you. I'm enjoying all of it *because* you're here, too. If not for you, I wouldn't have gone into that bookstore. And even if I had, I wouldn't have talked to Hendrik the way I did. Certainly wouldn't have made plans to meet up at the Christmas market." He shrugged. "I think everything is more fun and I'm more...I don't know...free? I feel more relaxed and more comfortable in my own skin and more...more inclined to seize every moment. To talk to strangers. Stay out late. Taste everything I can possibly taste." He stopped walking and turned to face her. "Make no mistake, Claire. I wouldn't be doing all of that without you here. I wouldn't be having these experiences, regardless. All of it is happening because of you."

Eleven

I f Jack's words had reassured her that he, too, felt a special connection between the two of them, they didn't exactly calm Claire down. Her heart was racing the rest of the walk back to the hotel, and her mind was doing the same.

What did that mean, exactly? What did the rest of the evening have in store for them, considering all that they had shared? Should they keep hanging out, maybe sit together in one of their rooms and watch a movie or make plans to meet up again once they were both settled back in the US? Claire wished there were someone she could talk all of this through with...and that's when she remembered.

"Oh, shoot!" She slapped her forehead with her palm. "I'm supposed to talk with my agent tonight. I totally lost track of time."

They had entered the lobby and were making their way to the elevator. Jack glanced at his watch and frowned. "Surely she'll understand if you need to reschedule. Can it wait?"

Claire shook her head, feeling some of the career panic that she had shoved down earlier start to resurface. "It's, like...career stuff, you know? She said she had to tell me something, and I'm honestly just dreading it. I feel like it's going to be bad news, and the longer I anticipate it, the worse it gets. If she just tells me tonight, then at least I'll stop eating myself up wondering what it is." Her hand found its way to her stomach, soothing in its touch. "Maybe I'll stop having constant stomach aches once I have some clarity about what's about to happen."

Jack pushed the button for the third floor as the elevator doors began to close. "But why would it be bad news? It doesn't take an expert publishing eye to see that you're successful, Claire. And as far as I know, agents don't fire their successful clients unless they're complete fools. Is your agent a fool?"

"She definitely isn't. She's wonderful, actually. I owe my whole career to her, or at least all the successful parts of it." She worried her lower lip with her teeth. "It's just something about this trip, though. The fact that she wasn't here for it, that she's been way less communicative than normal during it. It makes me wonder if there's something uncertain about the future. I don't know if it's my future, hers, or the publishing company's, but either way, it makes me nervous as hell." She shot a glance at Jack. "I shouldn't have said that to you. Forget I said it."

He frowned. "Why? Because you're speculating about the future of one of the big New York publishing houses?" He lifted a reassuring hand, waving it in front of him. "Rest assured, I don't have any reporters on speed dial who would just be dying for a tip off like that. And keep in mind that it's not exactly insider information, either, Claire. It's just a feeling. And before you can argue, I'm sure you're an intuitive person and often the things you feel are almost eerily perceptive. It's what makes you a good writer, and to the untrained eye, it might look like you have some kind of mind reading skills. Or you're a witch with psychic abilities." He winked at her then. "But I know the truth."

"What's that?" Claire gulped, her throat feeling dry as he continued to study her.

Jack stepped closer to her then. "The truth is, that sometimes your intuition is correct about something, and sometimes it's wrong about other things. You focus on the ones that were correct, especially in a moment like this. But can you think back to *any* other moment in your life when you just *knew* something was about to happen...and then it didn't?"

"P-probably," said Claire with a small shrug. At that moment, she couldn't think of a single moment from her entire past, not with Jack standing that close to her.

"What about today?" he asked, his eyes still on hers. "What about me? Oh, it's not exactly the same thing, but didn't you have some feeling about me right from the beginning? Some snap judgments about the kind of person I am, how little you would want to spend time with me, how boring I would be to talk to?"

"Tech Bro." She said, nodding. "That's how I referred to you when I texted my friend Emma. And you're right. You did surprise me. Although I did get the 'bro' part right. And I guess the 'tech' part, too. It's just when you put them together that they lose their meaning and no longer accurately describe you."

Jack's smile was small as he lifted a hand to tuck a few loose strands of hair behind her ear. "If I could surprise you like that, is there any chance that your agent could surprise you, too?"

Claire shook her head. "Lightning doesn't strike the same place twice, does it? You were the best surprise I could imagine, and I couldn't even imagine you. So now what? Bianca is going to tell me that I've been nominated for a Pulitzer? A Nobel Prize? I'm getting my own talk show? They're naming the auditorium after me at my university?"

A frown crossed Jack's face. "Would you want any of those things?"

"Not really." Her voice sounded small even to her own ears.

"Why can't it be something wonderful and something you can't even begin to guess? Why not just stay open to that possibility of something good?" He licked his lower lip and her eyes darted there to track the movement. "Or, barring that, you could at least acknowledge that everything is an unknown. All of this anxiety and worry, and she might just be calling to tell you that she didn't come along on the tour because she developed late-onset motion sickness." Jack shrugged. "It could happen, you know."

"You're right," said Claire, "And I'm a big enough person to admit that. I don't know what's about to happen and...yes, it's entirely possible that I'm *not* going to lose my job. This might have nothing to do with me at all."

"Exactly," Jack agreed. "And it might even be wonderful."

The elevator dinged to announce their arrival, pulling them apart and propelling them out the doors toward their rooms.

As Jack unlocked his door next to Claire, he turned to her again. "If you want to talk after your call, you know where to find me." He smiled. "I'm sure it will all be fine, but I'd still love to hear it from you."

"Thanks, Jack," she said with a forced smile. "Good night."

Was it her imagination, or had Jack's smile faltered at her words? "Good night, Claire."

Inside the room, Claire leaned against the closed door and let out a deep sigh. She wanted Jack to be right. Of course she did, even if she didn't dare hope he was. She wanted a lot of things where Jack was concerned, as it turned out. She stepped away from the door and into the room, pausing in front of the adjoining door between their two rooms. He was right there, right on the other side of the two doors. If she opened her door now, all that would separate them was his door. Would he open it? Was it already open?

She felt a thrill rush up her spine at the image of his door open, just waiting for her to open hers and discover it. Those two doors, open on either side of the tiny space separating them, just the thickness of the wall, would turn their two rooms into one large shared space if they were open.

Claire dug her phone from the pocket of her coat, smiling at the image of her cozy room turned into a large shared suite of sorts. She had no intention of being the first one to bridge that gap, didn't need to see the horrified look on Jack's face if she knocked on that door and burst the bubble of whatever this thing between them was. Sure, he liked her. That much was clear. But would he still like her if the walls literally came down, and they lost every semblance of mystery and privacy?

There was no way that was going to happen.

Claire sent a text to Bianca. "It's late, I'm sorry. But I'm here now if you still want to talk tonight. Let me know when you're free."

She reclined on the bed, scrolling through the apps on her phone while she waited for Bianca's call. Her dear agent was nothing if not devoted to her clients, and she had the unfortunate habit—well, it was only unfortunate if you were her friend, but it was *very* fortunate if you were her client—of being glued to her phone. It was bound to be just a few moments before she called. After all, Claire had been on the other side of this plenty of times—Bianca answering her phone during lunch, firing off a quick text with one hand while holding up a finger in the middle of Claire's sentence.

In the end, though, Bianca must not have called because Claire woke up in the dark room with her phone on her chest, still fully dressed. She groaned and checked the time on her phone—it was well after midnight now, and she needed to get some decent sleep if she was going to weather the journey tomorrow.

She hauled herself out of bed, peeling off her jeans and flinging them in the direction of the dresser. Her bra was next. It was only when she was digging her toothbrush and toothpaste from the bottom of her bag that she remembered her promise to share the toothpaste with Jack.

"Aw crap," she muttered. It was late. He was probably asleep. But she *had* promised he could borrow it, even told him not to bother buying his own tube. And if he was awake and could hear her rummaging around over here, wouldn't he wonder why she hadn't bothered about him?

At the same time, though, he might not be awake. She hadn't been, not until just a moment ago.

Claire picked up her phone again. She wouldn't dream of knocking on the door between their rooms, and she certainly wouldn't be venturing out into the hallway half dressed...but she could at least send Jack a text.

"Are you up? This isn't a booty text. I was just wondering if you still needed toothpaste. I fell asleep and forgot about it until just this very moment."

There was no immediate response from Jack, so Claire shuffled into the bathroom and splashed water on her face, before squeezing the toothpaste onto her brush and setting to work on cleaning her teeth. Her phone buzzed then with a message from Jack.

"Yes, please. Want me to come over and get it?"

She looked down at herself in horror, cataloging the sheer expanse of leg that was visible now that her jeans were ancient history. She hadn't thought this through, had she?

She wrote her response quickly, panic at the thought of hearing a knock on the door, speeding her fingers along. "Why don't we just open the adjoining doors a crack and I'll slip it to you? I'm not exactly dressed for the occasion, so definitely don't come over."

The sound of the text slipping through hyperspace to the room right next door had her rereading her words and slapping her forehead again. Did she really need to create a mental picture for Jack of what "dressed for the occasion" meant? Semi-consciousness was clearly not the best state to be writing impromptu messages in, and especially not ones where you had any interest in preserving some sense of mystery and mystique at all.

Claire spit out her toothpaste and rinsed her mouth, aware of the click of Jack unlocking his door, followed by a soft tap on hers. She screwed the cap back on her toothpaste, unlocked her own door and opened it just a crack, making sure to hide as much of her body behind the door as possible.

"Hi," she said, just her face and an arm extended to offer the toothpaste visible. "Sorry again for falling asleep. I really should have given this to you before all that happened."

"Not at all," said Jack, and he looked amused as he accepted the toothpaste. "Do you want me to give this right back to you?"

"No need." Claire waved a hand. "I'm going to sleep now, anyway." She let out a rueful laugh. "I'm dressed for it already, so I might as well."

Jack swallowed. "Yes, um...well. The way you're hiding behind that door there is making my imagination run wild. I'm thinking you're either wearing an embarrassing t-shirt that has a picture of your eighth-grade school photo or...orthodontic headgear?"

"I wish, but just remember that I'm the loser who didn't pack a change of clothes in my carry-on." She gestured to Jack, who was wearing a white t-shirt and a pair of sweatpants. "So I'm full-on Winnie the Pooh-ing it with a shirt and no pants at all. A. A. Milne would be so proud."

"Right," said Jack with a gulp. He held up one finger. "Hold on just one second, okay? Don't close the door."

He closed his own door until it was just ajar and disappeared. When he returned a moment later, he held out the toothpaste and another white t-shirt, which Claire accepted. She gave him a puzzled look, her eyebrow climbing her forehead.

"I borrowed some toothpaste, but I figured you would need it again in the morning. And you won't feel fresh tomorrow if you sleep in the same shirt you're wearing again. I had another one—a clean one, of course—and figured you might want to borrow it."

"Oh, that's...really nice. I'd give you a hug, but...well." She felt her cheeks heating just a bit and chuckled softly at herself. "Good night, Jack. I'll see you in the morning."

"Good night, Claire." His grin was wide. "What time are you getting up? We can go get breakfast together."

She rubbed her eyes. "I actually, believe it or not, didn't even set an alarm before I fell asleep. I was waiting for Bianca to call me back, but..."

"Right." Jack grimaced. "I didn't even ask about that. No call?"

Claire shook her head. "No call and not even a response to my text, so things are looking just *super* in my little world." She stifled a yawn. "Will you just knock when you wake up?"

"Of course."

They smiled at each other before closing the doors behind themselves. Claire lifted Jack's shirt to her nose and sniffed it, wondering what the inside of his luggage must smell like if an unworn t-shirt already carried the scent of his shampoo, his soap, and his presence. She chucked off her own shirt, letting it land with the rest of her discarded clothing before sliding Jack's shirt over her head. She flicked the lights off, collapsed onto the bed, and sank into a deep sleep.

...or at least she tried to.

But it was at least an hour before Claire's eyes closed for the night. As comforting as Jack's presence was in the form of his soft, cozy shirt, her mind was running through all the possibilities of what Bianca ignoring her text message could mean. It could be bad news for Velvet Leaf, of course, a possibility she never failed to consider. It could be bad news for her personally. But what if something had happened to Bianca? What if she had been mugged on the sidewalk, her purse stolen?

It was in the refrain of "what ifs" that Claire finally exhausted herself and fell fitfully into something resembling rest. She couldn't unearth the meaning behind Bianca's silence, no matter how many angles she approached it from in her mind.

Twelve

It took a moment for Claire to find her bearings in the morning, to make sense of the dull knocking sound coming from somewhere just beyond her feet. In her dream, someone was building one of the booths from yesterday's Christmas market, and the hammering was incessant.

"Enough!" she yelled, eyes popping open as she wrestled herself out of the blankets and finally realized where she was. Her hand flew to her mouth in embarrassment. "Oh shoot. Sorry, Jack! I thought you were a carpenter!"

Jack's deep laugh echoed through the door. "I will take that as a compliment, I guess. For what it's worth, I only knocked a few times."

"Ah." She had found her feet and was walking to the door now to talk to him through it. "In my dream, the hammering had been going on for hours, but I guess ten seconds in real life is the approximate equivalent of *ages* in dream time." She yawned and stretched.

"Want to meet in the hallway in ten minutes or so? I'm *dying* for some coffee. All that wine caught up to me, and I need caffeine injected straight into my bloodstream."

"Sounds good." She smiled to herself as she began gathering her clothes, preparing to clean herself up and get dressed for another day of travel. Jack hadn't even suggested opening the door between the rooms and she warmed at the thought. It was like he knew it would be too much, an intimacy that they didn't dare share to see each other with sleep-rumpled hair and puffy eyes. With a washed face, freshly brushed teeth, and at least a swipe of deodorant, they could reconnect in the hallway without the sheepish feelings that were inevitable when the situation felt too much like a sleepover.

Claire fluffed her hair, shrugging at her expression. "That's as good as it's going to get, I guess." She grabbed her coat and her purse and slipped out the door just in time to find Jack doing the same.

"Good morning, Claire." As her eyes met his for the first time that day, her heart lost time and then sped up to make up for it.

"Good morning, Jack." She smiled at him and he, naturally, smiled back. "How did you sleep?" They stepped away from the doors, slipping their keys back into pockets and purses.

"Very well," he said. "How about you?"

"Okay," said Claire, and Jack shot a look at her. "Okay, you caught me. I did sleep eventually, but it wasn't an easy journey to get there."

His smile was sympathetic as they started to make their way toward the elevators. "No word from Bianca?"

Claire shrugged, already reaching for her purse to retrieve her phone. "No calls came through last night, and I didn't even check yet to see if there was a text or an email." She groaned as she read the notifications on the screen, holding the phone out for Jack's inspection. There was just one message, from Bianca of course, and judging by the preview, it was disappointingly short.

"'Sorry I missed you,'" Claire read out loud. "'There's a lot going on here, but I'll update you when we talk again. Safe travels today!' You see?" She turned to Jack. "She isn't exactly trying to reassure me that nothing's wrong. I mean, what does 'a lot going on' even mean?"

Jack pursed his lips as he pushed the button for the elevator. "It could mean it's Christmas in two days and everyone is running around picking up last-minute gifts and dry cleaning their ugly sweaters. Or it could mean the office has been invaded by highly intelligent and incredibly lifelike robots and Bianca is trying to save the future of humanity without being found out and replaced by a droid that looks just like her."

"Now I think it's you who should write science fiction." Claire stepped into the elevator, shaking her head at Jack. "Would that story have a happy ending, though? Or would it end with the extinction of humans? Because I think I'd need to know that before picking it up."

"Hmm. Good question. Do you always know how your books are going to end before you've written them? Because, if I may be honest and confess a deep dark secret here...I *just* thought of that story idea. I haven't even perfected my"—he gestured around them, grimacing at the cheesiness of his joke—"*elevator* pitch yet."

Claire groaned. "That was terrible. Just terrible. And it feels like a crime that elevator pitches are called that because the journey is so short and you have to be concise...and yet somehow this journey feels like it's taking ten thousand years, thanks to your dad jokes."

"What can I say?" Jack shrugged. "I may not have any children, but I think I'd be a natural based on my sense of humor alone."

"Oh sure, that's definitely the most important qualification." As the door finally opened, Claire stepped out. "I'm not sure your question really needed an answer, but I'm going to pretend you're dying to know anyway, if only to create some distance between us and that joke."

"Absolutely." Jack nodded fervently. "For what it's worth, I *was* actually going to follow up and get my question answered, but I think I lost some brain cells back there in the elevator."

Claire walked through the doorway into the hotel's breakfast room. There was an array of dishes arranged for a buffet, and only as the smell of eggs and sausage reached her did Claire register just how hungry she was.

"I don't know the details of how a story will end, not always. But that's the thing about genre expectations, though. I always know there's going to be a happy ending, a happily ever after. So as long as the story works towards that, even if everything gets messed up along the way and it seems like our main characters will never find happiness...it all works out in the end."

They had picked up large empty plates and were slowly making their way through the line, piling on a little bit of everything. Jack looked thoughtful, taking a slice of brown bread for himself and offering one to Claire. "So you're never tempted to turn the story into something totally different? Like...the male main character turns out to be a crappy boyfriend and so the female main character plans the perfect crime to kill him and dispose of all the evidence? Or, if not that dark, at least to get him framed for something that will lock him away for years?"

Claire chuckled. "When I was going through a breakup, it was pretty hard to write all the ooey gooey feelings and warm fuzzies. I was definitely tempted by the revenge fantasy. But people don't pick up a Claire Davis book for revenge and murder, and I wouldn't even know where to begin writing something like that. To say nothing of the fact that my publisher would literally have kittens if I turned in a manuscript like that."

"That sounds like all the more reason to do it," said Jack. "Well, I should clarify. Would you get to keep the kittens? Because if so, I say go for it."

Her laugh was bigger now. "I would have to check the terms of my contract. But really, though, I love my little happy endings. And as much as it might be therapeutic for someone like Hazel to read them, it was probably just as good for me to write one at that point in my life. It wasn't like it made me believe in love again or anything like that..." She paused, tongs full of cheese poised in midair over her plate as she pondered her next words. "I think it was probably just helpful for me to remember that, even if my heart was a little broken, the world was still continuing. And also, the male characters I write are just *light years* ahead of my ex. It was hard to be sad about him when I was writing about one of them."

"Ah yes, is that the whole 'men written by women' thing? Hazel is always saying that about actors, characters..."

Claire nodded. "Yeah. The female gaze, I suppose."

They had made their way to an empty table by then, setting their plates down to claim spots and immediately making a beeline for the beverage station. Considering that it was a travel day, caffeine was more a necessity than ever. They fell into step, and Jack waited while Claire poured a cup, collecting packets of cream for the two of them. Without even asking, she took the mug from his hands and filled it, and he poured a packet of cream into her mug.

"Is one enough?" he asked, immediately opening another packet at the scowl that had appeared on her face. "Two it is then. Three? Really?"

When both cups were perfectly doctored—or at least as perfect as hotel coffee could be—they took their seats and dug in. After the easy conversation of the morning, they shared a comfortable silence, only breaking it to warn or encourage each other about the various elements on their plates.

"What do you think?" Claire asked as she leaned back in her chair, one hand flying to her stomach in appreciation of all the best parts of the meal she had just eaten. "Should we head to the airport pretty soon, then? How early do you normally like to get there?"

Jack shrugged, his posture mirroring hers as he sipped his second cup of coffee. "You probably do this traveling thing more than me, so I'd defer to you. I think they say, what, two hours is usually sufficient?"

"Three for international flights," said Claire with a nod. "And considering what happened yesterday, the fact that we don't have our luggage, and all the other extenuating factors..." She worried her lower lip with her front teeth. "I mean, yeah, I'd rather wander around Munich some more, maybe check out another cafe, but..."

"Say no more," said Jack. "I'd be stressed and worrying the whole time, too. I don't think there's a ton of room for enjoying a good cup of coffee if you're checking your watch every couple minutes to make sure you aren't missing your flight. Plus, we might find some decent coffee at the airport once we're through security."

"Sounds like a plan." Claire forced a smile, but now that they were talking about their travel plans for the day, the end was in sight. There was a part of her that was still pleasantly surprised to hear that Jack wanted to drink coffee with her at the airport, rather than parting ways as soon as the shuttle dropped them off at departures.

You really need to get a grip, she reminded herself with a sigh.

It was quick enough to pack up their things, at least—that was one perk of having only the bare minimum of luggage available. Claire folded up the t-shirt she had borrowed from Jack, then knocked on the door between their rooms.

When he answered, she smiled up at him and held out the shirt like an offering. "Thank you for this," she said. "And on behalf of whoever sits next to me on the plane, thank you again that I got at least a few hours off from wearing the same clothes."

Jack smiled back, but he didn't reach for the shirt. "Well, I hope and assume that I'm the one who will be sitting next to you, so thanks, and you're welcome at the same time." He dipped his head towards the shirt. "You're welcome to keep it, if you'd like. I know good sleep shirts are hard to come by."

She hesitated just long enough for him to chuckle and keep speaking. "I don't mean, for example, that I'm afraid of cooties and don't want to take the shirt back now that you've touched it. I gladly will." He leaned down then, bringing his nose close to the shirt and taking a deep inhale, much to her embarrassment. "It smells like you now, which is a perfectly delightful turn of events. If I take it back and wear it, it'll be the perfect role reversal." He straightened up then, his smile sincere. "Seriously, you're welcome to it. And I will support you, whatever you decide." He scratched the back of his neck. "I was under the impression that women love to steal men's clothing, though I'm ready to admit that there's more nuance to that situation than I am aware of."

Claire barked out a laugh. "I mean, yeah. We don't generally go around stealing men's jackets while they aren't looking or...I don't know, instead of pick pocketing, like, pick pantsing? Swiping your pants right from under your very eyes without you even noticing? It's mostly boyfriends' hoodies, actually." She wrapped her arms around herself, closing her eyes and smiling at the feeling she had just conjured. "There's nothing cozier or more comforting than a man's hoodie. I don't know why, but

I swear they're made of softer material than any I've ever bought in the women's department."

Jack cleared his throat and Claire opened her eyes at the sound. "That's all duly noted," he said. "And I realize a travel buddy's t-shirt isn't quite on the same level as a boyfriend's hoodie, but—"

"I'll keep it," she interrupted, pulling the shirt close and moving to shut the door between them. "Let me just tuck it in my bag and then we can head down? You about ready?"

Jack nodded, leaning against the door frame. "Ready whenever you are."

The trip back to the airport in the shuttle was uneventful, yet Claire's thoughts were flying a mile a minute as she stared out the window. How was it possible that in the time since she had been in this vehicle, since she and Jack had shared their first words, everything had changed between them?

Less than 24 hours before, she had been on this shuttle with a stranger, one she had judged from first sight that she had no interest in getting to know. She had looked out the window at the city and envisioned very little of what had actually transpired there. No, if Claire had been left to her own devices, she might have ventured into the heart of Munich to visit a cafe and not much more than that. She certainly would have missed out on the Christmas market, likely spending the evening crashed out in her hotel room eating purse snacks and flipping channels on the German television.

The time she had spent with Jack had enriched her stay in Munich immeasurably. More than that, though, it had quickly and easily become the highlight of her entire European trip.

That was dangerous thinking, though. That way led thoughts like, *"I've never had a better travel companion than Jack"* and *"I bet* anything *Jack and I share would be pure magic—what if we were* more *than just travel companions?"*

One day at a time. That was her mantra—*had* to be her mantra—even when the previous day had been one of the best in a long time. Let today bring whatever it would bring and let tomorrow worry about itself.

Jack, who was sitting next to her this time rather than being across the aisle, bumped her with his shoulder. "You okay?" he asked. He nodded towards the window, where she had been staring for the past ten minutes. "It seemed like you disappeared there."

Claire shrugged. "Just thinking, I guess. It's always a little weird right before a long travel day, but this has all been so unexpected. I think I'm trying to wrap my head around it still."

Jack reached for her hand, gave it a quick squeeze, and replaced it on her knee. It all happened so quickly that Claire wasn't sure if she had imagined the gesture. "Don't overthink it," he said. "For what it's worth, though, I kind of wish we were staying longer."

Me, too, Claire thought to herself.

Thirteen

The often slow-moving stages between arriving at the airport and finding the right gate for departure were all moving seamlessly that day. It seemed mere minutes between the shuttle drop-off and their arrival on the other side of the security line, with Jack tucking his laptop back into his carryon bag while Claire checked her phone for new emails. At the airline check-in counter, they had been assured that their bags were waiting to be loaded onto the plane and that their boarding passes had already been issued.

When the counter agent had gone to print the boarding passes, Jack had interrupted. "Is it possible for the two of us to sit together, by any chance?" He glanced over his shoulder, down at Claire with a quick nod, as if to confirm that was what she wanted.

Of course she had. If she had been asked for a seat preference, she wouldn't have cared if her options were window or aisle or even business class or economy. The only thing that really mattered in that moment, the only secret desire she would have dared voice to a genie, a wizard, or a fairy godmother, would be to spend the day as close to Jack as possible.

"That's no problem at all," the counter agent had said shortly before handing them back their passports, boarding passes tucked inside. "Have a nice flight."

Once they had confirmed their gate by sight—it was empty, after all, considering just how early they had arrived at the airport—they had plenty of time to kill before anyone would be getting on their plane. In fact, it hadn't arrived yet, but Claire reminded herself that it was bound to be there with plenty of time to spare. As much as she might have enjoyed the idea of fate intervening to grant her some extra time in Munich with Jack—"all the flights were canceled, Mom! I swear I tried everything in my power to make it back home for Christmas but it looks like I'm stranded her until New Year's at the earliest"—her rational mind didn't actually believe that was a possible outcome for the day. And if she was to be spending the day traveling back to New York, then the least the universe could do was make sure there were no delays and smooth travels. If she could make an extra request and ask for no turbulence and all the passengers waiting patiently to deboard rather than crowding the aisles as soon as the plane landed, then she'd take those as well. After all, she had done a good thing the day before by giving up her place on the plane. It must be a law—of karma or of nature—that doing a good deed like that entitled her to an extra special travel experience today.

"Coffee?" Jack asked after they had stared at the gate for a solid minute. "Snacks? A beer? Pretzel? Sausage?"

Claire groaned. "As much as I would love to eat all the things and squeeze *at least* one more delicious German meal into our time here...coffee, it is." She felt a small smile forming at the corner of her mouth. "Okay, and maybe something from the bakery. Twist my arm, why don't you?"

The first cafe they found was a Starbucks, but Claire just shook her head and kept walking. "It's about to be all Starbucks, all the time. Let's at least pretend to try to find something German. Vaguely European, even. Just not the best coffee Seattle has to offer."

Jack raised his eyebrows. "I think Seattle's Best would take exception to that remark." He tilted his head towards a small cafe further down the concourse. "Think that will meet your needs?"

"There's only one way to find out," said Claire as she started walking more quickly in the direction of the cafe.

Half an hour later, when the last drops of coffee were gone—Claire had opted for a latte while Jack had tried the cafe's drip coffee and appraised it positively—and the crumbs of the three pastries they had shared were all eaten, Claire sighed. "That was definitely a good choice," she said. She nodded towards the empty plates, where their strudel and stollen had been. "Now if I could just find a cafe in New York that sells those, I won't spend every remaining breakfast of this lifetime being disappointed."

Jack recoiled slightly. "Yikes. No, we definitely don't want that for you. But even if there aren't any good German bakeries near you...I mean, that does sound more like a midwestern thing to me. Maybe it's time for you to take a trip to Frankenmuth? No, but even if you can't find a stollen that compares, maybe you could at least find a recipe."

Claire scoffed. "I am many things, Jack, but a baker is not one of them. Plus, when you make something yourself, it's never as good as when someone else makes it."

He tilted his head to the side in thought. "Really? That can't *always* be true. I mean, yes, coffee does often taste better when someone else makes it. Exceptions to that, of course, are hotels and a fairly long list of restaurants. I would take my homemade brew over that anytime. But even if I had an espresso machine, I suspect someone else's americanos and cappuccinos would always be superior. But what about homemade pizza?"

Claire shrugged. "I've never tried making it, so how would I know? I said I'm not a baker, and I wasn't kidding. I don't just mean I don't bake cookies…I mean I don't use my oven at *all*. Well, that's not true. I do use it for storage sometimes. Space is a premium in an apartment, after all. It's just a waste to have a perfectly good cupboard going empty."

"Yes, because it's *not* a cupboard. It's a very special receptacle that can withstand temperatures up to 500 degrees Fahrenheit. I hope you at least aren't filling it full of flammable things."

"Oh yeah, it's just full of hairspray and gasoline," said Claire with an exaggerated eye roll. "No, it's mostly pots and pans. Occasionally a loaf of bread, but I usually forget those are in there and it ends up being a gross mess. Don't look so horrified, Jack. I can't be the first person you've met who does this."

"You might actually be. I've seen apartments in the city that don't have ovens at all. A few that didn't even have kitchens. One that didn't have its own bathroom and was clearly using the word 'apartment' way too loosely. Maybe I should come visit you sometime and break that oven in for you."

Claire raised an eyebrow. "You bake?"

Jack wrinkled his nose. "Let's use the term loosely, and then I can say yes. I'm not much of a baker, but I do dabble from time to time. Mostly pizza. Hazel is the real pro, though. If you find a recipe for stollen, I'd give her a crack at it."

"Good to know," said Claire. She was schooling her expression, trying not to give away the full extent of joy she was feeling at Jack's suggestion that he come to her home, that his sister try out a recipe for her. All her fears about this thing between them evaporating as soon as they were back on American soil were in danger of vanishing if she didn't hold on to them more tightly. Time for a subject change. "So you really live in New York City and yet make your own pizza?" She shook her head. "What will people say, Jack?"

He held up his hands in mock protest. "I never said anything bad about a New York slice, and you can't pin that on me. It just happened one winter, one particularly snowy day when I was younger and my mom said there was too much snow and we couldn't drive anywhere. She suggested we make pizza, and I looked at her with just about as much skepticism as you're looking at me now." He shrugged. "But the end result was...well, the taste buds don't lie. It became sort of a family tradition after that, and we bake pizzas together every year. Usually sometime between Christmas and New Year." He exhaled a laugh.

"We Holloways may not bake Christmas cookies, but we bake a *fine* Christmas pizza."

Claire nodded in thought. "That sounds like a nice tradition, actually. Especially since it's in the week between Christmas and New Year and not yet another thing that has to be done before the holiday actually starts. The only tradition I get excited about year after year is my Christmas movie marathon with my friend Emma on Christmas Eve Eve, but that hasn't exactly been a thing since she moved to Ireland."

Jack raised his eyebrows. "I should think not. That commute would be a killer. Did you get to see her while you were traveling these last few weeks?"

"I did." Claire nodded. "And we got our marathon in, even if it was a little early."

"Will you still have your Christmas Eve Eve tradition on your own?"

"What, today?" She shrugged. "I mean, I guess it depends on how the day goes. If there is a selection of Christmas movies on the plane, then that's close enough. But I doubt there's going to be much of anything happening at home tonight that isn't sleeping."

"Should we...?" Jack gestured to their tray. "I don't know...walk and talk?"

"Yeah, sounds good." Claire got to her feet and took the tray to the receptacle by the trash bin, where they began sorting out their trash and dishes.

"Are you going to your own place tonight?" Jack asked, then flushed based on something he must have seen in her reaction. "I'm not inviting myself over or anything. Just wondering if you're going to be alone or if your family traditions are kicking off as soon as you arrive."

"My dad is picking me up," Claire explained. "Taking me to New Jersey. And when I crash and sleep for twelve hours, I'll be doing it in my childhood bedroom. It'll be nice to stay there for a few days while I readjust. What about you?"

Jack nodded. "Pretty much the same. Hazel wants to pick me up, but I haven't decided yet if I'm going to let her. And I'm doubtful that I'll be getting a ton of rest this evening. Once I'm actually there in person, I have a feeling there's going to be a *lot* of talking happening. At some point, though, I'll tell her to go read one of your books and call me in the morning."

"That sounds like the kind of prescription more doctors should give. And I'm not just saying that because if my royalties could rival the kind of money drug companies make, I'd be living a *very* different life."

"Of course you aren't," said Jack with a smile. "I know you believe more romance would make the world a better place. And"—he hurried to continue as she frowned at him—"I'm inclined to agree with you. I started reading *Serendipity Springs* last night, and I think I'm already hooked."

"Oh?" Claire raised an eyebrow. "I...well, I'll try not to read along over your shoulder if you pick it up on the plane, but I'm not going to lie, I'm *really* curious what you'll think about it."

He stopped and turned to face her, a slight frown on his face. "Why? Claire, you know you're good at what you do. You don't need my opinion—or anyone else's, for that matter—to assure you of that. *Plus*, I'm already sure I'm going to like it. It's not like I read a ton of romance to compare it to, for one thing, and for another thing, stories of human connection are universally appealing. If I read it and said it was just okay, that would be about me and not about you." He put a hand on her shoulder lightly. "That won't happen, though. Both because I already do like it and because I'm not a jerk. Just in case you didn't know that."

She chuckled softly as she shook her head. "I did have a sneaking suspicion that you weren't a jerk, but thanks for confirming it."

"Happy to be of service. Now..." He rubbed his palms together and looked around. "Since we've been talking about this book, I'm itching to do some more reading. Shall we make our way to the gate? Stop and get some snacks and water along the way?"

"Sounds like a perfect plan."

Claire had done her best not to be a passenger seat reader. She really had. But she couldn't help it that whenever Jack exhaled a soft sound of amusement, her curiosity got the best of her and she simply *had* to peek over his shoulder and see what had inspired the reaction.

She had tried to be subtle about it, but he had caught her in the act. As her eyes had been skimming the page, noting that this particular reaction must have been triggered by Hector's first attempt at convincing Isabel to go on a date with him, the words were suddenly obscured by Jack's long fingers. It took a second for her to realize that both pages were, in fact, covered by Jack's hands and that he was looking at her with a quizzical expression on his face.

"Ah," she said when their eyes met and her mouth pulled to the side in a grimace. "Right. Not supposed to do that, am I?"

But he just smiled back at her. "You can do whatever you want. I just wanted you to know you aren't as sneaky as you think. So if you're going to read over my shoulder, feel free to do it loudly and proudly. This is a great book, and I think you'd really enjoy it."

Claire shook her head at him and chuckled softly at herself. It was a strange yet welcome sensation to enjoy her own work like that. It had been so long since she had written *Serendipity Springs,* and so many other characters and plots had filled her mind and her days since then, that reading the words on the page had felt like visiting an old friend. She had almost no recollection of the agony of round after round of edits on that particular story, detached enough from it to enjoy it purely for its heart and humor.

It had been a journey to get to that point, of course. Claire had started writing as a natural next step after devouring more books in a year than many people did in a decade. That transition had led to all sorts of unexpected emotional landmines, from not being able to enjoy a movie because her writer brain was dissecting its structure to losing the old standby comfort of a good novel because she was so consumed by comparisonitis and imposter syndrome.

Thankfully, that was all more or less in the past now, thought Claire as she fished a thriller out of her carry-on bag and dove in. Mysteries and thrillers were her favorites for a travel day, stories that pulled her in and kept her guessing and striving to figure out the plot twists, without engaging her romance writer brain. There was a stack of recently released romance novels waiting for her on the nightstand at her apartment, though, set there with the specific intention that once her trip was over and she had a bit of time off, there was nothing on her agenda but copious amounts of hot chocolate and muscle cramps developing from sitting for way too long in the same position while reading "just one more chapter."

That was, of course, assuming that the upcoming weeks were actually "time off" and not "time after losing one job while frantically searching for the next one."

On that thought... Claire shook her head and cracked open her novel, glancing back a few paragraphs to remind herself where she had left off.

And that was when she heard it. There was the crackling of a microphone coming to life and then the words that had changed everything just yesterday. The sound was so familiar that she wondered if she had conjured it into existence. If her wishes to extend her time in Munich had willed it into being.

But, unmistakably, there it was: *"Attention passengers. Our flight today is overbooked. We are looking for two passengers to take the same flight tomorrow. You will be put up in a hotel overnight, and you will receive meal vouchers, as well as a payment of 500 euros. Please come see me at the counter if you are interested."*

Claire stared at her book for a moment, not daring to believe that the sentences she had just heard existed outside her head. Her skin prickled as if she were being studied, and she chanced a glance in Jack's direction to find him already looking at her, a smile blooming as soon as their eyes met.

"Are you thinking what I'm thinking?" he asked, holding out his hand to her.

Fourteen

But Claire was already on her feet, already feeling herself pulled towards the counter by the same magnetic force that had tugged her there the day before. Coming to her senses, she paused, looking back at Jack who was still gathering his things—as well as the book, sweatshirt, and water bottle she had left behind in her haste.

He joined her halfway to the counter, chuckling softly to himself.

"This *was* what you were thinking, right?" Claire asked as a thought suddenly occurred to her. "You weren't suggesting we should definitely *not* take the offer, right? Like, we should wait and see who would accept it and then give them some pointers for how to spend the day?"

He shook his head, nudging her forward to the counter. "Not at all. I didn't want this time to be finished, and I don't think you did either. And when life gives you the thing you've spent all morning wishing for, you'd have to be a fool not to accept it."

"That's true. So you're saying it's big of me to admit that I wanted this?"

"Absolutely. How else are you supposed to get it?"

They were in front of the counter now, the same agent from the day before greeting them with a smile and slightly quizzical expression. If she actually recognized the two of them from the previous day's attempted flight, Claire would be seriously impressed. Then again, it was probably to the benefit of airline employees and to the ultimate security of everyone at the airport for airline staff to be good with faces.

"Can I help you?" the agent asked, fingers poised on her keyboard.

Jack spoke up. "We heard the offer for two people to take the next flight tomorrow, and we wanted to accept it."

The woman behind the counter studied both of them more carefully. "Did you...?" she began, her eyes darting back and forth from one to the other.

"We both accepted the same offer yesterday. Alone. But then we became friends and spent the day exploring Munich together, and now we want to do it all again," offered Claire.

"Right..." The woman paused, as if she were thinking through the deeper implications of Claire's words. "You really want to stay again? The offer doesn't get any better, I'm afraid, the more days in a row you take it."

"Oh. No." Claire exchanged a glance with Jack and continued speaking. "We aren't planning on making a life or a career out of staying in Munich one day at a time. And I'm pretty sure we do both need to get back home before Christmas comes. But today?" She shrugged. "We can do today. One more day in Munich sounds like a fun adventure, and I don't think you could talk either one of us out of it if you tried."

"Very well then," the woman said as she began typing on the computer. "In that case, I believe you know how this all works. Please wait just a moment while we gather the vouchers for you and arrange the shuttle to the hotel."

"Oh! I almost forgot," Jack interjected. "Would it be possible for us to have our suitcases with us at the hotel? One day of living out of your carry-on is fine, but a second day is pushing it."

"You didn't have your bags with you last night?" The woman looked horrified. "I'm very sorry about that. That was an oversight on our part." A thoughtful expression crossed her face. "Let me just see one thing here..." She continued to tap away on the keyboard, her fingers flying so rapidly that Claire couldn't even begin to imagine what she was doing. Sending a newsy holiday email to her great uncle? That was possible. Writing the last ten pages of her thesis? Only time would tell.

"There," the woman said finally, a pleased expression lifting her features. "Everything is all taken care of. If you'd just have a seat over here, I'll have your bags here shortly."

Claire perched on the seat next to Jack, leaning into his space to whisper to him, unable to stop the grin from spreading wider across her face. "I am *so* freaking excited about this," she hissed. "Just *think* of all the fun we're going to have! We can go to the Christmas market again—"

"Duh," Jack cut in. "I couldn't even tell you what else I want to do today, but a second night at the Christmas market is a must. Should I text Hendrik and let him know?"

Claire bit her lip as a bitter feeling blossomed in her stomach. Was it selfish to want to keep Jack for herself on this bonus day? If so, why should she care? If the universe was in the business of granting wishes, then she didn't need to keep *any* of her desires to herself. "Don't," she said with a shake of her head. "Nothing against him or Jana, but don't you think it would be kind of fun to experience it, just the two of us?"

Jack nodded, looking pleased, but didn't say anything. Was it her imagination, or had his ears turned pink at the edges?

"We should let people know," she said, digging her phone from her pocket. "Make sure no one heads to the airport this evening to pick us up from a flight that we aren't on. And promise them we'll be there tomorrow."

Jack shot her a glance. "Can you really make that promise? If the same offer comes up again tomorrow, you won't take it?"

She grimaced. "I will probably want to take it...but maybe by tomorrow I will have gotten this city out of my system and be ready to breathe some New York air. Plus, we're cutting it dangerously close to missing the holidays entirely. And what's next once you miss Christmas? Will we be in Germany through New Year's Eve? Valentine's Day? St. Patrick's Day? Where does it end? Where do you draw the line?"

Jack was already tapping away on his phone, no doubt sending an update to Hazel and his parents, shaking his head at her at the same time. "I'm ignoring you," he explained, "because you're taking a perfectly legitimate concern and making it ridiculous. It's understandable if my parents or yours are worried about the meaning of a member of the family missing Christmas.”

Claire gasped in fake affront. “And you don’t think they’re entitled to feel exactly the same way about me sitting out President’s Day? Where is your holiday spirit, mister?”

She tutted her disapproval, then fired off a few text messages. There was a quick message in the group chat to her parents, letting them know her plans had been delayed by one more day, along with a similar message to Bianca. She refused to acknowledge the unspoken elephant in the room that was eating up all the oxygen…if Bianca wanted to talk to her, she would figure out a way to do it that didn’t involve teasing and torturing Claire.

The final message she sent was to Emma.

“So, guess who’s once again jumping at the chance to take the next flight tomorrow and spend a fun and frisky day exploring Munich? I’ll give you a hint: it’s not just me, but I feel a lot differently about the other person than I did at this time yesterday.”

Emma sent back a solid line of exclamation points, followed by another line of question marks. “What do you mean? Can’t the airline get their shit together and get you back to the States? Or is something brewing between you and Mr. Tech Bro? Blink twice if you need to be rescued. I can be there in, like, 8 hours.”

Claire sighed as she wrote back. “I definitely could have flown back today if I wanted to. But Jack and I both thought it sounded like more fun to have an extra bonus day in Munich, on top of the bonus day we already spent here.”

"Okayyyyy...so you're not being held against your will?"

"Not even a little bit. And in case you were wondering, though apparently you weren't, I'm not holding him here against his will either."

That earned her an emoji rolling its eyes skyward. "As if anyone 'stuck' spending a day with you could do it against their will. I'm totally jealous of Tech Bro, by the way. I wish it was me getting to hang out with you all day. Are you going to allow him to participate in Christmas Eve Eve today?"

Claire pursed her lips in thought, tapping her nails on the edge of the screen before writing back. "Good question. I suppose I could put the offer on the table. Considering that you let Connor participate from the very first week you met him, I don't think I'd be violating a sacred contract or anything like that."

More eye rolls. "Not why I was asking, but good to know. Just...have fun and be safe and get home eventually, okay? And let me know when you do."

"Would I ever not tell you something like that? For all the mundane details of my day-to-day life that I readily share with you, I think you can rest confidently knowing I'll share any transatlantic flight details with you."

She sent one final message before tucking her phone back in her pocket: "By the way, if you and Connor want to come crash Christmas Eve Eve at the hotel, you'd be more than welcome."

Emma's response came quickly enough that the phone vibrated before Claire had even released her grip. She pulled it back out and smiled at the message. "I would in a heartbeat. But something tells me that this little two person party you have going on with Tech Bro definitely doesn't need to be crashed." As if the meaning of her message weren't obvious enough, Emma had included a series of emojis, starting with a winking eye, then progressing to a kissing face, and ending with a face surrounded in hearts.

A uniformed man approached the bench where they were sitting then. "Mr. Holloway and Ms. Davis?" he asked. At their nod, he gestured for them to follow him. "I'll escort you to the shuttle. Your suitcases have already been collected and will meet us there. I believe you already have all your vouchers and compensation accounted for?"

"We do." Jack nodded, handing Claire her sweatshirt, water bottle, and book. A brief thought flashed through her mind, a question of how she had managed to travel for the past few weeks on her own without losing any of her possessions. Maybe she was just more careful when she didn't have someone else to lean on, but now that Jack was here, she could really just relax...and apparently come dangerously close to leaving half of her carry-on luggage behind when she walked away.

The shuttle was identical to the one that had carried them to the airport that morning, all the way down to the driver, who did a double take when he saw them.

"It's really us again," said Claire with a smile. "We just can't get enough of that hotel of yours." He looked puzzled and didn't say anything in response, but at least he returned her smile.

"It's nice to see this bad boy again," she said as she slapped the side of her suitcase and took a seat. "I think the first order of business, for me anyway, is a shower and a change of clothes. What do you think? Head out after that?"

Jack had taken a seat across the aisle from her again, both of them taking up the empty seat next to them with their suitcases. "That's a good plan," he said. "I can't say there's anything too specific that I'm dying to do in the daytime, either, so if you've got any ideas, I'm all ears."

Claire shrugged. "I think after I shower, I'll be searching on my phone for the must see places in Munich. Because off the top of my head, all I can think of is Oktoberfest and I am pretty sure that's irrelevant right now. Unless there's a Decemberfest that I don't know about."

Jack shook his head at her. "And you think my jokes are bad? How much more Decemberfest can you get than a full-on Christmas market, though? Maybe we could go to the English Garden and walk around a bit? Can't go wrong with a little fresh air before a big travel day."

"We have to stop talking about big travel days," said Claire, "Or I'm afraid we'll end up stuck in this weird travel purgatory where we're always getting ready to fly across an ocean tomorrow and yet tomorrow just never comes."

"It's too soon to say if just because we haven't been able to leave twice if we've actually found ourselves in some sort of *Hotel California* situation. Especially considering that we were both willing participants in our travel delays. In fact..." He gave her a meaningful look. "You might even say we *volunteered* for our travel delays."

But Claire just rolled her eyes at him and went back to looking out the window. It had a twofold benefit, in that she got to admire the passing scenery while also hiding the smile that had spread across her face. Of course they were both excited for the extra time in Munich, a little extra adventure, but that didn't mean she needed to be so expressive about it.

At the hotel, Klaus appeared completely unsurprised to see them—or else he had the best poker face Claire had ever seen. "Welcome back, Mr. Holloway and Ms. Davis. We received your reservation from the airline, and we have upgraded you to a suite per their request."

Ah. So *that* was why he wasn't surprised to see them. Of course he had already spoken with the airline staff, but...

Hang on a second. What did he say? Claire thought, but Jack was already speaking up.

"I think there's been a mistake, Klaus," he said, leaning in with concern. "We need two rooms, and neither one of them needs to be a suite. Ms. Davis and I aren't traveling together."

Klaus raised a skeptical eyebrow. "I knew this was happening yesterday, but still I played along with your whole role-playing charade. But when the airline called and said the two of you were coming back again and then asked for an upgraded room given that it was the second night in a row you would be staying here, the truth was revealed. I'm afraid the reservation is locked in the system and unless one of you wants to pay out of pocket for another room, then it's the presidential suite for you. Such a hardship, I'm sure."

Jack's hand reached for his pocket, but Claire put a hand on his forearm to stop him. "It's okay," she said with a small nod. "We don't need another room." She hated the thought of Jack spending his own money on nothing more than a bed to sleep in that night just as much as she hated the thought of whipping out her own credit card and letting Klaus run it through the machine. She looked back at Klaus then. "I'm sure the room—the suite, in fact—has at least two beds, right?" When Klaus nodded, she looked back at Jack. "Then it's fine. It's hardly any different from having two adjoining rooms like we did yesterday."

Klaus pursed his lips, but when neither of them raised additional objections, he began to speak again. "The presidential suite features a king size bed with an en-suite bathroom, as well as a kitchenette and living room with a fold-out couch. Will you be needing linens for the fold-out couch as well?" He raised an eyebrow as if he were asking the question of our mere formality, but Jack nodded.

"Yes, please," he said. "I'll sleep on the couch."

Claire smiled and nodded along, though she felt the vaguest flash of disappointment. It wasn't that she wanted to share a bed with Jack, necessarily, or that she was unaware of just how awkward it would be to do that—what, would they build a wall of pillows down the middle to ensure that no touching happened? It might be Jack's perceived resistance to being near her that was making her feel a bit off, or it might just be the fact that she was practically on the verge of living out one of her favorite romance tropes to write, only to have it pulled from her grasp.

"Only one bed" is way better on paper than in real life, she reassured herself. *In real life, it's all awkwardly positioned*

bodies, no rest for anyone, and it ends with morning breath and pre-caffeine conversation. At least this way we'll both get some sleep and still have the maximum amount of time to hang out as well.

Klaus handed them their keys, directed them to the already familiar elevator, and assured them that a housekeeper would be up with extra linens soon. Jack and Claire thanked him for his help and were silent until the elevator doors closed behind them.

As soon as the last sliver of the lobby disappeared behind the silver doors, she chanced a glance at Jack, only to find him already peeking in her direction. When their eyes met, laughs bubbled out of both of them and built until they had dissolved into a fit of giggles.

"That was…" Jack trailed off. "I'm not sure what that was. The pinnacle of awkward human interactions? Something that should only happen in the pages of one of your novels?"

Claire dabbed at her eyes. "I just don't know if I've ever been misunderstood that badly before. It's like, no matter what we say and no matter what we do, he is determined to believe that we're a role-playing couple who's been together since the very beginning, but we just like pretending that we're strangers. I mean, I know things like that happen…I'm just pretty sure they mostly happen in movies, I guess. Not at sleepy little hotels that should be closed for the holidays, anyway." She looked suddenly at Jack with a sober expression. "Do you think that's what it is? He's just bored and needs a little excitement? If so, who are we do deprive him of that?"

They approached the door of their room—their *suite*, Claire reminded herself—and Jack swiped it open with the key. As the light turned green, just a second before he turned the handle, Claire felt a flash of something stir inside her. Excitement? Nerves? Who could say which one was dominating? All she knew was that she was about to be alone inside this hotel room with Jack Holloway and there was no part of her that was prepared for what that might mean.

Fifteen

"This room is bonkers," Claire breathed as she emerged from her tour of the bathroom. "Have you seen the tub in there? It could fit at *least* two people." She cringed at the words she had just said before rushing to explain. "Not that I'm suggesting we should take a bath together. Or that we should pick up any randos to join us in the bathtub. I'm just saying, if the couch doesn't work out for you, I think you could be *very* comfortable in there."

Jack appeared to be studying her, a quizzical expression on his face. "I think the couch will be just fine," he said finally, "though if you insist that someone should experience sleeping in the bathtub, then by all means, be my guest."

She exhaled a polite laugh, then perched on the edge of the bed, looking around the massive bedroom. Despite all the space they had to share, it felt...close. Even though, if Jack sat on the couch and she sat on the bed, there would be no clear line of sight between them, it was still as if everything they did in this room was a shared activity.

Claire wouldn't be curling up in bed with a book, leaving Jack to fend for himself. She wouldn't even be taking a quick nap in her room while he did his own thing in his room...because they were in the same dang room.

"I'm going to take a shower," said Claire, jolting suddenly to her feet. "Unless you need the bathroom first?" She raised her sentence into a question, checking to make sure that Jack had not, in fact, been intending to bolt to the bathroom at that precise moment. At his reassuring nod, she wrestled her large suitcase towards the bathroom, silently cursing the one wonky wheel that kept snagging on the carpet.

Could she have made things easier on herself by opening the suitcase in the bedroom and sorting through her clothes there?

Of course.

But did that bring with it the potential of exposing Jack to a peek inside the mad world of a suitcase that had been hastily packed at the end of six long weeks of solo travel, equal parts dirty laundry and humorous souvenirs?

...Maybe.

The fact was, there had to be some clean underwear tucked away in there, and there was no way she wasn't going to find it. But if she could search for it in a way that didn't expose Jack to the sight of her open suitcase looking as if it had defied the laws of physics by closing in the first place, then all the better. This was, after all, why most people didn't bring their literal baggage along with them on a second date.

Or whatever this day was.

Clearly, yesterday wasn't a date, and neither was today. It was somehow simultaneously less than a date and so much more than one. She and Jack had shared more intimacy than any first dates she'd ever participated in, and they'd been clear enough about their interest in each other, which went against all the rules of the dating game she was aware of.

But, at the same time, they still didn't have the clarity that came along with a date. The part where you promised to call later, to "do this again sometime," the pause where the possibility of a kiss goodnight still hung in the air, before that question had been answered. But there had been no kiss goodnight last night, only a tube of toothpaste and a worn t-shirt shoved through a crack in the door. They were either acting like platonic friends or an old married couple.

Claire picked a change of clothes from her suitcase, turned on the water, and stepped inside the shower. If life was fair at all, the hot water streaming over her head would wash off some of these unfamiliar anxieties that had cropped up and she would be free to enjoy another day with Jack without her brain needlessly complicating things.

By the time each of them had showered and prepared for the day, shockingly few words exchanged between them as it all unfolded, Claire was feeling more positive about the hours ahead. This was Jack, her instant travel buddy, and the two of them were sure to walk and talk and laugh and eat and drink until they were so exhausted they each collapsed onto their respective beds and any potential nighttime awkwardness didn't even stand a chance at making a toehold into their day.

Jack had emerged from the bathroom fully dressed, which must have been an act of mercy, because his wet hair, the towel around his shoulders, and the drops of water clinging to the sharp lines of his face had provided more than a preview of what she might have seen if he had instead exited the bathroom with only a towel wrapped around his waist. As it was, that tousled wet hair and the scandalous drops on his surprisingly long eyelashes...whew. She stopped short from fanning herself.

But, of course, Claire didn't give away just how twitterpated she was feeling inside on the outside. Instead, she looked up slowly from her phone, blinked once at Jack, and asked with a practiced nonchalance if he would be ready to head out soon.

Jack nodded. "To the English Garden? It's a little farther, but we can either suck it up and do it or take a taxi."

"We can walk," said Claire, with the confidence and assurance of someone who had checked the distance on a map rather than someone who simply preferred any activity that was more likely to render them too exhausted to feel awkward when the night rolled around.

"Fair enough," Jack agreed. "As long as we wear practical shoes, we should be good."

"Right. And when we get too tired and just want to give up, remind ourselves that tomorrow is going to be a long travel day and our muscles will thank us if we at least use them a little bit today."

"Exactly."

As Jack nodded again, perching on the edge of the couch to slip on his socks, Claire gritted her teeth. This walk, this outing had better be the cure for whatever this stilted interaction they were having was. She offered up a silent prayer that the awkwardness existed only in the hotel room, that as soon as they were outside the door, away from the large bed that practically screamed, "I am a romance novel plot device," things would go back to normal. She could only hope that was the truth.

By the time they were almost ready to leave, things had only gotten worse. After Claire had ducked into the bathroom to put some sunblock and lip balm on, she and Jack had done that halting dance when he had approached the bathroom to...well, to do something that she probably shouldn't even know about, should she? Whether he was putting on deodorant, brushing his teeth, or using the toilet, all of it was too intimate for a friend to be just on the other side of the door for. It was probably thanks to that being on her mind that she had first stepped to the left to get out of Jack's way, only to nearly collide with him there, then stepped to the right side to repeat the same thing. It had taken three near collisions before Jack had chuckled, held up his hands, and pointed to the right, the shortest distance between himself and the door, and announced, "I'll go this way."

Claire had laughed at herself and nodded, retreating to the kitchenette, the furthest she could get from the bathroom—and Jack—without actually leaving the room. When she was confident he couldn't see her, she gritted her teeth and muttered under her breath, "Are you freaking kidding me, Claire? Was this all a huge mistake, or are you going to get your shit together at some point?" If things didn't improve, it would have been a much better use of their time and energy to just take that day's flight to Newark. Maybe Munich was the kind of place where you could only have one fun-bordering-on-romance day with your airplane crush. Maybe the second day was cursed. Maybe that had deprived some other star-crossed strangers at the airport from having their rightful experience today.

But it was too late to worry about that, wasn't it? Those strangers who would have become something more were already well on their way to Newark, and whether they had a meet cute of their own in line for the plane's bathroom or not was entirely up to them.

Claire couldn't think of a less romantic place to meet a potential special someone than the hallway just outside an airplane's bathroom. "Unless it was business class," she mumbled to herself. "Not sure what those bathrooms are like, but surely the ambiance and smell have to be at least a *little* more conducive to romance."

"Are you talking to yourself about the mile high club?" Jack had entered the room, apparently, and it was also apparent that the volume at which Claire mumbled to herself wasn't as low as she might have thought.

"Something like that," she said as she turned around to face him. "Imagining where a meet cute would happen on an airplane. Because that's the fantasy, isn't it? Every time you fly, you kind of wonder if you're about to have something absolutely thrilling happen to you." She shrugged. "Or that might just be how my brain works."

Jack took a step closer, dangerously close to entering her bubble. "I can't say that's something I ever wondered about. I'm much more of a pragmatist than that. Generally, I'm hoping the seat next to me will be empty and I'll have some extra room to stretch out, not hoping my soulmate is going to sit there."

"Sure." He had come even closer, and Claire was about three inches away from bolting for the door. "I was wondering if by taking the delay option two days in a row if we deprived someone from a magic meeting of their own. I was consoling myself with the idea that they could meet in line for the bathroom on the plane instead, but I can't think of a stinkier or more awkward place to meet."

Jack was studying her face. "Are you nervous, Claire? I could listen to you talk about just about anything and consider it an honor to get to be the one whose ears are hearing your words, but..." He tilted his head to the side, a small smile playing at the corner of his lips. "Well, it's a bit more bathroom talk than I expected."

She was the first to break eye contact, looking down at her feet. "It's weird, isn't it? I didn't think sharing a room would change things, but I was wrong. It's too strange." She grimaced as she looked back up at him. "I should go beg Klaus for another room, talk him into not charging me for it. We can go back to how things were yesterday, no need for any awkward dances around or weird silences or..."

With one final step, Jack was close enough to touch, and he took both of her hands in his. "You don't need to do that. It's going to be okay." He took a deep breath and let it out. "I think we just need to be clear about a few things, okay?" When she nodded, he continued. "I am very interested in you, in every way that I already spelled out for you." Claire gulped at the force of his tone.

"I won't bore you with the details," he continued.

Please, she thought, *bore me with the details.*

"But nothing is going to happen, today, tonight, or anytime that we're in this room. That doesn't mean I suddenly stopped finding you attractive once I heard you pee—yes, that bathroom door is just as thin as you were afraid. It *does* mean, however, that I'm serious about how captivating I find you and that I value a longer-term potential future with you much more than any short-term fun. Does that sound okay to you?"

Claire couldn't stop herself from barking out a nervous laugh. "I...what? Really? You're telling me, essentially, that I should settle down because nothing is going to happen between us?"

Jack nodded, just once, not breaking eye contact. "That is exactly what I'm telling you. I believe, considering that it is your actual job for you to have an active imagination, that it is in our best interest to be abundantly clear about our intentions."

"Right." It was her turn to nod, though she looked back down at her feet as she did so. "And you *are* interested. So it's not a lack of interest that's making you say this?"

"Not at all." He exhaled something like a laugh. "I would do something to prove that I'm as interested as I say I am, but I'm afraid it would defeat the whole purpose of this conversation."

She peeked up at him through her lashes. "So...why not just say, essentially, that what happens in Munich stays in Munich and spend the rest of the day in bed with me?"

Jack's eyebrows had climbed sky high. "It's not that the thought hadn't crossed my mind. The problem, though, is that I know I wouldn't want it to 'stay in Munich.'" He shrugged. "So if that's how this thing works, then I have to choose something different. A little old-fashioned, some may say, but slow and steady wins the race."

"Well, uh." Claire's mind was a complete blank, her next words not coming to her. "Thanks. That's good to know."

He chuckled at her. "You're welcome. I hope that helps you feel a little less"—he gestured towards her vaguely—"however you've been feeling. It would make the next day unbearable if we couldn't feel relaxed together."

"Yeah, totally." She nodded, going through the motions. How was she supposed to feel relaxed around Jack now? Sure, he'd made it plenty clear that there was a zero percent chance of anything romantic happening between them tonight. But the fact that he'd had the audacity to make it plainly clear that he *did* have an interest in something happening in the future—and something more *long-term*, at that? While it surely wasn't his desired effect, his words just might leave her second guessing every word, every movement, every thought and decision. There might be no physical expectations for today, but clearly there were hopes and dreams for tomorrow hanging in the balance.

Jack shook his head at her. "I think I just scrambled you up even more, Claire." He let go of her hands to place his palms on her shoulders, his grip reassuring and steady. "Just focus on today, okay? Today and the *nothing* that's going to happen between us in this room. Or anywhere else in this city, for that matter. We'll go out and explore and then when we come back it'll just be like two friends or roommates hanging out and watching movies. Just like you and Emma." He shot a glance at her. "There's no sexual tension between you and Emma, right? Because I'm definitely not trying to make things worse by comparing myself to one of your friends who's the one who got away or anything like that."

That got a genuine smile out of Claire. "Emma, though she is beautiful and wonderful and everything I wish I could be, is a safe choice for a friend comparison if you're looking for a totally platonic friend whose shoes to step into for the night." She shot a sideways glance at him. "What's this about watching movies, though? We've got a city to explore again today, mister."

"And we will do that. I just know myself well enough to know that two days of non-stop exploring is not my idea of a good time anymore." His lips curved down at the corners in thought as he weighed his next words. "In hindsight, it may never have been my idea of a good time, but as a younger man, I definitely put a lot more pressure to see it all, do it all, soak up every last drop. For today, if you're game, I'm thinking a little walk around the English Garden, another visit to the Christmas market, and not much more besides that. When you were in the shower, I checked the TV channels and found some English ones that are due to play Christmas movies tonight."

Was it Claire's imagination, or was Jack looking sheepish? Almost vulnerable, even?

He continued then. "I don't want to insert myself into your traditions." He winced. "And my apologies for that word choice." He shook his head. "Think, *then* speak, Jack. But anyway, if you'll have me." He grimaced. "If you're up for it, I'd love to join you for a little Christmas Eve Eve movie marathon tonight. If you don't think Emma would mind."

Claire clapped her hands as a genuine grin spread across her face. "Oh my gosh, I would love that so much! I wish it was movie time already." She pulled Jack in for a quick hug before thinking better of it. Judging by everything he had just told her, that was the last thing he wanted right now. She let go and stepped back, her cheeks pinker than before. "Shall we?" she asked, gesturing towards the door.

Sixteen

The English Garden, as it turned out, was only a fifteen minute walk from the hotel. They enjoyed exploring the paths in the park, and Claire could only imagine how beautiful it would be with spring blossoms or fall foliage. They paused at a river for quite some time to watch the ambitious and adventurous surf a standing wave there, Claire and Jack both tucking their hands deeper into their pockets against the cold as a new surfer tumbled off her board.

By the early afternoon, Claire could feel her energy levels flagging and nothing sounded better than a nap. She shot a furtive glance at Jack, pleased to catch him in the middle of a yawn. She grabbed his hand then, clasping his gloved fingers in her mittened ones.

"You're tired, aren't you?" Before he could say a word or even nod, she plowed on. "What do you think about heading back to the hotel for a bit? We can get some snacks, maybe a hot beverage, and go start the movie marathon a little early?" She held up a hand, though he still wasn't speaking. "I know what you're thinking. If we head back now, will we even make it out again later for the Christmas market? But I have faith in us, Jack. And you should, too." She smiled up at him then. "So? What do you think?"

His smile was indulgent, stretching across his face. "While I am nowhere near as confident as you are that we will, in fact, leave the hotel room again, I will do just about anything you ask. Let's go, then."

She raised an eyebrow at him. "Just about anything?"

"We've been over this," Jack scoffed. "No matter how nicely you ask, there will be no funny business this evening. *That* I can promise you."

As they walked back to the hotel, Claire felt a lightness that had been missing for quite some time. Perhaps it wasn't even a *lightness*, so much as the absence of heaviness. Sure, she was aware in the edges of her consciousness that she hadn't heard from Bianca that day, that there was a big unspoken Something waiting for the two of them to have a discussion. But in that moment, she wasn't rehearsing her fears of what might be about to happen. She was simply enjoying Jack. Basking in the warmth of his presence beside her, enjoying the surreal feeling of being the sole recipient of his undivided attention.

He had made his interest in her so abundantly clear that she couldn't even let doubt creep into the back of her mind. There was simply no room for misunderstanding, nothing he had said that she could have wondered if he intended differently, no thoughts that could possibly torment her.

And it was with that thought—and a perma-grin fixed on her face—that Claire took his hand and tugged him into a small market about halfway back to the hotel. When

Jack gave her a raised eyebrow and a look of confusion, she explained. "Snacks, remember? That's how you do Christmas Eve Eve, after all. Snacks on snacks on snacks." She shook her head at him. "It's not a 'calling room service for a proper meal' kind of event."

"Right." Jack nodded. "And it's a good idea to have a stash of sustenance available when we inevitably decide not to go out again for the evening."

She shook her head at him. "Oh ye of little faith." She grabbed a basket and stepped closer into the shop, which appeared to be set up for a one-way flow of traffic. "I'll readily admit that on a normal day, in normal circumstances, with my regular options available to me..." She picked up a box of cookies, scanned the packaging until she saw the familiar word "gingerbread," shrugged, and dropped them in the box. "If I were at home and it was cold and dark and my friends wanted to meet up for drinks, if by some bizarre turn of events I even said yes in the first place, I guarantee I'd be canceling those plans. Blanket. Couch. Popcorn. Jim jams." She gestured around them, tossing a bag of what looked like corn puffs but had pictures of peanuts on the front into the basket. "These are not normal circumstances. And while coziness and comfort almost always win over adventures out in the wider world, this is the rare exception." They had stumbled onto the selection of chocolate, and Claire grabbed bars and tossed them into the basket with abandon. "No such thing as too much chocolate. They can be gifts, stocking stuffers, if there are any left over."

"'If there are any left over...'" Jack muttered. "There are approximately four pounds of chocolate in that basket, Claire, plus all the other things you're tossing in—"

"And why aren't you tossing anything in? Hmm? This is a group project, buddy, and I am not into the idea of doing all of my work *and* all of yours."

"Fair enough." Jack nodded, grabbed a few packages of gummy bears, and added them to the basket. "It'll be fun to repack our bags in the morning and add a bunch of half eaten junk food into the mix, just to keep it interesting."

"What better souvenir is there than something you can eat?"

"I'm pretty happy with the books I bought yesterday." Jack looked thoughtful. "Really enjoying my first romance read so far."

Claire's lips pulled into a grimace. "I...I'm glad you're reading it, and I hope it will help you understand your sister—"

"I'm not reading your books to understand my sister," he cut in. "I'm thrilled that they helped her figure her shit out...or are in the process of helping her figure it out, at least." His gaze found Claire's, his eyes so intense she couldn't hold eye contact. "But it's you I wanted to know, wanted to understand."

"Ah." Claire's teeth found her lower lip, worrying it. "Good to know. That won't make me more anxious when I see you reading it *at all.*" She forced a smile then. "Just...don't read into it too much, okay? Remember that it's just a story, that I'm not interchangeable with the main character and that the hero isn't my dream man or anything like that."

The expression on his face was puzzled. "You mean the basic concept of a work of fiction? Yeah, I think I got it..." He put his arm around her shoulder, pulling her in for a quick side hug before letting her go and returning to perusing the shelves. "It's just about appreciating your talent, Claire. I swear, every word I read in that book makes me feel a little less worthy of even having a conversation with you." He grabbed some cheese and placed it in the basket, before noticing just how full the basket was getting and taking it out of her hands. "I mean, the things that are clearly going on in your mind to be able to create something like that...well, let's just say I'm not even sure there's a passing resemblance between that genius machine in your head and the meat blob in mine."

Claire laughed at him, her head tipping back to let her amusement flow more freely. "Oh, Jack. If you only knew." She wandered in the direction of the produce, picking up a few apples to balance out their snack selection with a little fiber. "There isn't one sentence that I write in a first draft that I think is any good. It just flows onto the paper and the main job I have is convincing myself not to delete it all and go find a real job. Of course, after it rests for some time, when I come back and read it again, some of it is actually pretty good. That's what I think a lot of creative work is about, though. Getting past the doubt and criticism and just doing the thing. I'm pretty sure anyone could do it."

Jack was staring at her, his mouth open as he began to shake his head slowly. "Don't minimize it like that. You're clearly good at what you do, even you can't deny that. Not with all those 'bestseller' titles attached to your name."

She paused before responding. "I'm grateful for all of that. I just bristle when people make it sound like there's something special about me that they couldn't possibly be or do or have." She shrugged. "I don't write because it's easy for me. It's anything *but* sometimes. I write because it's important to me and I have stories I want to put out into the world and because I don't really know how to do anything else. But I'm not tapped into some magical source of inspiration that drives me out of bed in the middle of the night because I simply have to do it. I just write when I can and probably spend more time convincing myself to write most days than I actually do writing."

Jack nodded, looking deep in thought, but didn't say anything further.

Claire eyeballed the shopping basket, then looked up to meet his eyes. "Should we quit while we're ahead? I know it goes against the core values of Christmas Eve Eve, but I think we've already got more than enough to get us through the rest of the day."

"I'll second that." He lifted the basket a few inches, then lowered it again, testing its weight. "There's some serious mass here, and if we don't make a dent in it tonight, then our suitcases are going to be over the weight limit tomorrow."

Claire scoffed. "Don't be an amateur, Jack. We've got the time, the movies—at least I hope we've got the movies. If we have to watch YouTube clips on my phone, I'm going to rage. Anyway, the conditions are perfect. Cozy room, entertainment, a wide variety of sweet and salty treats. We'd never need to leave the room again, at least not for a few days." She held up a hand. "Yes, I know we already have plans to leave the room again this evening, and I'm not going back on those. I'm just saying, we're perfectly set up for a holiday movie marathon that lasts days. But that if we don't actually have days to execute it, we can crank up the intensity a bit for the next few hours at least."

"I'm not sure what cranking up the intensity means, but as long as you aren't going to have two movies playing simultaneously side by side or turn up the speed to finish more in a shorter time, I'm completely up for it." He nodded in the direction of the cash register, then began making his way there after Claire agreed that she was ready to go.

One final stop on the way to the hotel, and they were fully equipped for the afternoon. They had carried their groceries and treasures to a cafe close to the hotel, stopping there to pick up coffee.

"Ooh, and two hot chocolates, too, please," Claire had interjected. "Extra hot, please." She shot Jack a look. "We'll drink those after the coffee, so hopefully that will help them stay warm."

"Of course," Jack answered with a look of amusement on his face. "Good thinking, because without those extra drinks, we might have gotten thirsty. Or hungry. Or had a chocolate deficiency."

She glared at him. "I know you're teasing me, but that's just because you don't know how terrible it is to watch the small town love story unfold and see the characters drinking their hot chocolate covered in whipped cream or marshmallows and have nothing more than a bottle of water beside you. It's almost as bad as watching a Korean drama when the characters sit down to a great meal with all the side dishes and everything looks so delicious and all you have is an almost empty bag of pretzels."

"Ah." Jack nodded. "So you're a bag-half-empty-of-pretzels kind of gal, not bag-half-full?"

Claire paid for the drinks, then moved to the end of the counter to wait for them. "I'm not even dignifying that with a response, as I believe I *clearly* stated the bag was almost empty. Would you look at a glass that had a few sips of water left at the bottom and describe it with the word 'full' or 'empty'?"

Jack smiled at her. As the barista slid the drinks across the counter in a cardboard tray, he picked them all up, thanked the staff, and made for the door. Claire just shook her head at him. Why was it so fun to tease him, to jump on every little comment and pick a completely unserious fight about it? Maybe it was all the energy that would otherwise be directed towards the sparks between them finding a different way to express itself. As long as they were both having fun, and as long as they could still have a serious conversation when the need presented, she didn't figure it would be a problem.

It was a quick walk to the hotel, both because the distance was short and because they had picked up the pace considerably. Jack seemed to be on a mission to preserve as much heat as possible in their drinks, and the two barely talked as they traversed the remaining blocks. Only when they were back in the lobby did Jack slow down long enough to make sure they were good, that no treats or shoes had been left behind in their hurry. Claire just nodded at him, tipping her head in the direction of the elevator.

"We're all good," she said, catching her breath. "Almost there!"

Back in the suite, Jack plopped onto the couch, picking up the remote to switch on the TV. "Let's see what we can find," he said. "Here's hoping we can find something up to your usual standards."

But Claire just looked at him with an expression of disbelief on her face. "What are you doing? Out here?" She shook her head. "No way! Christmas Eve Eve marathons have to be conducted in the ultimate of comfort." She gestured in the direction of the bedroom. "There's a TV in there, too. Come on, put on your jim jams and join me."

"Uh. What?" Jack balked, his expression uncomprehending. "You...want me to put on my pajamas—"

"Jim jams, but yes," Claire interrupted. "Don't you even dare think about wearing your"—she gestured towards his shirt and jeans—"outside clothes in the bed." She shuddered with disgust. "I will get no sleep at all tonight if I'm lying there wondering what you might have brought into my bed and left there to fester. Some kind of jean-loving bacteria or something."

But Jack was still standing in place, still looking at her with the same expression. "I just...well, I fail to see how the two of us climbing into bed together is a good strategy at *all*, especially considering the promises I've explicitly made you about today."

Claire waved a dismissive hand at him. "Oh please, I'm not trying to seduce you or anything. Now if you'll excuse me, I'm going to go change into the unsexiest jim jams possible and I'll meet you back here in ten. Deal?"

Jack gulped, but nodded. "Deal."

Seventeen

When Claire exited the bathroom, cozy in her worn sweatpants and favorite old sweatshirt with only a hint of the Jaws movie poster remaining on it, she smiled at the neatly made bed. The conditions were perfect for Christmas Eve Eve. There might be the slightest doubt in the back of her mind that she would be trading her sweatpants in for jeans again, that she and Jack would actually make it to the Christmas market...but for this moment, at least, she didn't need to worry about that.

She glanced over her shoulder, noting that the door between the bedroom and the living room was closed. Jack must have closed it to change his own clothes there, and she smiled at the thought. He was so careful not to cross any lines, and even if there was a part of her that wanted him to throw caution to the wind, to kiss her like he meant it and then see what might happen next, there was an even larger part of her that was turning cartwheels at the thrill of waiting. The opportunity for the two of them to enjoy spending time together without any pressure to see what might come next was confusing and exciting and frustrating all at once.

It was clear the interest was there—it was undeniable on her end, and Jack had made it plenty clear that he definitely felt *something* for her—and yet it was as if it was all too precious, all too delicate for any rash actions or quick decisions.

Claire glanced down at herself and frowned. It wasn't as if she had intentionally dressed herself in the least enticing outfit she could find—she didn't exactly travel with a lacy negligee, oddly enough. And she wasn't interested in living out a cliche, dressing herself up like an elaborate gift to be unwrapped, just to entice Jack into breaking his word.

Still, though. It might have been nice to find a happy medium in between temptress and hibernating forest crone. Perhaps something with just a hint of shape, rather than these comfortable yet completely unflattering sweats.

There was a soft knock on the door then, and she smiled. "Come on in," she called to Jack as she tossed herself onto the bed, settling back into the pillows.

He entered a moment later, the door opening with a slight pause that suggested he was just as unsure and hesitant as she was—or apparently more so, judging by the way he stopped, eyes on her, and swallowed with discomfort. Jack was also wearing sweatpants—gray ones, which any romance reader or appreciator of the male form would know should be illegal—and a very familiar white t-shirt.

Claire smiled at him and patted the bed beside her. "Come on," she said, as she picked up the remote. "Time to get cozy." He paused for a moment, studying her, his eyes flashing down to take in her complete look, which made her entire body heat at the attention, then moved into the room. When he took his seat next to her but not within arms' reach, still without having spoken so much as a word to her, she passed him his coffee from the night-stand, then leaned down to pick up the shopping bag that was still full of treats and dropped it on the bedspread between them.

That got a laugh out of Jack. "Oh," he began, "I see how it is. I'm not allowed to wear my 'outside clothes' into your bed, but this bag, which has been exposed to just the same elements and germs as I have been...well, I guess the rules don't apply?"

She leveled a look at him for that. "Can you not see how it's different? For one thing, I'm not rubbing this bag all over my pillow, and I'm certainly not going to let it get under the covers." She frowned at the look that flashed on Jack's face, then continued. "And for another thing, it's totally different material. The plastic of this bag, well...it's, like, slippery, isn't it? But denim is porous. Anything can stick to it."

Jack shook his head, then lifted his cup to his lips, a smile playing there for the first time since he had entered the room. All the tension that had been building up between them was gone with that simple movement of his mouth. "While there's some truth to that, I think it's more about hard surfaces. I'm no epidemiologist, though. Maybe all we need to do to prevent the spread of disease is cover our-selves with plastic bags throughout cold and flu season." Jack exhaled a small laugh. "Don't know why no one ever asked you to come up with a solution to communicable disease."

Claire scoffed. "I know you're teasing me, but seriously. I know for a fact that if we all covered our heads with plastic bags, there would be no way to spread disease." She paused a beat, then continued deadpan. "I mean, that would be because we had suffocated and died, but still."

"I'm not even going to dignify that with a response," said Jack, nodding towards the television. "What have you found for us to watch, anyway?"

Rubbing her hands together, Claire let out a scheming laugh. "Oh, you are in for a real treat, mister. Turns out the hotel gets the *perfect* channels for a Christmas Eve Eve marathon. We can choose between a channel that appears to have nothing but Hallmark movies on it..."

"And?" Jack asked with a slight wince. "*Die Hard*? Please tell me the other option is *Die Hard*."

Claire shrugged. "It might be. But I'm not sure if it matters because the other option is dubbed movies. Mostly Christmas ones by the looks of it, but my German isn't that good. Does *Stirb langsam* sound like the German version of *Die Hard*?"

"Beats me." Jack took another sip of his coffee. "And as much as I enjoy *Die Hard*, my German skills are nonexistent. Hallmark it is then, I think."

Switching on the TV, Claire nodded at him. "That's what I was thinking, too. Though we can always give ourselves a little German immersion experience if we get tired of the small town country mouse showing the big important city mouse the meaning life and love."

"And the meaning of Christmas," added Jack. "You can't forget about the kindly old man who is actually secretly Santa Claus. That's an essential element of the story, too."

Claire turned to look at him, a suspicion playing in the back of her mind. "Aha!" she crowed, "So you're not a Hallmark newbie at all. Seems like you might even be a bit of an expert, judging by how well you know the tropes."

"We might not call it Christmas Eve Eve, but Hazel and I are no strangers to the Hallmark channel. If I want to hang out with her during the holidays, it's pretty much guaranteed that one of these movies is going to be playing in the background." He shrugged. "Okay, and sometimes not just the background. If the story gets going, we usually end up dropping whatever we were talking about and just watching."

"And you like them? The movies?" It was hard to explain what Claire's chest was doing at that moment. She already knew Jack was a good brother, that he cared about his sister and her happiness more than she had come to expect from most of the men in her life. But he just kept taking things to a new level, raising the bar higher and higher of her expectations for the male species.

"Of course," he said with a nod. "Not all stories are equally good, of course. But the story pulls us in, no matter what. Some evolutionary mechanism or something. It's like we're sitting around the campfire learning about our origins again."

"Right," said Claire with a roll of her eyes. "It's all about oral tradition and evolution and nothing whatsoever to do with the uniquely gifted writers who work for Hallmark." She narrowed her eyes, studying him. "Or is it the small town romance thing? You're a sucker for a love story set on a Christmas tree farm in danger of being sold to build luxury condos. Ooh, or a bed and breakfast about to get bought out by a hotel. Hmm, or let me guess? Uh...a tractor dealership that's going to start selling sports cars instead?"

Jack leaned forward, picked up a bar of chocolate and tossed it right at Claire. It smacked her lightly on the upper arm and then dropped into her lap. "That's enough teasing from you. Don't tell me you're a snob about Christmas movies or the people who love them."

She glared at him then. "Is it even possible for that to be true? Let's consider that this was my idea *and* that I write what many people might consider cheesy love stories for a living. The last thing I'm going to do is be snobby about a happily ever after, no matter where it comes from."

"Okay then. So we agree." Jack opened a box of cookies, held it out for Claire to take one, and then leaned back against the headboard. "Enough talking. Time to watch."

Four hours later, Clare yawned and groaned as she stretched her arms above her head. Her gaze fell on Jack, who looked just as bleary-eyed and exhausted as she felt.

"I never thought I'd say this," she said, as she leaned forward on her knees to start gathering up the snacks that had spread across the comforter, "But I think it might actually be time to get out of this bed." She held up one hand in response to the protest she imagined Jack was making. "I know, I know. You could stay here all day and never get tired of it—"

"I could," he said, with a serious note in his deep voice that made her stop what she was doing, turn and look at him. "I know you're kidding, and I know you're mostly talking about the quality of our entertainment. But given the option of staying in this bed with you for a whole day, a whole weekend..." He shook his head. "I would be a fool to say no to that."

Claire gulped. This was the most they had spoken since the movie marathon had begun, one and a half Christmas movies and one German-dubbed *Die Hard* ago. They had laughed, exchanged a comment here and there, but for the most part it had been a comfortable silence. They had moved closer too, under the pretense of more easily sharing the box of cherry cordials, but Claire hadn't moved back to her side of the bed even after they had both stopped eating.

She took a moment to weigh her options of how to respond to Jack. She could tease him, play it off as a joke, dispel the tension. Or she could respond to his vulnerability, his honesty, with a little bit of her own. It was almost Christmas, after all. Didn't she owe him that much?

"I...really like it, too," she said, only able to hold his eyes for half a second before her gaze dropped down to her hands. "It's so fun, so comfortable, to just *be* with you. Not at all what I expected." She darted a glance towards the television, her teeth finding her lower lip. "I just feel like I'll regret it if we don't go out and enjoy the Christmas market one last time while we have it. And I don't want to mess up your Munich trip by depriving you of it, either."

"Hey." There was that serious tone again. Claire looked up to find Jack looking at her with an intensity that almost made her shiver. "I don't care what we do next, as long as we do it together. If you want to go to that market, I'll be right there by your side. And if you want to sit here for another six hours, I...well, I can't promise I'll stay awake for it, but I'm not going anywhere. So...it's really your choice then. Go see some Christmas lights and drink some mulled wine, or stay right here where we are and wake up in the morning after unwittingly falling asleep together in the same bed." He winked at her then. "Your call, Davis."

I want both, Claire thought. *I want it all. I want to go wherever you go, too. I want to see and experience and taste all that life and this city has to offer and I want you to be there for it, too. And then I want to fall asleep next to you and do it again the next day.*

She didn't know how to say all of that to him, though, because surely it was too much. It sounded more like a proposal or a vow, and she'd only met the guy yesterday.

So she chose the safest option. The one that didn't have the two of them snuggled up against the same headboard, only moments away from falling asleep under the same cozy blanket. Claire bolted to her feet then, focusing her attention as far away from Jack and the equally cozy pillows and chest that were already beckoning her back to the bed.

"Christmas market!" she cried, digging through her open suitcase to gather her clothes. "We should go." She was speaking to Jack over her shoulder, still not looking at him. "I don't want us to regret missing it. It's not like there won't be movies on the plane tomorrow, but I doubt they'll have mulled wine." *That, and out there I won't be tempted to rest my head on your shoulder. Won't think about how you would react if I kissed you. Won't feel all this tension between us so thick you actually* couldn't *cut it with a knife. A chainsaw, maybe.*

Claire could hear the sound of the mattress shifting, but she still didn't look. She didn't raise her gaze from her suitcase until Jack was almost to the door separating the bedroom from the living room. "Sounds like a great plan, Claire. Just give me a couple of minutes to get ready." She looked at him then, but his calm demeanor gave nothing away. If he knew how wildly her heart was beating, if he had the faintest idea what was going on underneath the surface—or right out in the open for everyone to see, judging by how good Claire was at playing it cool—then he was giving nothing away. She shot him a quick smile before he closed the door, then she bolted for the bathroom with her own clothes.

She took the next few moments not only to dress herself for the chilly December day but to stare herself down in the mirror while delivering a silent pep talk through the intensity of her gaze alone.

Just...be cool. Don't make this weird. Yes, you know he likes you. And yes, that is all sorts of terrifying, mainly because you like him, *too. But tonight is not the night. No matter how romantic it gets out there and no matter how much mulled wine you both drink, it's not going beyond flirtation. Not tonight, and maybe not ever. And no, you don't know why he had to make all these rules, either.* She shook her head at her reflection. *Yes, you do. He doesn't want this to turn into a one-night stand. A one-night city. One-night country. And you know yourself well enough to know just how quickly you would manage to sabotage yourself if things* did *progress like that tonight. By tomorrow morning you would have convinced yourself that there was no future, that you had made a huge mistake, and you would spend the whole plane ride home freezing him out and avoiding him. Is that what you want?*

Claire exhaled a sigh at her reflection and spoke her next words out loud. "No. I don't." *You win this one, brain.*

Eighteen

Approaching the Christkindlmarkt was like stepping into one of the small town Christmas movies they had just watched, and even though they had been there just the day before, Claire felt her breath catch at the sight of the lights, the smells of cinnamon and nutmeg that were wafting her way.

"Why?" she breathed, her eyes finding Jack's.

"Why what?" he asked, looking concerned.

"Why is it like this? Why does it feel so magical?" She shook her head. "I...I can't explain it, not really. It just feels like a Christmas from my childhood. Like anything is possible, even a flying sleigh appearing right over our heads."

That earned her a soft smile from Jack. "Don't look now, but—" He wrapped an arm around her, pulling her into his side. "No, I won't kid with you. There is no sign of a flying sleigh, but I agree that the magic does feel just about powerful enough for that to happen."

"Why is it like this?" They were walking through the stalls now, an unspoken decision to take in as much of the market as they could rather than making a beeline for the glühwein stand. "Why does it feel so different? Have the Germans figured out something we haven't?"

Jack shrugged as he sighed. "I don't think it's that simple. I think the magic of the season is everywhere, even in New Jersey. It's just about whether or not you're free enough to appreciate it. Back in the States, you would probably be scrambling to get your last minute shopping done, but you don't have that pressure on you here." He gestured around them. "And I'm sure there are people here with mile-long to-do lists, too. Although, maybe with the whole month of December to enjoy the Christmas markets, they're a little more on top of their holiday to-do lists."

"Valid points," said Claire, gesturing towards the line for the glühwein stand, then beginning to walk there at Jack's nod.

"Of course, there's also the fact that it's a little easier to find the magic when you're out of your normal environment." He gestured to the crowd around them. "I'm sure some of these people appreciate the spirit of the season...but all of them? Do you think the Germans have somehow mastered the art of savoring the Christmas spirit, or...?" He trailed off, giving her a meaningful look.

Claire sighed. "Or do I think that people are basically the same everywhere and there are stressed out Germans here just like there are Americans who are enjoying the holiday season just as much as I am here?"

Jack shocked her then by reaching forward to boop the tip of her nose with his finger. "Ding ding ding," he said, then grimaced. "Sorry, I don't know why I just did that."

But she only smiled. "No, don't be. I kind of loved it." The gesture had been so natural and so intimate that it was easy to imagine the ease between them was the ease of an established relationship, that his reaching out to touch her lightly on the nose was something he did all the time, either to punctuate a point he was making or to surprise her in the middle of a disagreement or simply because he knew it would make her smile.

The gesture seemed to have embarrassed him, though, because he wasn't quite meeting her eye now. "I just think about that a lot, I guess. When people go to Italy for a week and come back raving about how everything there was so much better than back home, you know? Suddenly, they're grumbling about everything they loved a week before. And sure, nobody does pizza better than the Italians. But you loved a New York slice last week and suddenly it's garbage now?" Jack shook his head.

"It's easier to find the magic when everything is new and different, but if we put in a little effort we'd see it around us, even back home?" Claire looped her arm through his. "Is that what you mean?"

"I guess so." Jack was nodding. "There's something about the whole idea of the grass being greener on the other side that really irks me."

Interesting, thought Claire. She was tempted to dig a little deeper into that, but thought better of it at the distant look in Jack's eyes. If he wanted to tell her, he would. And if he didn't, then maybe it wasn't any of her business after all. She stayed silent then as they took their place at the end of the line for mulled wine, taking small steps forward every few moments.

But the silence seemed to invite Jack to continue, and when he spoke next, his vulnerability surprised her. "That was what happened with my ex. A work trip, meeting someone new, and suddenly everything about me was old and tired and wrong and everything about him was new and fresh and just the perfect match for her. It didn't happen immediately, though. It wasn't like she came straight home and dumped me." He shook his head, blowing out a mirthless laugh. "No, she kept me around even though everything I did seemed to either annoy or embarrass her. And she started talking about the new guy, her new work friend, every chance she got. I could see there was something there, even if she didn't want to admit it."

"So she dumped you for him?" Claire winced as the words came out.

But Jack was already shaking his head. "I ended things when I figured out what was going on. No need to stick around until she was well and truly sick of me."

"And are they together now?"

"I don't know. She even denied at the time that there was anything there, but it was so clear. So obvious. I told her I didn't want to be anybody's second choice, not even hers." His smile was small and sad. "I really loved her, and I would have stuck around. Would have contorted myself into trying to make her get her feelings back. But it doesn't work that way."

"That's why you're so determined to help your sister," Claire breathed, her voice barely a whisper.

Jack nodded. "Yeah, it was seeing Hazel go through it that made me realize what I needed to do. I did it for both of us."

Claire leaned in to Jack's side, overcome with affection for him. How could anybody not love him? Get tired of him? Meet someone new and think that they even compared to him, let alone were a better choice than him?

It all made sense then, especially his hesitation to take things too quickly with her. He wanted to hold on to her, to the feelings long enough to be sure that they were real.

And even as much as she wanted to push through that, to insist that they were different, that they could do whatever they wanted and be together forever no matter how things began between them...she understood. She respected his wishes, his need to take things slowly.

And if she was honest with herself, she probably needed that slow pace, too. It wasn't as if she'd never been scared off by things getting too real too quickly. She was no stranger to the art of self sabotage.

At that thought, an awareness washed over her. Was that what was happening right now with Bianca and Velvet Leaf? Was her career, in fact, doing better than ever—hence the European tour—and the last thing her agent was about to do was give her bad news? Was she only worrying herself about it because it felt like things were *too* good and such a feeling could only mean the other shoe was about to fall?

But Claire shook off the thought and turned her attention back to Jack, just in time for the two of them to step up to the counter. If, by some bizarre twist of fate, her career survived until the end of the year, she would celebrate that news with Jack in New York.

•❤•❤•❤•❤•❤•

It was possible that huddling around the cozy heater, insides warming from within with every sip of mulled wine, had created an infinitely more cozy and tempting atmosphere than staying in bed in their sweats.

Given that Hendrik and Jana had been with them the day before, Claire had inaccurately predicted what the environment would be like this evening. While she had expected friendly laughter and good food, maybe a little bit of shopping, instead she had stepped right into a scene that felt like it came out of a movie.

Bundled in her coat and hat, only her eyes and the tip of her nose peeking out as she smiled up at Jack, it was all Claire could do to stop herself from batting her eyelashes at him. And when he reached over and tugged the collar of her coat even higher, she nearly swooned at the action and at the care with which he handled her.

"Food?" he asked, studying the bottom of his empty mug. "Or more wine?"

"Food," she responded, even when all she wanted to say was "bed" or "forever" or anything and everything in between.

Jack tucked her mittened hand into the crook of his elbow and slipped his hands into his pockets. He guided her toward a stand with sausages that they had noticed the day before, stopping on the way at a small booth that had caught his eye.

He picked up a small ornament, a heart filled with bookshelves covered in books, and held it up to her with a twinkle in his eye. "Do you think Hazel would like this? A little extra Christmas present, a souvenir from the trip where I met her favorite author?"

Claire nodded, beaming into her scarf, where Jack couldn't see. What was it that tickled her so much about the image of him giving a present to his sister that the two of them had picked out together? Was it the fact that couples in many stages of their relationships did just the same thing whenever holidays and birthdays rolled around? That it felt like she already knew his family, even if she hadn't even known Jack himself two days ago.

Jack finished his shopping and paid while Claire was looking at some ornate Christmas pyramids, layers covered with wooden figurines with what looked like fan blades at the top. They were spinning from the heat rising from the candles at their bases, and she was briefly hypnotized by them—on second thought, food was a necessity. That had been more wine than she had realized. The pyramid was an impressive work of craftsmanship, and it stirred up vague memories of something she had seen in her grandparents' house as a young girl, but the fact that she could lose track of time enraptured by it suggested she needed some sustenance.

"Claire?" Jack broke into her reverie, following her gaze to the Christmas pyramid. "You like that?"

She just nodded, still transfixed.

"It would make a great souvenir, wouldn't it? Something to look at every Christmas and remember the days here?" Was it her imagination, or was there something unsaid in his question…she had noticed the lack of pronoun, that he hadn't specified that *she* should look at it every year, so maybe he had meant to suggest that *we* could look at it every year.

But Claire just shook her head. "I love it," she said, "But there is no way that's surviving the journey in my suitcase and I don't have the heart to take a chance on it."

"You mean opening your luggage up to find it smashed into a million little pieces wouldn't make you want to write glowing five-star reviews for the airline's baggage handlers? Weird." Jack cast an appraising glance back over the wares for sale at the booth, then tipped his head towards the food stand, his hand that wasn't carrying the bag of ornaments coming to land on Claire's lower back.

They both decided on bratwurst in a bun, opting out of having one last German beer in favor of one more mug of glühwein before retiring to the hotel. Claire took a bite, looking around to see if there were any areas of the market that they hadn't managed to investigate yet.

Just as she was about to point to a distant corner and suggest walking by there when they were done eating, she turned back to Jack to find the bag from his purchase placed on the table in front of her.

"What's this?" she asked, raising her chin towards it.

"It's not much of a surprise," he said, "but open it."

She reached into the bag and pulled out the bookshelf ornament he had purchased for Hazel. "I...am confused. Were you just asking me if I liked it to test out a gift idea for me? Because you didn't have to..."

Jack pulled an identical ornament out of his pocket, then replaced it after she had seen it. "I got one for each of you. Do you like it?"

Claire nodded, her fingers trailing over the surface of the ornament, taking in all the details. "This is handmade, isn't it? The craftsmanship is just..."

"I know." Jack was watching her, a smile in his eyes. "Put it on your tree every year and think about this trip." He looked around then. "The Christmas market, Munich, the airport...me?" His last word was tentative, rising into a question as his eyes found hers.

Claire reached across the table, placing her hand on top of his and smiling at him. "I...well, I hope this isn't too bold, but whatever. Here goes. I hope you'll be with me next year when I hang this ornament on my tree. And we'll talk about our time in Munich and how we met there and whether or not we'll go back again someday."

Jack's eyes had lit up as he listened to her speak. "You'd like that?" When Claire nodded, his grin stretched impossibly wider. "I'd like that, too." He shot a meaningful glance at the ornament. "It's only fair to that piece of craftsmanship, after all. I doubt it's going to make it onto the tree this year, is it?"

Claire shook her head, chuckling softly. "I have no intentions of spending Christmas Eve—that is to say, the one small part of Christmas Eve that I *don't* spend on an airplane—driving all over the tri-state area trying to find the perfect Christmas tree and then decorating the bastard." Her fingers trailed over the surface of the ornament. "But I'll sneak it onto my parents' tree. And then take it off again when I leave for my apartment. It's the perfect start to my own ornament collection."

"Your first ornament?" Jack's eyebrows had climbed up his forehead. "If I'd known it was your first, I would probably have put a little more thought into it. Are you sure...?"

But Claire was nodding, picking up the bookshelf ornament to turn it over. "I love it. And I have other or-

naments...in my parents' collection, I mean. My grand-
ma always gave us an ornament for Christmas every year,
something that represented the year. I haven't bothered
to sort through the box and pick out the ones that are
mine because my parents and I always spend Christmas
together. I've never even had my own tree."

"But you want to next year?"

Claire shrugged. "I think it would be nice. My older
sister took a bunch of ornaments out of the collection after
moving out and getting married. And I can be my own
little family instead of just a branch on my parents' family
tree, you know?"

"You can," said Jack with a nod. "There's nothing
wrong with enjoying spending the holidays with your parents, of course. But making your own traditions, too...I
think there's something really special about that."

"It's like accepting the adult mantle, I guess." Claire
tipped her head to the side, weighing the pros and cons of
the dilemma. "Of course, I haven't missed having the daily
chore of sweeping up all the needles that fall off the tree
every night."

"Some would say that's why God made artificial Christmas trees," he responded with a small shrug.

"But does a fake Christmas tree smell like pine?"

"I see your question, and I'll raise you another one.
Does a fake tree have needles that stab your fingers with
a violence equivalent to avenging its own murder? And in
that same vein, how many trees have to die to get a fake
Christmas tree into your home?"

Claire smiled. "Well, the answer probably isn't zero,
considering that trees are cut down everywhere all the time

for all sorts of different purposes. But I hear your points and I will take them into advisement."

Jack squinted, studying her. "And I'll see next year what you land on?"

That set off a flutter of butterflies in Claire's lower belly. "I guess you will."

Nineteen

"Come on," Claire said, tugging on Jack's hand as she nearly slurred her words with exhaustion. "Let's go home."

Jack let himself be dragged along behind her, almost as if he were enjoying nothing more than her hand in his, her taking charge of the situation.

After their meal, they had walked one final lap around the Christmas market, picking up some roasted chestnuts at the booth in the far corner Claire had noticed. They had toasted the evening with one last mug of glühwein, savoring the drink until it was cold enough to have lost most of its flavor and charm, but both seemingly unwilling to let the evening end.

"It's not the last time we'll drink mulled wine," Claire said, as much to herself as to Jack. "And not the last time we'll be in Germany for Christmas, if I have anything to say about it."

"You would bring me here again? You wouldn't be too afraid of getting sucked into the weird airport vortex again and never escaping?"

Claire elbowed him softly in the side. "You know I would. And if there exists some kind of *Hotel California* purgatory dimension where it's just you and me and Munich and there's no means of escape..." She shrugged. "Well, that doesn't sound bad at all."

They finished their short walk back to the hotel in comfortable silence, feeling more like an established couple who didn't need words to communicate than two people who had been strangers not 48 hours before.

It was only when they were back in their hotel room that any of the day's earlier awkwardness and tension resurfaced. The bed, where they had spent most of the day, was right there, along with a temptation in the back of Claire's throat to just squeak out an invitation for Jack to join her there. *I don't mean that, you know...anything should happen. It's just...well, isn't it silly for you to spend the night on a couch when there's a piece of furniture this comfortable?*

But she didn't say it out loud. She reminded herself of all that he had shared with her that day, the hurts he had sustained in his previous relationship as well as his confident assertion that the path between the two of them must only be walked slowly. And instead, she offered first use of the bathroom to Jack and then settled herself on top of the covers with a book.

When Jack emerged from the bathroom in those damn sweatpants again—she should have made a rule against them if he was going to insist that things remain platonic—his eyebrows raised at the sight of her. "Sitting on the bed in your outside clothes?" He shook his head, tutting in mock disapproval. "What will people say, Claire? You're going to have to boil those sheets in disinfectant now. I don't know how you're going to fall asleep there when there's just so much potential for vermin creeping and crawling all over you." Jack shuddered then. "Better you than me. I'm confident no one has ever sat on my bed in their jeans."

"Of course not. Who would sit on a couch in their jeans? It's unheard of!" She gestured down to her attire. "If you must know, though, I thought this through. I put that extra blanket—the one that I'm already planning to toss on the floor because I don't know if they wash them—back on the bed so that's all my outside clothes are touching. Plus, it was better to do it this way than to change my clothes out here and risk you coming out of the bathroom and catching me in the act."

He walked closer to her then, his pupils growing darker and his gaze never leaving hers. "Why do I not believe that you really mean that?"

Claire shrugged. "I wouldn't have minded, that's true. But I'm just trying to respect your wishes. Or, I should say...not trying. Actually respecting them. I'm not going to force anything on you that you don't want. I understand your feelings, and I think they're totally valid and worthy of respect."

"That's good." Jack's gaze dropped to Claire's lips. "What would you think if I gave you a kiss goodnight and then left? Closed the door between our rooms and promised not to see you again until the morning?"

"I...would think that's very good." Claire gulped. "The first part, especially. The first part sounds very good to me." Her tongue darted out to moisten her lips. "But, like...don't feel any pressure on my account. I...uh...am totally okay with taking things as slowly as you want."

"Great," said Jack. And with that, he closed the distance between them, leaning down until his face was just a breath from Claire's, his eyes all she could see. His hand came up to cup the back of her neck, and then she was closing her eyes, leaning towards him, and all she could feel was the warmth radiating off of him and all she could smell was...him. His toothpaste, his soap, and something underneath it all that was cozy and inviting, intriguing. He smelled like the cinnamon and nutmeg in the air at the market had clung to his hair, layered on top of the body wash or cologne or whatever it was that smelled like cedar and lime.

And then his lips were on hers and Claire was in another world. An explosion of light and heat and warmth in the middle of a sea of darkness, like a spaceship exploding in deep outer space, if such a thing had even been possible—her rational mind, which had almost completely checked out but was still ever so slightly on-line knew that oxygen was necessary to feed a fire and that made loud, fiery explosions surrounded by nothing but stars impossible.

But still. That was what it felt like, and that was what the image in her mind was, and if there was ever a time *not* to be literal, then wasn't this it? She let the last part of her conscious awareness, the one that was acting like a science fiction fact checker sign off then, losing herself only in the sensation and emotion of the moment.

And what a moment it was. Jack was gentle, tentative at first, but then more confident as the moment stretched, the kisses deepening and lengthening. And then, just as Claire was about to pull back to catch her breath before diving in for another round, it was over.

She felt his absence like a broken window on a winter day. Where there had been warmth and passion and his enticing smell, now the air was cold and empty. She opened her eyes to see that Jack had stepped back and was looking down at her from a short distance away, his pupils still blown and his breaths coming more quickly than they had been when he had first come out of the bathroom. Claire could see his pulse racing in the soft, stubbly skin just below his jaw and felt a thrill of something like pride low in her belly.

I did that, she thought. *It's my presence that's creating this reaction in that gorgeous man. How did I get so lucky? And how the hell am I supposed to fall asleep* now?

"Well then," Jack interrupted her thoughts, a smile appearing on his face that matched the joy dancing through her veins. "I should leave." It was clear he didn't want to, judging both by the way his gaze hadn't left hers and the fact that his feet were unmoving.

"You probably *should*," said Claire, "but I understand if you don't want to." She darted a gaze to the empty spot on the bed beside her.

That seemed to sober Jack, who nodded once. "You're right, I should. Good night, Claire. I'll see you in the morning. Get some sleep."

She watched him leave, disappointment at knowing she wouldn't see him for almost eight hours filling her being. *This is ridiculous*, she told herself. And yet, as the door closed behind him, she couldn't deny that no matter how absurd it was, she missed Jack.

In the morning, Claire woke with a smile on her face. She had kissed Jack the night before, and it had been a good kiss. Good enough to occupy her thoughts far past her normal bedtime and good enough for her to attempt some midnight telekinesis and see if she could get the door between them to open—or vanish altogether—by sheer force of will.

It, of course, hadn't worked, but at least it had led—*eventually*—to Claire falling asleep, exhausted by her invisible effort.

As she turned around in the comfortable bed, reaching for her phone to check the time, she heard sounds of stirring from the living room and her smile stretched even wider.

"Good morning," she called towards the door.

"Morning," came Jack's voice, even deeper with lack of use. "Mind if I come in there to use the bathroom?"

"Be my guest," said Claire, throwing the blankets aside as she stretched and yawned, all nervous energy at the excitement of seeing Jack again after being separated by a thin wooden door for the duration of the night.

The door handle turned, and in walked Jack, his hair mussed and eyes still looking only half awake. Claire's pulse tripped over itself.

"Hi," she said, her voice feeling and sounding small as she pushed herself up to lean against the headboard.

"Hi," he replied with a dip of his head. "Sleep well?"

Claire nodded and murmured her agreement. "You?" Why did this all feel so awkward again? Was it because of the kiss the night before, or was it merely that being in that vulnerable morning state with someone was always awkward when you had known them for less than a week? In a month, it would be normal, in a year completely unremarkable. She never felt awkward waking up in the same house as Emma or her family...not even with Connor, the first time she had slept over at Emma and Connor's place.

That's because of the lack of sexual tension, goofball, she chided herself, watching Jack's back disappear into the bathroom. *If Jack were my best friend's husband, I never would have let myself feel this way about him. Plus, she would be here too. No, it's all just entirely too weird. This is, like, established couple level of intimacy, not flirtatious friends who've kissed exactly once.*

She hauled herself out of the bed then, digging through her suitcase for a change of clothes and to get ready for the day. If this morning went anything like yesterday morning, she and Jack would be having breakfast downstairs before heading to the airport. And this time, they would *definitely* be claiming their rightful seats on the flight.

"Oh, right!" Claire cried when she heard the bathroom door open. "Merry Christmas Eve! I forgot to tell you that when I woke up, but...I mean, yeah. Today's the day."

Jack had walked over to her, rubbing his hand on her upper back softly as he passed by on the way to the window. "Merry Christmas Eve to you too, Claire."

She came to stand beside him and they looked out at the view of Munich together. A light dusting of snow had fallen since they had entered the hotel the night before, and between the buildings and the trees, all of it covered in what looked like powdered sugar, it was the perfect vision of a gingerbread Christmas village.

"It feels a little strange, doesn't it?" she asked him finally as she turned to meet his eyes. "Christmas Eve in a hotel, I mean. And soon on an airplane. I can't say I've ever spent a holiday quite like this before."

"I haven't either." He smiled at her. "And I think if I were with anyone else, I could feel sad about it. Missing my family, missing the appropriate festive feelings in just the right intensity..." He reached for her hand and she let him take it. "But being here with you, even in a nondescript hotel room, with nothing ahead of us but a mediocre breakfast, a shuttle ride, and a long flight...it feels entirely festive enough." He lifted her hand to his mouth, pressing his lips to her knuckles. "It might be *too* festive, actually. I'm already afraid that next year won't possibly be able to compare."

Clare could feel her cheeks heating at the intensity of his attention. "Don't say that. Who's to say next year won't be even better than this year? I like to believe that such a thing is possible." She cleared her throat. "And I'm inclined to think that sleeping on a more familiar mattress with linens whose cleanliness I can vouch for with 100 percent confidence will stack the deck in next year's favor."

"So you definitely want to be at home in your own apartment next year? I'm just making mental notes, I mean. Want to be prepared, make sure our calendars align."

She smiled. "I didn't say that. *Familiar* could mean all sorts of things." Claire shrugged. "It could even be as simple as a hotel room I booked myself rather than one an airline booked for me."

"That's true. Of course, a familiar could also mean, like, a witch's animal companion. But I know you didn't mean it that way." He tapped his temple. "Context clues, you know."

"You're ridiculous." Claire huffed out a laugh, ready to change the subject. They could talk about their plans for next year some other time, perhaps after they'd known each other for at least a week and when they weren't still waking up and trying to hide their morning breath from each other.

"Should we get ready to head down for breakfast?" she asked. "I figured we should get to the airport early today, so we don't run the risk of checking in too late and losing our seats."

Jack had to laugh at that. "First of all, we were there plenty early yesterday, weren't we? I mean, is it possible to be at the airport more than three hours before your flight departs? If so, I can't wait to experience it. But also, they can't boot us off the plane. That's how we ended up in this situation in the first place. If the airline could just pick people at random—or by the order in which they checked in—and tell them they were grounded, I doubt very much they would have paid for a hotel room for the two of us."

"Three hotel rooms, actually. Just if you want to get technical about it." Claire grinned at Jack, teasing him. "But I get what you're saying. And you're right about the three hours thing, too, I guess. So...give me twenty minutes and we can go downstairs?"

He nodded. "Perfect."

The events of the morning unfolded in such an eerily similar way to the previous morning that Claire experienced a brief moment of panic, wondering if she and Jack were living out some kind of *Groundhog Day* scenario. And that particular panic triggered another, even briefer one, where she wondered if, in fact, only *she* was living in that *Groundhog Day* scenario and Jack had no memory of their kiss the night before because they were about to live that same day over again.

It helped that she remembered his comments about going to the airport "yesterday" and also that he hadn't remarked about waking up in a strange room, trading in his familiar hotel room for a suite seemingly in his sleep.

It also helped that there was snow on the ground, which hadn't been there the day before.

Okay, so there are actually plenty of indicators that time is continuing to pass in the normal manner. The only thing that had Claire second guessing herself was that kiss. She was pretty sure she hadn't dreamed it and all signs pointed to a new day dawning that morning, which meant it wasn't in their shared future but in their shared past...and yet the thing that kept her doubting it was the fact that they hadn't acknowledged it. Not after the fact, and certainly not this morning.

Jack wasn't drunk last night, was he? Claire wondered. *He certainly didn't seem drunk...or heck, he didn't taste like mulled wine. Maybe he was sleepwalking. Yeah right, sleep-walking from the bathroom, where he had been sleep-brushing his teeth and sleep-washing his face? That can't be how that works.*

Claire managed to push it from her mind enough to enjoy one more hotel breakfast with Jack, mediocre coffee and all. Following that, they had returned to the room, repacked their suitcases, and they were on the shuttle to the airport and all the way through security before it totally landed on her what the day had in store.

They were going home.

Twenty

As much as a small part of Claire had wished for yet another act of divine intervention to grant her and Jack one more day together, one more day before they had to reenter the real world and see if the tentative thing blooming between them would survive, that didn't happen.

The gate had been emptier that morning than any of the two previous mornings. "That's what happens when you fly on Christmas Eve, I guess," Jack had said. "All the people who care about spending the holidays with their family had the decency to arrive, oh...yesterday?"

Claire had just nodded. His words had stirred up a feeling of guilt, both for so casually depriving her family of her company over the holidays...and for the airline staff who were having to work today. She bit her lip as she surveyed the area surrounding the gate.

"What are you thinking?" Jack asked at her expression.

"All of these people are working today because of us." She nodded towards the counter, then the admittedly smaller number of shops that were still open.

"Not just us," said Jack, gesturing to the passengers around them. "All of these people are flying today, so even if you and I had skipped the flight, it would still be running." He reached over and placed a reassuring hand on her knee. "Plus...not everyone celebrates Christmas."

"I know that," Claire retorted a little too sharply. "It just feels, even if it's not *your* special holiday, that on a day when almost everything is closed and almost everyone is at home with their loved ones, having to go in to work would be such a bummer."

"Maybe. But maybe people like the camaraderie of being part of a smaller crew." He nodded towards the flight crew, who were smiling and laughing at the counter. "They look like they're having more fun today than they did yesterday. Plus, I'm sure that holiday overtime helps."

"You might be right," she admitted. "Still. I won't make a habit of flying on holidays. Lesson learned."

Jack looked at her carefully, studying the expression on her face. "You don't regret taking the next flight, do you?"

"Not at all." She smiled at him, then placed her hand over his and gave a light squeeze. "I'm gladder that we met than I have been about anything in a long time. I'm just feeling a little strange about missing Christmas Eve."

"Well, it's..." He checked his watch. "It's just after three a.m. in New York right now, so I doubt you're missing much of anything. And assuming everything is on time today, you'll be there in plenty of time to join the Christmas Eve traditions. Let me guess...singing carols? More mulled wine?" He frowned. "You aren't one of those families that opens their gifts on Christmas Eve, are you?"

Claire recoiled in mock horror. "How could we possibly do that when Santa hasn't even come yet on Christmas Eve? No, with the Davis family, it's mostly about the meal, the music, and sitting around the tree with no other lights on in the room, just chatting and enjoying each other's company. It's nice."

"You'll be there for it." Jack nodded. "And we'll enjoy today, too. I promise."

She wondered how he could make any promises about what the day held in store for them. Jack wasn't exactly in charge of anything that was about to happen, from the weather that could delay their flight to the choice of in-flight meal, but she wouldn't tell him that. If he wanted to believe that Christmas Eve in the air was a fun and exciting adventure, then she could give him that, at least.

Claire briefly entertained the idea of going in search of something to make the day a little more special—some snacks or holiday-specific entertainment—but let herself relax in her seat, leaning in to Jack's arm. *Sometimes you just have to go with the flow and be open to whatever happens,* she told herself, *especially if you're solely to blame for finding yourself in that situation in the first place.* After all, if it had been so important to her to be home in time for Christmas, she wouldn't have thought twice about taking her flight home the day before. She had signed up for this, and it was inevitable that there would be consequences to her actions.

Naturally, there had been no announcement seeking out volunteers to take the next flight. The first time the speaker had crackled to life, Claire's heart had leaped in anticipation of that offer coming her way again, of how much excitement it had brought into her life in the previous 48 hours. But when the flight crew had instead wished everyone a merry Christmas and hinted at some unusually festive plans for the transatlantic journey, Claire relaxed back into her seat. *So. This was it. They were really going.*

They had again asked for their seats to be assigned together, and Claire felt warm under his gaze when Jack turned to her to ask if she wanted the aisle or window seat before the counter agent printed their boarding passes.

"It doesn't matter to me," she said. *As long as I'm sitting next to you, I'm happy.*

Finally, it was time to board, the waiting passengers lining up eagerly in anticipation, in what Claire feared was a preview of what was bound to happen within moments after the plane landed in Newark. She shot a glance at Jack and then tipped her head towards the line. "You don't...?" She trailed off when she saw understanding pass across his face.

"Oh, no." He shook his head. "Get in line for a seat that's already reserved for me, on a flight that—by the looks of this crowd, anyway—is going to have a bunch of empty seats, anyway?" Jack wrinkled his nose. "Nah, I'm good. Unless you want to get in the line. In which case"—he let out an exaggerated sigh—"I will gladly follow you, just happy to be in your company."

Claire laughed as she elbowed him in the ribs. "You are ridiculous." She shot a nervous glance at the line that was continuing to grow in length. "I'm not going to lie. There's a certain kind of FOMO that crops up when I see a line like this. Like if I'm not in it, then the plane is going to leave without me. Which I know is ridiculous. It's probably actually therapeutic for that FOMO if I just sit here with you until it's time to go to the gate. As long as you don't make me wait so long that they start looking like they're going to close up the jetway and leave us behind."

"You realize there's plenty of middle ground between those two extremes, don't you? We'll get in the line soon, I promise you. As soon as it gets a little shorter."

True to his word, it was less than ten minutes later that Claire and Jack were making their way onto the plane. He had steered her in front of him with his hand on her lower back, and Claire was glad to not be in danger of making eye contact when he had her in that position. What was it about the simple gesture of that reassuring palm, the heat that she could feel through her shirt, the clear *togetherness* that it implied?

It wasn't as if she didn't know where to go, as if she needed to be steered...and yet the reminder that he was right behind her, that he quite literally had her back filled her with an ease that she didn't normally experience on a travel day. *I could get used to this...*

They found their seats on the plane, two seats by themselves on the left side—one aisle seat and one window seat, nice and cozy. Jack paused then, looking at Claire with a raised eyebrow. "You're going to have to decide," he told her. "And don't be polite or make your decision based on what you think I want."

She nodded. "Okay, then, if you insist." She ducked in first, taking the window seat. When she flew by herself, she always opted for an aisle seat, so averse to disturbing the person next to her if she needed to get up and use the restroom or simply stretch her legs. She had a feeling, though, that Jack wouldn't mind. She certainly would feel more comfortable tapping him on the shoulder and asking a favor than she had ever felt with a stranger sitting next to her, no matter how friendly they had been.

When Jack was seated, they both settled in. Claire filled the seatback pocket in front of her with her water bottle, headphones, and her e-reader, and she noted with some pride that Jack had slipped his copy of *Serendipity Springs* into the pocket in front of his seat. Catching a glimpse of his bookmark, which seemed to be marking the rough middle of the book, she recoiled lightly in surprise. When had he found the time to read it?

She dismissed the thought. It might not even be marking his page. Maybe it was just a receipt he was saving for later—for taxes? business expenses?—and the middle of the book had seemed like a good place for safekeeping. Considering that Jack was a self-confessed spine cracker, it was entirely possible that he had marked his place in the book with a dogeared page. Claire suppressed a shudder at the thought.

Once the flight was boarded and the cabin crew announced that the doors would soon be closing and that everyone should take their seats, Claire looked around. There were empty seats scattered around their section of the airplane, and she could see her fellow passengers surveying them as well. If Jack wanted to get up and claim a different seat somewhere with a little more space, she wouldn't hold it against him. His knees were pressing into the back of the seat in front of him, and she didn't begrudge him seeking out a little more comfort.

He shot a quizzical expression at her. "What's up? You're looking around an awful lot. Are you a nervous flier?"

Claire shook her head. "This flight is pretty empty, especially compared with the previous two flights to Newark." She nodded her head towards a bank of four empty seats. "Do you want to move there? Get some more space to stretch out?"

"Do...do you want me to? If I move there, then you'll have these two seats to yourself. Would that be more comfortable?" He shook his head. "What am I talking about? Of course that would be more comfortable." He moved to unbuckle his seatbelt, but Claire stopped him with a hand on his arm.

"I'm not telling you to go for me. I just want you to be comfortable, not squished into this seat here with me."

Jack studied her, his eyes squinting slightly as if he were trying to read the fine print across her irises. "It's an airplane seat, Claire. Unless they upgrade me to business class, it's pretty much a guarantee that it's going to be uncomfortable." He glanced over at the bank of seats she had pointed out. "It looks like some other folks are having the same idea, and I don't particularly care to fight a battle royale over some airplane seats. Do you mind if I stay here?"

She shook her head earnestly. "Of course not. I'd prefer to have you stay here, if it were up to me. I...I was just trying to be considerate."

He smiled at her then. "Well, stop that right now. I'm staying here with you for the next eight hours, and there's nothing you can do about it."

Claire smiled, settling back into her seat. *I wouldn't have it any other way.*

The flight crew had truly gone out of their way to make that day's journey as festive as possible. First, there were the Santa hats that many of them wore, and then there were the treats they had distributed once the flight took off, gingerbread for all the passengers and small Christmas stockings for the children branded with the airline's logo. Prior to serving the first meal, they had come around with a special cart and offered all the adult passengers a mug of mulled wine, which made Claire suppress a giggle into Jack's arm.

"What are you smirking about over there?" he asked in a soft voice as he accepted their two mugs from the flight attendant with a smile.

"I'm just imagining that we're all about to break out into Christmas karaoke mayhem, like some kind of festive singalong straight out of a movie." She accepted the mug from him with some amount of trepidation. "It also seems *very* early to be getting into the mulled wine."

"Ah, but you're forgetting." He gestured around them. "Time isn't real on an airplane. It's like we're in limbo between two different worlds and no rules apply." The corners of his lips dipped down in thought. "Actually, I think it begins at the airport. That's why you see people drinking beers at the same time other people are inhaling coffee and a croissant trying to wake up. You can eat or drink anything at any time, and you can close your eyes and sleep for hours straight any time the urge comes over you. It might be barely ten o'clock in the morning in Munich, but they're probably going to serve us dinner and cut the lights soon."

"That's super weird, though, isn't it? If we fall asleep now, it's going to be like we slept through Christmas Eve."

"And yet, when we arrive, it will still *be* Christmas Eve." Jack wiggled his eyebrows. "At least if you sleep now you'll be rested for it."

But Claire had no interest in sleeping, in spending her remaining hours with Jack unconscious. They chatted, read their books, even picked up where their movie marathon the day before had left off and watched *Die Hard 2* together, hitting the play buttons in sync so that they would experience it all at the exact same time.

At some point, and against all her wishes, Claire drifted off to sleep. When she woke up, her head was on Jack's shoulder and his hand was gently squeezing her knee, trying to get her attention.

"What's up?" she asked, wiping a hand across her face to remove any evidence of her recent unconsciousness.

"They're coming around with a final meal service before we land in two hours." His small smile was apologetic. "I didn't want to wake you up, but I also didn't want to decide for you that you were going to skip this meal."

"I appreciate it. I could definitely eat." She lifted her hand to stifle a yawn. "What time is it? How long was I asleep?"

"You were out for a while," said Jack, lifting up the book—*her* book—that was on his lap. "Long enough for me to finish this masterpiece, which was just the tiniest bit challenging, considering that my arm was falling asleep a little bit."

"Oh! Sorry." Claire lifted her head from Jack's shoulder then, sitting upright and putting some distance between them. "You should have just pushed me off."

Jack chuckled softly. "Never. It was nice. It's not like I was in pain. I just had to figure out how to hold my book and turn the pages with one hand without giving myself a crick in the neck. Turns out that's why they invented these handy tray things." He reached forward and patted the tray.

Claire was silent for a beat. Finally, she asked the question that was weighing on her. "So you liked the book?"

He nodded. "I really did. It kept me turning the pages, wanting to know what was going to happen next. And even though I've heard you and Hazel both talk about happily ever afters enough to know that one was coming, I was still feeling anxious to see what was going to happen to Hector and Isabel." He shook his head. "I mean, it's crazy. Those two started off hating each other, but by the end of it, it was so clear that they actually loved each other. And that some of that was there all along...I think I'm going to read it again and see if I can pick up on the hints that I missed the first time. And I liked that it wasn't just about the love story either, but that they both learned something about themselves, too." He tapped the cover of the book lightly. "I can definitely see the appeal of a book like this, and I'm looking forward to reading the others."

Claire was practically vibrating with joy. She rarely asked friends or family members what they thought of her books. If one of her friends happened to mention that they were reading one of her books, she never followed up, always figuring that if someone liked it enough to tell her, they would. And if she never heard another peep, well maybe they were subscribing to the "if you don't have anything nice to say, don't say anything at all" belief.

Or maybe they have entire lives that don't revolve around you, a voice reminded her in the back of her awareness. *Maybe you don't need to take it personally at all.*

She simply smiled and thanked him, settling back into her seat. She could try appreciating a compliment for a moment, rather than immediately justifying to herself why she might not deserve it. Even if it was just this once.

Twenty-One

It was as if Claire blinked and the remaining two hours of flight time had passed in the brief pause while her eyes were closed. Too soon, the captain announced that they were beginning their descent towards Newark, and she was making sure her seatbelt was buckled and her seat was upright and...

"You okay?" Jack asked, concern wrinkling his forehead.

Claire nodded. "Yeah. It's just...wow. It's over. Or, almost over, at least."

He reached over and grabbed her hand on the armrest. "This part is almost over. But we'll see each other soon, I hope. What are you doing the day after tomorrow?"

"The...day after tomorrow? What day is that, even? What day is it today?"

Jack smiled. "I mean the day after Christmas. Boxing Day, I believe it's called."

"Oh. Uh...nothing? I mean, my little brother likes to go shopping that day, but I like to do anything I can to avoid getting dragged along."

"So that means you would be up for meeting up with me? I don't know...we could go into the city, maybe? Do something cliche like ice skate at Rockefeller Center or go up to the top of the Empire State Building or something cheesy like that."

Claire squinted at Jack. "Are you playing this off as cheesy because you're self conscious about it? I mean, the whole Empire State Building thing might be a cliche, especially if we do a full-on *Sleepless in Seattle* reenactment and only allow ourselves technology from the 90s."

"You want me to page you when I'm there? I'm not sure if there's a payphone on the observation deck," Jack deadpanned.

She shook her head at him. "I definitely *do* want to spend Boxing Day with you. And I'm curious if there are any Boxing Day traditions I should know about. Why don't we plan to meet at whatever time we think we'll both be awake and then play it by ear?"

"That sounds good." Jack shot her a look. "So I'm guessing that's why we already exchanged phone numbers, rather than leaving our meeting to chance?"

Claire rolled her eyes. "Exactly." She settled back in her seat with a smile, thrilling at the idea of seeing Jack again in just two days. She had believed—or at least *wanted* to believe—that they would meet again, but that it was happening so soon had her grinning with joy and anticipation.

They didn't part ways for as long as they could possibly avoid it. Claire remembered her initial flight to London six weeks before, and the older woman sitting next to her, who had struck up a friendly conversation once they were landing. The two of them had wished each other pleasant stays in the city...and then exited the plane one after the other, still in the prime positions to keep the conversation going. And yet, since they had already said their farewells, it felt awkward to do more than smile and nod. Their time together had ended, and there was no need to extend it beyond its natural deadline.

Of course, it wasn't like that with Jack. They left the plane together, and Jack waited for her when she ducked into a bathroom, just as she had hoped he would.

"Is someone picking you up?" Claire asked, as the baggage carousel began to turn.

Jack shook his head. "I told them I'd take a cab. Insisted upon it, actually."

"Oh." Claire's mouth turned down at the corners. "My dad is coming to get me, and I'm sure he wouldn't mind dropping you off at home." She looked up, feeling hope course through her veins at the thought of just a few more moments with Jack.

But he was still shaking his head. "I do really appreciate the offer, but it's not necessary. I promise." He looked at her with warmth and kindness in his eyes. "It's Christmas Eve, Claire. The sooner you and your family are cozy and comfortable, the better. And the same for mine. And I promise I'll tip the driver well." He winked at her.

"Right." She nodded, distracted from her next words by the sight of her suitcase sliding down the ramp onto the conveyer belt. Her pulse picked up at its approach, the end of this time with Jack rapidly coming to an end. Claire stepped forward as the bag approached, but he slid up behind her and reached one long arm around her, grabbing the handle and lifting the suitcase easily.

"Thanks," she said with a smile. "I'll wait for yours to come around."

"No, please don't." Jack gave one more small shake of his head. "Your dad is waiting and there's no need, really. It'll be out soon, I'm sure." His lips moved into a smile as his hand came up to tuck her hair behind her ear. "I'm going to see you soon, Claire. Don't forget that."

"I know. It's just..." Her pulse was still racing, anxious feelings increasing with every passing moment, every second that brought them closer to parting ways. "It just feels weird to say goodbye to you."

"It shouldn't." Jack frowned. "Two days ago, you didn't even know me." But he smiled then, before leaning forward to place a soft kiss on her forehead. "Bad joke, I know. It feels weird to me, too. I don't want to let you go, and yet I know that abandoning your family to spend Christmas with someone you just met is, like, a major red flag. If Hazel was doing that, I would definitely be pulling her aside to have a little chat. And it's too soon for you to meet my parents or me to meet yours, so..." Jack leaned back and shrugged. "What choice do we have? It's just one day. Which I realize is actually half of the length of our entire relationship." His chuckle was small and sheepish. "But don't wish tomorrow away, okay? Enjoy the day."

"I will." Claire wrapped her arms around him and squeezed, her ear coming to his chest. "And you have a merry Christmas. Say hi to Hazel for me."

His laugh rumbled under her ear. "I will. And I'll text you on Boxing Day."

"You'd better."

"If I don't, then it's a sign that I've been kidnapped. So you'd better text me, send the police to my house, hire a private investigator..." His tone was deadpan. "Do what you have to do, Claire, to avenge me."

She chuckled and squeezed him tighter. "That was dark. But I accept the challenge." She let herself enjoy the feel of his arms around her for a beat longer and then, at the sensation of her phone vibrating in her pocket, she pulled back. It was time.

"See you soon, Jack," she said with a smile that was braver than she felt. "Get home safely."

He nodded. "I will. Merry Christmas, Claire."

"Merry Christmas, Jack."

She could feel his eyes on her as she wheeled her suitcase away and towards the exit. She turned back one last time before walking through the automatic doors, smiling at the sight of Jack waving at her. Boxing Day couldn't come soon enough. As soon as she'd had the thought, though, she chastised herself. Christmas was always a special day in the Davis household, and she owed it to her family, especially to her parents, to be as present for it as she could be.

Outside the door, she braced against the cold wind, wrapping her coat more tightly around her body. There were horns sounding in a few different directions as she searched for her dad's sedan, but his voice bellowing, "Claire Bear! Over here!" was unmistakable. Claire grinned, waved, and slipped into a jog at the sight of her father.

Doug Davis was standing next to his car, hands in the pockets of his parka and a wide smile on his face as Claire approached. He pulled her in for a bear hug, giving her a tight squeeze. "Hey there, kiddo," he said when he released her and began wheeling her suitcase towards the trunk. "Welcome back. And hey! Merry Christmas!"

"Merry Christmas, Dad," said Claire. She reached for her suitcase, attempting to resume control of the maneuvering that was about to happen, but Doug pushed her away and nodded towards the passenger seat.

"Get in the car, kid. It's cold out here. Your mom sent along a travel mug with some hot chocolate for you. She didn't put any schnapps in it, though, so don't get excited."

Claire chuckled, shaking her head. "Yeah, good call, Mom. We don't need to get in trouble for breaking open container laws on Christmas Eve, do we?"

Her dad gave her a skeptical look. "And why exactly do you think I would be getting pulled over on Christmas Eve, anyway? You'd better not be doubting your old man's driving skills."

"Never." Claire opened the door of the car, but waited for her dad to join her at the front of the vehicle before climbing inside. "So, how's the day going? Is everyone at home?"

Doug nodded as he put the car in gear and began to drive. "Gang's all there. Your mother has been cooking up a storm. Jeremy's no help at all, of course. And your sister arrived last night with the whole family. It's been non-stop ever since they all turned up." He shot her a warm glance before redirecting his eyes back to the road. "Hasn't been the same without you, though, so I'm really glad you're here. We all will be."

Claire's smile was perfunctory. So often, when the whole Davis family was gathered, there were complicated feelings. Insecurities that bubbled to the surface that never would have bothered her on a normal day left her fake smiling and drinking one too many glasses of wine on many a Thanksgiving. The tension with her sister had been a fixture for years, and it showed no sign of evaporating anytime soon. Was it the fate of middle children everywhere to suffer the same?

But something felt different this year, even if it was only the fact that she had missed out on nearly half of the time they spent together for Christmas. But Claire felt like the guest of honor, the one arriving fashionably late, in the middle of a celebration that had surely been awaiting her arrival. And it wasn't as if she were arriving late because she'd been playing video games—she had been on a European book tour. If her siblings were ever going to be impressed by her, now was the time. Even the idea that her absence had been felt was enough to warm Claire from the inside out.

"I'll let you rest a bit," said her dad. "I'd talk your ear off about your big tour, but I know everyone else is going to want to hear it, too. Plus, you might need a minute to catch your breath before the kids descend on you." He glanced at her again. "Was it a good trip? Meet anyone nice?"

"It was great," she admitted with a nod. "A bit long, but those extra days in Munich were actually really fun.

The perfect ending." She felt wistful as she gazed out the window, the familiar sights not as comforting as she would have expected them to be a few days ago. Instead, they only served to remind her just how far she was from Munich—and from the reality she had lived in there with Jack.

"Yeah, I was wondering about that. You surprised us with that first text about coming home late, and then two days in a row?" Doug shook his head. "You should call the airline about that. That's some pretty terrible customer service, if you ask me. You should send them a Twitter or something, get some attention on it."

Claire shook her head. "It's really okay, Dad. I volunteered both times, and they compensated me for it. It was just fun to be in Munich, and we wanted a little more time there."

Doug's glance came with a wrinkled brow. "Who's 'we'? Someone else was there with you? I thought Bianca stayed behind?"

Claire's stomach twisted at the reminder of her agent. She hadn't heard so much as a peep from her since that last message, still had the uncertainty of whatever Bianca had so desperately needed to talk to her about hanging over her head. Not that she would be calling her tonight or tomorrow—even agents deserved to have a day or two off for the holidays.

"I made a friend in Munich," Claire explained, not offering more than she was comfortable sharing. If her parents and her siblings knew that there was a man in the equation, then she would either need to be prepared for incessant teasing—"Claire and Jack sitting in a tree..."—or the disapproving head shakes that would come when they realized she had stayed, had deprived them of spending Christmas Eve with her, because of him.

"That's nice. I'm glad you weren't there alone. We all missed you like crazy and were hoping you would be alright on your own, not feeling too homesick in your hotel room. It's good to make a friend. You gals explored the city together?"

Claire gulped. She should have guessed her dad, old-fashioned as he was sometimes inclined to be, would assume that she had only bothered to strike up a conversation with a friendly stranger because they were both women. But she couldn't lie to him. She braced herself and went for the briefest explanation she could. "Yeah, Jack and I explored Munich together, and we both flew back today. His family lives in the area, too."

Doug nodded, but he was quiet, thoughtful. Claire offered up a silent prayer that her dad would refrain from offering any advice or comments about her relationship—or lack thereof—with Jack, and her wish was granted. He simply switched on the radio, already set to a station playing non-stop Christmas songs, and hummed along as he drove the remaining twenty minutes to the Davis house.

As soon as the garage door opened, before they had even turned into the driveway of her childhood home, the front door had flown open and Davises were swarming out onto the yard and driveway. Claire's mom was leading the pack, a spatula in one hand and an apron tied around her waist. Alison's kids were right on her heels, and Claire thought she heard their small voices crying, "Auntie Claire! Auntie Claire!"

Claire got out of the car with a smile on her face, and she was engulfed by hugs immediately, the kids, Wendy and Amelia, holding on around her calves while her mom pulled her into her arms. "Hi, sweetheart," said Laura Davis, pulling back to take in Claire's appearance. "I'm so glad you're home."

"I told you I wouldn't come home without her," called Doug from the other side of the car.

Claire hugged her mom again and then crouched down to hug both of the kids at the same time, whispering that she had a surprise for them in her suitcase. Getting back to her feet, Alison, her older sister and the mother of those two adorable young people, gave her a quick smile and even quicker hug. "Glad to see you, Claire. Merry Christmas. Come on inside, kids. You don't have coats on." She shuffled off with the children, her wife Trish giving Claire a quick hug of her own and an apologetic smile before taking off after them.

Jeremy, her younger brother, was waiting to greet her a bit further back from everyone else, his eyebrows raised and full of meaning when Claire finally looked his way. She chuckled at what she saw there and nodded, closing the distance between them to pull him in for a hug and to mutter, "Some things never change, do they?" into his ear.

As she looked up at the house, the handmade wreath hanging there like every year before, the same one that Laura had purchased at a craft fair while visiting Claire at NYU years before. She caught a glimpse under a dusting of snow of what looked to be melted jack-o'-lanterns left over from Halloween, probably carved by Wendy and Amelia, and smiled at the sight. Even if there was a part of her that longed to be some place else, she knew she was home.

Twenty-Two

The evening passed in a flash, thanks to Claire's late arrival. The whole family had eaten a few hours before she arrived, a fact that they were all apologetic about, though Claire assured them that she didn't mind.

"I ate on the plane, I promise," she said, eyeballing the spread her mom had left arranged on the countertop, "but if you all don't mind watching, I'll definitely take a second meal. Believe it or not, Mom, this looks way better than airplane food."

Laura swatted her lightly with a kitchen towel. "It wasn't just me. Alison and Trish brought all the veggies."

"Alright then." Claire gave an impressed nod, taking a little bit of everything on her plate, despite the faint protestations of her stomach that was both disoriented by the time zone change and still discombobulated from all the pressure changes of takeoff and landing.

The kids were in the living room, watching a Christmas movie and eating popcorn under the watchful eyes of their mothers, who had to intervene a time or two to ensure that Pepper, the family dog, didn't end up eating more popcorn than both children combined. Claire joined the rest of her family at the dining room table, the open living room-dining room combination still keeping them all together despite the difference in mealtime activities.

"So," began Laura, "tell us all about your trip!" She gestured to Claire's plate. "I mean between bites, of course." She pulled a face. "Sorry. Want me to tell you about our day instead?"

Claire nodded as she chewed a mouthful of Brussels sprouts. "Please do," she said, when she had swallowed. "I don't even know where to begin."

"Claire Bear mentioned something about a new friend she made in Munich," said Doug, his eyes twinkling and his eyebrows climbing his forehead. "And apparently he's from New Jersey. What do you all think about that?"

"I'd like to know more!" called Trish from the living room, before shooting Claire an apologetic look. "Sorry, Claire. I'm just...a sucker for a good holiday meet cute, I guess."

"It's true," chimed in Alison with a serious nod before darting a look in the direction of the kids, whose attention was focused on the movie, but could be diverted without even a moment's notice. "Of course, if it's not a kid-friendly story, can we save it until these two conk out?"

Claire closed her eyes and shook her head. "This is what I get for telling the biggest gossip of the family my juicy news." She opened her eyes to level a playful glare at her dad. "Anyway, it's too soon to say what it is, but I did make a new friend and we did have a fun time together." She shrugged. "I'm going to meet up with him in a couple days, so maybe I can tell you more after that. I might see him again on this side of the Atlantic and realize I made the whole thing up."

"Oh, please." Jeremy scoffed. "Claire, you write love stories for a living. Surely you aren't impressionable enough to develop a crush on someone simply for being in the right place at the right time. I doubt very much that there are any rose-colored glasses that are about to fall off and reveal an ugly truth to you."

Claire was quiet after that, as the rest of her family chuckled and raised their eyebrows at Jeremy's comments before changing the subject. What could you say in response to such wisdom? But that was Jeremy...quiet, most of the time, but when he did have something to share, he was more than happy to do so, no filter needed.

The kids went to sleep soon after, with promises of full stockings and presents under the tree, making it almost impossible for them to close their little eyes and settle in for the night. Claire had joined Trish for the bedtime routine at Amelia's request, flipping through the pages of an old copy of *The Night Before Christmas* that had been in the Davis family at least since Claire had been the same age as the kids.

As Wendy's yawns became more frequent and Amelia couldn't keep her eyes open any longer, Trish nodded towards the door and she and Claire tiptoed out of the room, switching off the light on their way before closing the door almost the whole way.

They walked down the stairs to rejoin the rest of the family, and Trish leaned towards Claire, dropping her voice. "We're all really glad to see you, even Alison. I know she doesn't always express it that well, but she really does care about you."

It was all Claire could do to stop herself from scoffing. Warm fuzzy feelings between herself and her older sister hadn't exactly been in abundance since they were teenagers. It wasn't as if either of them were to blame, Claire knew, but simply that such differences in personality and disposition weren't exactly conducive to a blossoming friendship. If they weren't related, they wouldn't even know each other, that much was clear. Alison would be immersed in her work, her mission to singlehandedly eradicate housing inequality, and Claire would still be playing around with her "stories," devoting too much of her time to an endeavor that Alison considered a nice hobby at best, but not something you could trot out at dinner parties and expect to impress anyone.

It would be one thing if those were simply Claire's ideas of what her sister thought of her. If that were the case, then maybe she could talk herself out of it with some nice affirmations, maybe even reading a few positive reviews of her bestsellers.

But the unsurmountable obstacle between them was probably the fact that every terrible thing Alison thought about Claire, she had said to her on one particularly eventful Thanksgiving.

It had been a few years prior, the year before Alison and Trish got married, and whether it was fueled by too much to drink or pre-wedding nerves or a third thing that Claire couldn't even fathom, once the words had come out, they couldn't be unsaid. Claire had made a point of booking publicity-related travel in late November and early December ever since, though this was the closest she had ever come to missing Christmas.

She gave Trish a small smile and the barest of nods. "I'm glad you're all here," she said, hoping that how strongly she meant it about the kids could cover over the awkward feelings between herself and Alison. All she needed to do was get through these few days, and then they would go back to their own worlds, their own lack of communication and sharing. The family group text chain, where birthday wishes and holiday greetings were shared, was just about enough as far as Claire was concerned.

Unless she thought about the way things had been before. Back when she and Alison were kids, living at home and sharing their disparate wardrobes and talking about everything under the sun. Alison would give Claire advice about the classes—and tips about how to impress the teachers—she had taken three years prior, and Claire was always a captive audience when Alison was reviewing flashcards or practicing for a debate.

Things change, Claire thought to herself as she slipped onto the couch next to her mom, who was crocheting what appeared to be a sweater for one of the children. *I can appreciate the relationship Alison and I had without expecting we can ever get back to it.*

Jeremy was setting up the chess board, waiting for Doug, who was making cups of tea—Earl Grey for Alison and peppermint for everyone else, if Claire had to guess—in the kitchen.

Claire glanced at her phone, willing it to show her a message from Jack, some inside joke or a selfie with Alison or a note about how much he missed her, but there was nothing there, and she didn't want to be the first one to reach out after their arrival back in the US. Not yet, at least. If she hadn't heard from him by the next evening, she would send a message just to make sure they were still on for the meeting.

When she dropped her phone in her lap, she looked up to find Alison looking at her, her expression unreadable. Claire held her gaze for a moment, seeing something there that opened up a question in her mind. There was a vulnerability, something that looked almost like longing. But no, that couldn't be it. Claire darted her gaze away, focusing her attention on her mom.

"Should I put on some music? A movie? Something in the background?"

There were glances exchanged around the room, and Claire had the feeling that they all knew something she didn't. Had they been talking about her while she was gone? Frustration threatened to bubble up, but she shoved it down. Now wasn't the time to make a scene, and in fact, was there ever a time for that? Far better to just leave things alone and process it later with Emma. Emma was a safe person to be vulnerable with. Alison? Not so much. Not anymore.

"What's up, guys?" Claire asked. "Something to share with the rest of the class?"

Naturally, Jeremy was the first to speak up. "They were all talking about you today." He pointed at their parents and Alison. "Concerns about your future plans, stability, blah blah blah. I wasn't totally listening, but I heard enough to get the gist of it." He nodded at their older sister.

"Go on, then. If now's the time to have an intervention, then intervene away."

But before Alison could speak, Claire's words poured out of her. "Are you kidding me? Of all the times, when I just finished an *international book tour*, you have the audacity to express...what? A concern about my 401K? My retirement account?" She exhaled an indignant sigh. "You have some nerve, Alison, to act like you care at all what happens to me." She shook her head, disappointment and frustration coursing through her veins even as a voice was screaming at her in the back of her mind to stop, to not ruin Christmas, to not say what couldn't be unsaid. "You barely talk to me, you don't care even the tiniest bit about my life or my happiness...but some illusion of financial security? *That's* what matters to you? Please. It's just an excuse to show how, once again, you come out on top. I'm a failure, and you're the golden child. But spoiler alert, Alison: that's not new information. We all already knew that."

There was a stunned silence when Claire finished speaking, before all of her family members rushed to respond at once.

"Claire Bear—"

"Honey, no—"

"That's not—"

But she didn't want to hear any of it. Not now, and possibly not ever. Claire got to her feet, raising a hand. "I probably shouldn't have said all of that. I'm tired and jet lagged and I have no filter. Just...just forget I said it." She gave a weak smile, knowing it looked just as insincere as it felt. "Have a good night, everyone. Here's hoping I'll wake up in the morning with a personality transplant."

No one laughed at her weak joke, but they gave her tentative smiles and soft wishes to sleep well and have sweet dreams as she made her exit from the room.

When Claire closed the door to her childhood bedroom behind her, she slid down the length of it to sit on the floor, overcome by the shame of her outburst and the embarrassment about Alison's concerns. Her family didn't even know how accurate those concerns were. She hadn't so much as hinted at the tumultuous future of Velvet Leaf Publishing, and if she had been afraid of what their reactions might be, now she had confirmation that it was even worse than she had feared.

Parents—and even older siblings, apparently—just wanted to know that their children were okay, were going to be set for the future because they had made good financial decisions and actually thought about their futures. That wasn't going to be the case for Laura and Doug Davis, though. Their daughter—*their middle child*, Claire thought with scorn, as if her birth order was the reason for her impending failure—had chosen a creative career, so disillusioned and disconnected from the real world as to believe that such a thing was possible.

She was tempted, for just a moment, to blame her parents. How dare they let her believe in this elaborate fantasy of hers? Why hadn't they insisted she study business or engineering or medicine at school rather than that overpriced and unnecessary English degree?

But she knew it wasn't their fault. She would have always fought for her impractical career, had always ignored any advice to the contrary. She'd had the persistent belief that things were going to work out for so long that it was only lately that she had realized just how dangerous that was. All of her eggs were firmly in the basket of books and writing and Velvet Leaf, and that basket wasn't even in her own control.

Claire sighed as she mustered just enough energy to flop herself onto the bed, still in the clothes she had worn while traveling. The realization that she was wearing "outside clothes" on top of her blanket made her want to text Jack so badly that she couldn't ignore the impulse. Regardless of whatever she had told herself shortly before, she grabbed her phone and fired off the message.

"I miss you. Let's do the cliche thing and meet on the observation deck of the Empire State Building. I could use the mood boost. Meet there at ten?"

Clare dropped the phone on the nightstand, groaning at the realization that she would have to get on her feet again to switch off the light. She was suddenly so tired that it felt impossible. She took off one sock and balled it up as tightly as she could, then flung it at the light switch.

Nothing.

She repeated the process with her next sock, managing to hit light switch this time, but the light kept shining brightly. Claire groaned as she got to her feet and shuffled across the room. She couldn't even turn off a light from the other side of the room, which suddenly felt like nearly as colossal a failure as her soon-to-be-sunk career.

Once she was in darkness, lying on her back and staring at the nothingness above her, Claire felt an almost crushing sense of loneliness. It was bad enough that no one in her family really understood her, but to have them voicing her own fears out loud to her as failures? It was almost too much.

She briefly contemplated getting dressed again and ordering a taxi to take her to her apartment, disappearing into what was surely a cave of dust and clutter that would perfectly match how she was feeling on the inside.

But just because her Christmas was ruined, did she have to ruin it for her mom, too? After all, Laura hadn't been the one expressing her "concerns" with such "care." It hadn't been her dad or her brother, either. And Trish was innocent. So were the kids. It was only Alison who deserved any kind of punishment, and Claire wasn't petty enough—or at this moment, she wasn't awake enough—to be the one to give it to her.

Tomorrow will be a new day, she thought as she rolled over, tucking into her pillow. *Maybe it'll be better.*

She reached for her phone, checking to see if there was a response from Jack, a message she had missed in her efforts to turn off the light with as little energy as possible.

As it turned out, he had "liked" her message with a heart, but...she opened the message to check. No, he hadn't said a word. A little cartoon heart was all she had gotten from him. She tossed the phone onto the carpet, letting it slide out of her reach.

She knew it was ridiculous to wish Jack would have said just the perfect words to make her feel better about a situation he wasn't even aware of, but it was her right to be as ridiculous as she wanted to be when her career, her family, and the wall she had firmly in place to keep the two apart were all crumbling.

Twenty-Three

The next day didn't dawn as miraculously as Claire had feebly wished it would the night before. She woke up feeling slightly more refreshed, even if the first time her eyes opened it was 4 o'clock in the morning, pitch black outside, and so cold she would have gotten up to adjust the thermostat if she weren't painfully aware of the scolding she would get, even as an adult, for doing that. Instead, she had burrowed deeper into the blankets, forcing her eyes shut and willing herself back to sleep, despite the fact that her brain, still on German time, was already racing with reminders of the previous day.

She may not have slept any more after that initial wake-up, but Claire stayed in bed, blankets pulled up to her chin and eyes squeezed tightly shut, going through a mantra in her head that sounded something like, "Alison...the nerve...Bianca...my job...Jack..."

When she heard the heat come on in the vent in her bedroom, she couldn't take it any longer. She jumped out of bed, pulling on a sweatshirt and shoving her feet into a pair of slippers her mom had left there for her the previous day. Claire stumbled down the stairs, finding her way into the kitchen by the light of the Christmas tree, which had been aglow all night.

The sight of the strands of lights reflecting off the baubles hanging on the branches, combined with the glow of white coming in through the window, the streetlights illuminating the snow, pulled her out of her misery meditation, even if just briefly. *Everything* wasn't terrible, she could admit to herself, even if most things were. No, even that was an exaggeration. She had a family that loved her, for the most part. Alison might be an exception, but the odds were still in her favor. *Three out of four immediate family members agree that Claire Davis is a tolerable companion for the holidays.* And it was even better when she added Trish and the kids into the mix as well.

Claire was still staring at the lights when a sound from the kitchen island caught her attention. As her gaze swung in that direction, she started at the sight of Alison there, a glass of water in her hand and an uncomfortable look on her face, as if she had been summoned by Claire's thoughts and sincerely wished she were anywhere else.

Alison had the decency to look uncomfortable, Claire noticed with a small amount of satisfaction. "I...just getting some water," she said in a small voice, looking as if she wished she could teleport back to her room upstairs.

Claire raised her hands. "Hey, no need to explain yourself to me. If you're thirsty, you're thirsty."

A pained expression crossed Alison's face, much to Claire's annoyance. "I...can we talk later, Claire?"

"It's Christmas, Alison. Can't we just enjoy some festivities without getting into the drama?" She huffed out a mirthless laugh. "Or, I don't know, at least let the sun come up before we start opening the old wound?"

"I'm sorry." Alison's voice was small. "You're right. It's too early, and it's not the time. But I do want to talk to you sometime, if you'll let me."

"I'll think about it." Claire was almost too shocked by two such rare statements from Alison—"I'm sorry" and "you're right" weren't exactly frequently used in her vernacular—to remember to keep up her gruff exterior. She shuffled towards the coffee machine while she heard Alison's feet padding away on the carpet.

"Do you think the two of you might be able to keep things civil today?" Laura's voice rang out in the silence, though she had spoken quietly. Claire hadn't heard her enter from her own bedroom with Pepper at her heels, but she winced at the question.

"I'm sorry, Mom." She chewed on her lower lip as she turned to face her mom. "I don't know why I'm so on edge with Alison. Like...I don't want to bite her head off before I've even had a cup of coffee, but..." She threw her hands in the air in exasperation. "I just feel so frustrated every time she opens her mouth."

Laura was walking towards Claire, nodding. She opened the cupboard and removed a bag of coffee, beginning to measure scoops into the coffee maker. "It's not a mystery to me," she said. "There's always been this dynamic between the two of you, and I've just been watching it play out. Sure, things were different when you were little girls. At least then the two of you could play together nicely sometimes. But there were always these moments where it was like the two of you were competing about...well, about anything. Everything. Grades at school. How high you could jump. Artistic ability. You name it."

Claire frowned. "I don't remember that. I thought things changed when she moved away for college."

Laura shook her head. "Isn't that the way it goes, though? Of course you don't remember every interaction you had as kids...you were children. The highlights rise to the top and everything else fades into the middle distance." She gave Claire a small smile. "But I was an adult then, and I saw it all. And it was so obviously something, some dynamic that the two of you were going to have to figure out, that I couldn't just swoop in and tell you both to cut it out. It was more than a little challenging, I don't mind telling you."

"I'm sorry," Claire said automatically, but her mom was already shaking her head.

"Don't be. I'm not looking for sympathy. Just telling you what I saw. I can't explain it either, why things were like that with the two of you. It wasn't as if your dad and I were comparing you to each other. She was three years older than you, so of course she was better than you at most things."

Claire nodded, unsure of what to say next. In her silence, her mom continued to speak.

"She's changed, though. These last few years. Maybe she hasn't let you see it, but I've seen it. Maybe it's about the kids...parenting has a way of humbling people." She let out a small laugh. "I think she's finally accepting the areas where you've outstripped her, where she has nothing to offer but pride in her little sister's accomplishments."

A laugh barked out of Claire's lips before she could stop it. "You're kidding, right? Alison has *never* been proud of me."

"But she has." Laura gave a small, sad shake of her head. "We all have, Claire. Of course we have. Do you know what a courageous thing it is to put your art out into the world the way you have been? To try something that so many of us say we'd like to do but so few of us ever actually attempt? I think writing a book is on the bucket list of just about anyone who's inclined to make a bucket list. And you haven't just done it once, either."

Claire's eyebrows had climbed up her forehead. "I...I'm not sure what to say. I'm genuinely surprised to hear that anyone in this family...okay, fine, I know *you're* always going to be proud of me. But the rest of them? I don't have the corner office, the house, the flashy car, the family with 2.5 kids—"

"Do you think that's all any of us want for you?" Laura interrupted with a frown. "All a parent wants for their child is for them to be happy and healthy. And happiness looks different for you and Alison and Jeremy." She let out a small chuckle. "Look at your brother. Do you think he'll ever get his own place, stop living with four roommates? If all Alison cared about was financial stability and keeping up with the Joneses, wouldn't she be on his case, too?"

"No." Claire shook her head. "You said it yourself. It was always me. The competition was always about the two of us, the two girls. Jeremy got to just be the cute little baby of the family who could do no wrong, and I'm the one who gets the passive aggressive comments and unsolicited life advice."

As she said it, she knew it wasn't entirely fair. Alison hadn't been a large enough part of her life for the last ten years to give her any advice. But Claire had seen the looks sent her way, the furtive glances and frowns, and she had interpreted them in the only way that made sense to her.

Laura's exasperated sigh, so heavy with exhaustion, kicked up uncomfortable guilty feelings that had Claire itching to bolt for the door, to disappear until at least Easter. "I don't know what to tell you, Claire," Laura said finally as she poured coffee into mugs for them. "This is something you and Alison should talk about at some point, and I hope you'll be open to that. I know it's pretty much asking for a Christmas miracle, but..." She shrugged. "Well, if there was ever a time to ask for a Christmas miracle, wouldn't it be today?"

Claire winced at her mom's tone, her lack of faith in that wish of hers coming true. "You're right, Mom. And merry Christmas. I know we didn't start the day off in the most festive way, so...can we start over?"

Her mom nodded, and Claire followed her to the couch, where the two of them sat facing the tree, Laura tucking a blanket over their legs. "How are you feeling this morning?" Laura asked, and Claire had never been more grateful for a subject change. "Jet lag kicking your butt?"

"Oh, totally," she answered, taking a sip of coffee. "I'll definitely be napping today, but I'll try to save it for a time when I won't miss anything."

"Late afternoon?" Laura's voice raised with the suggestion. "We'll eat early and then there will probably be some football on or something—those poor players, having to work on a holiday. But you won't miss anything."

Claire smiled at her mom's comment, remembering her conversations with Jack about people having to work on Christmas. "I bet the players still get to celebrate with their families. Wouldn't you work around a family member's schedule if they had to work, especially if they were getting paid as well as a professional athlete?"

Laura pursed her lips in thought before giving a slow nod. "You're right. It doesn't really matter what day it is, as long as everyone is together." She reached over and patted Claire's knee. "I'm glad you're here, sweet girl. Glad you made it back and didn't get stuck in Munich for yet another day. It was like that city was never going to let you go."

She turned to look at her mom. "You know that was my decision, though, right?" The warmth of the room and perhaps the darkness that was obscuring her features somewhat gave her the courage to continue speaking. "I just wanted to spend more time with Jack. At least the second day, that's what happened. The first day, well..." She could open up to her mom about Jack, if Laura were interested. But sharing her concerns about Velvet Leaf Publishing and her financial future hardly seemed like the ideal topic to broach on Christmas Day before the sun had even woken up for the day.

Happily, Laura knew just what to say. "Tell me about this Jack character. Are we going to meet him?"

Claire recoiled slightly but caught herself. "Well, first of all, hopefully *I'm* going to meet him again tomorrow. If things go well, I'm sure he'd want to meet you all at some point." She peeked at her mom out of the corner of her eye.

"I've only known him for a couple days, after all. That's hardly the appropriate time to meet the parents, is it?"

Laura took her time to sip her coffee, and Claire thought she saw a smile hiding behind the mug. Finally, her mom held up her thumb and forefinger, separated by the barest of spaces. "Maybe," she admitted. "Just a little soon, I guess. You dodged my first question, though. Tell me more about him." She nudged Claire's knee with her own. "It's not like you to hold out on me."

Claire's fingernails clinked on the edge of her mug like an influencer showing off products in their skincare routine. "I'm not sure what to tell you," she said after a beat. "He's a computer engineer, and he has a sister—"

Laura held up a hand. "You know I'm not asking you what he does for a living and what his savings account looks like. Why did you like him in the first place? I was already surprised that you took the deal that first day and stayed gone for an extra day. I would have expected you to spend that day just vegging out in your room and ordering room service when you got hungry. Weren't you peopled out by the end of your tour?"

Claire nodded. Her mom knew her well, that much was undeniable. While she had been gone, she had kept the family updated on her tour through the group chat—or at least through a group chat with her parents, trusting that they would share any relevant information with her siblings. It wasn't that she didn't want to include Jeremy in the messages; it was just that doing so would make it that much more obvious who—which *one* remaining family member—wasn't being included. Claire wasn't trying to be mean by excluding her sister, so it was easier just to keep both of her siblings on the outskirts of her life updates.

"It was exhausting," she said in response to her mom's question. "And no matter what spontaneous impulse it was that had me agree to take the next flight, it was unlikely that I would do anything other than exactly what you just suggested." She paused as she shrugged. "But...then I met Jack. I had noticed him at the airport, but had gotten totally the wrong impression of him. In the shuttle on the way to the hotel, we started talking for some reason and then we just...never stopped." She pushed out her lips. "Well. I mean. Obviously, we have stopped by now. But while we were in Munich, we were pretty much inseparable."

Laura raised her eyebrows but didn't say anything.

"At first, I tried not to read into anything too much," Claire continued, laughing at herself. "But you can imagine about how well that went, I'm sure. Jack, though, he was great. He was the one to say that there was something...*there*. Something between us that was maybe worth exploring. What?"

Laura was cringing, worrying her lower lip. "I'm sorry. I don't mean to be the one who casts doubt on the magic of your new man, but how does that *not* sound like a line to you? I know you write romance novels, honey, and that might make you think that all men are secretly capable of being the heroes in one of your books, but...well, in real life, sometimes they say whatever it takes to get you into bed and then they disappear."

Claire was aghast, jaw dropped as she shook her head at her mom's words. "I don't believe you, Mom. You would really just...what? Assume the worst of a man you don't know, sure. But of me?" She made to stand up, but stopped and faced her mom. "I was trying to spare you the nitty-gritty details, but *nothing happened* with Jack and me. And not for lack of opportunity, either. We shared a hotel room the second night, for Pete's sake. But you're right, I'm sure he's just a scum bag who was trying to seduce me and then disappear."

"That's not what I was saying." Laura placed a hand on Claire's forearm, keeping her in place on the couch when all Claire wanted to do was sprint back to her bedroom and slam the door shut like a dramatic teenager. "I...well, I'm happy to know that you were being safe with your heart and your body and all of that, of course. But I'm not just talking about sex, honey. Oh, don't cringe. You can handle hearing me say the word. I'm just advising a little caution, okay? Have you and Jack chatted since you've been back?"

"We've made plans to meet up, but those are just text messages." Claire spoke through gritted teeth. "And yeah, I'm worried that he's not going to show up. That I invented the whole thing in my head. That he *will* show up, but nothing will be the same. But just...for today, at least, I want to hold on to the dream a little longer. Can you withhold any questions that put that dream in danger, just for today?"

Laura pulled Claire closer and put her arm around her. "Of course, honey." The air was heavy between them with the unspoken weight of all that had already happened that morning, and there still wasn't even a hint of sunlight breaking over the horizon yet.

Twenty-Four

Christmas was the best with little kids around, that much was clear. Whatever awkwardness had been dogging Claire ever since she got out of bed that morning evaporated the moment Wendy and Amelia appeared downstairs, their eyes round with wonder at the presents under the tree, the bulging stockings hanging from the mantel, and the smell of cinnamon rolls permeating the air.

After Claire and Laura had sat in front of the tree long enough that the weirdness between them had dissipated, Claire offered to help her mom with whatever needed to be prepared for the day. That was how she had ended up elbows deep in yeast dough and cinnamon goo, trying her best to flip the worn recipe card to the other side without smudging it beyond recognition. She had to hand it to her mom, though. While plenty of families would be starting their days with cinnamon rolls, how many of them would be homemade, and not even popping out of a can?

"Of course," Claire grumbled, "it *is* slightly less impressive when you consider that she hasn't done any of the work herself."

"What's that?" Laura raised her voice over the sound of bacon grease splattering in the pan. While she may have been all too willing to pawn off the cinnamon roll preparation, that didn't mean she was a slouch in the kitchen.

"Oh, I was just waxing poetic about what an unstoppable force you are in the kitchen," she called back with a smile. "And also how impressively you bend others to your will." She lifted her hands and spread her fingers to show just what a mess had formed there.

Laura laughed with abandon. "You offered to help! Let that be a lesson to you to not offer what you don't want to give."

A long look passed between them, and Claire was warmed from within at the joy of working side by side with her mom. That was all they had needed, after that morning, just to get out of their heads full of worries...and stick their hands in some dough.

It was funny how that worked. Laura's concerns about Jack were long forgotten, at least as far as Claire was concerned, though that didn't mean Claire's own concerns about him were gone. She was aware of her phone, which she had left upstairs on the carpet wherever it had landed the previous night, as if it had its own gravitational force, fighting down the urge from moment to moment to rush upstairs and check it.

Had Jack had more to say than just "liking" her previous message? And if not, was he that unenthused about the thought of meeting up with her at the Empire State

Building? Or did he simply have the texting etiquette of someone who was newly acquainted with the internet and didn't understand the need for exclamation points and emojis, GIFs and memes to convey tone where the written word so clearly lacked it.

Though, to be fair, it wasn't so much the lack of tone that was the problem. It was more the fact that he hadn't even said a single word that was bothering her. That they could go from sharing everything from the profound to the inane, with a heaping dose of comfortable silence thrown in for free to...this?

It was more than a little concerning, and Claire wished for the first time that she hadn't even mentioned him to her family. If whatever had existed between them in Munich was destined to fizz out within sight of the Eastern Seaboard, then it would have been better if she could have spared herself the embarrassment. Wouldn't it have been less embarrassing to admit that she stayed in Munich because she needed the extra cash that the airline offered than to reveal her true nature as a hopeless romantic, destined to fall too hard and too fast for her own good?

That was what she had done, after all. At the first sight of a good man who was handsome and caring and enjoyed her company, she had thrown herself out of an airplane without even bothering to grab a parachute, so sure was she that he was going to catch her.

Claire forced the thoughts from her mind. If she didn't want to talk about Jack with her family, then the best thing for it was to stop mentally talking about him with herself, wasn't it?

"How does this look?" she waved her mom over to look at the long snake of dough and filling she had made on the counter top.

"It looks good," said Laura with an approving nod, poking the snake here and there. "Now slice them and get them in the pan as quickly as you can. They take a while to bake, and you know as soon as the kids get up, they're going to be hungry."

"Yes, ma'am," said Claire with a playful side-eye at her mother. "But you can't tell me that just because it's Christmas morning, you're going to let those two eat sugar first thing in the morning." She was slicing the dough and arranging it in the pan. "You raised me, after all. So I *know* that wouldn't fly."

Laura looked innocent—*too* innocent, Claire realized.

"Wait, is this one of those things where grandparents are so much more permissive and lenient with their grandkids than they ever were with their own kids?" But all Laura did was shrug, so Claire plowed on. "Mom, you will suffer...we will *all* suffer the consequences of your actions if you go through with this. Wendy and Amelia aren't going home tonight, making their sugar high a problem only for their parents to deal with. They'll be here, and we will all bear the brunt of it."

"My goodness, you are dramatic. You get that from your father." Laura picked up the tray and slipped it in the oven while Claire washed her hands. "But if you must know my whole plan...no. Cinnamon rolls are not a complete breakfast. But if those kids eat a little bit of protein first, then who am I to deny them a special treat?"

"Hmm." Claire nodded in agreement. "That's probably a metaphor for life—something about balancing out the sweetness of life with a bit of the...well, whatever protein is in this metaphor." She lifted her wet hands in a shrug. "Hey, man, I'm jet lagged. You can't expect me to be good with the...word stuff."

Laura was chuckling as she wiped her hands on the kitchen towel. "You might be jet lagged, but you still make me laugh. Why don't we get dressed for the day before the kids come down? You can go first, I'll keep an eye on the rolls."

Claire looked down at her pajamas. "I...was not aware that there was a different dress code for this event. Afraid I left my pearls at my apartment." She lifted the collar of her shirt towards her nose, bending down to take a quick sniff before recoiling. "But you're right, I did travel all day yesterday and then pretty much just crash. For all of our sakes, I should at least take a shower. Before I put on a different set of pajamas, of course."

"That sounds like a great plan, dear." Laura was wiping down the counters now, effortlessly restoring the kitchen to its pre-cinnamon roll state in practiced movements that seemed like an elaborately choreographed ballet as far as Claire was concerned.

When she returned downstairs half an hour later, Wendy and Amelia were perched at the island countertop, barely keeping their bottoms in their chairs as they wolfed down their breakfast, the clear majority of their attention on the packages under the tree that were waiting to be opened.

"Merry Christmas, Auntie Claire!" they chorused, earning them a smile, a squish, and kisses on the cheek from their aunt.

"Where are your parents?" she asked.

"Still sleeping," said Amelia. "We were really quiet when we left."

"Sure...that's nice." Claire exchanged a look with her mom, communicating with no words just how much faith they had in the children's ability to do much of anything quietly. If she knew Alison at all, she and Trish were staying in bed out of sheer force of will, eyes clamped tightly shut as if doing so could stave off the morning just a little longer.

"Mommy said last night we have to wait for everyone before we open presents," said Wendy, a bite of egg balanced precariously on her spoon. "Is that true? Or is that one of those things they tell little kids"—she shot a look at Amelia before turning her attention back to the adults—"like about Santa Claus and stuff? I mean, can we open just *one* present before everyone gets up?"

"Well, I'm sure I have *no idea* what you mean about Santa Claus," said Laura with a wink, "but your mommy was right about waiting for everyone to open presents. When you're done eating, you can help me." She slipped on an oven mitt and brought the tray with the cinnamon rolls closer, still out of reach of the little fingers. "Auntie Claire baked these, and when they're a little cooler, you can put some icing on them. Can you do that for me?"

Wendy and Amelia were both nodding so furiously that Claire was poised, ready to leap forth at a moment's notice to catch the morsels of food on their waiting spoons before they hit the kitchen floor. "We will!" cried Wendy. "And then can we eat them?"

"We're all going to eat them," said Laura. "What's the point of making cinnamon rolls if you don't eat them?"

Wendy and Amelia's shrugs were exaggerated and Claire and her mom exchanged smiles as they waited for them to finish their breakfasts.

In due time, the rest of the Davis family shuffled out from their rooms, sleepy eyes and pillow-styled hair all around. The Christmas music began playing from the stereo as soon as Jeremy, the final straggler, appeared, and the kids were barely restrained from making a beeline for the stockings and tree at the sight of his first sock on the stair.

When all the greetings and holiday wishes, cups of coffee and dashes of cream had been dispersed, the Davis family assumed their positions on the couches, chairs, and carpet, with Laura taking the first round as Santa's Elf to hand out gifts. It was the role of honor, and they all took their turns playing it, hamming it up to the taste of the elf who was in the spotlight at any given moment.

Claire sat back, sipping another mug full of perfect coffee with a small pile of presents at her feet as she watched the children tear into the gifts they had so eagerly anticipated. Amelia's eyes grew as big as saucers at the sight of a stuffed dragon that was clearly the stuff of her wildest dreams, bolting from her seat to hug both of her parents in gratitude. A similar dynamic played out as Wendy unwrapped a paint set that just kept going...first there were paints, then brushes, then paper, then an easel, then a couple of blank canvases...

She got to her feet with a smile on her face and answered the question on everyone's lips—"Who's it from?"—by calling "Santa!" over her shoulder as she dove into first Trish's arms and then Alison's.

"Well, if the jig isn't up for Amelia yet, I think it will be soon," Laura muttered to Claire, who bit back a laugh.

The warm glow of the lights from the tree, the laughter from the kids, the smells from the kitchen…all of it was enough to pull Claire from any lingering feelings of frustration or sourness. It was Christmas, and she was home with her family and it was every bit as magical as those nights in Munich had been. Whatever she had believed at the time, the spirit of the season wasn't lost forever, something she could only revisit by having a new experience on the other side of the ocean. It was right here, if she only paid attention enough to the joy of the children, tried to see things through their eyes. It helped, too, if she put aside her own pettiness, her drama with her sister, the ways in which she had let herself feel left out and on the outside of her family…

Well, that was a tall order. You couldn't expect a little cinnamon in the air and a few festively wrapped packages to undo years of sibling comparison and competition. It couldn't make up for all the unsaid things that had built up a wall between the two of them, that much was clear. Every darted glance exchanged between Claire and Alison carried so much tension, so much expectation. As much as Claire would prefer to continue kicking that particular conversation down the road, it seemed unlikely that she would be allowed such a mercy. If anything, Alison's gazes were increasing in their frequency, and Claire wondered if that meant she was working up her nerve to broach the subject.

Claire excused herself when things had settled down a bit, all the wrapping paper and gift bags collected for recycling and the kids playing on their own with their new toys. Claire's phone, in a turn of events that unfortunately didn't surprise her at all, contained no new messages or even reactions from Jack. It did, however, have a message from Bianca.

"Merry Christmas, Claire! Any chance you'll be in the city tomorrow to meet up for coffee?"

As she began to craft a response, Claire paused. How likely was it that Jack would turn up tomorrow? She was going to the Empire State Building in the morning, that much was clear. He deserved at least one last chance to disappoint her, to deposit the final nail in the coffin of whatever illusion of a relationship had existed between them. But should she tell Bianca she would be at her office 15 minutes after her meeting time with Jack? Or should she err on the side of him actually appearing, the two of them spending hours chatting and admiring the skyline from the observation deck and and and...

"Merry Christmas, Bianca! I'll be in the city in the morning. I can meet you at 10:30."

Half an hour. That was more than enough time for her to see if Jack had bothered to show up and to say what needed to be said. It was bound to be a morning full of unpleasant experiences, though, if the meeting with Bianca lived up to her expectations. Better to rip the bandage off all at once. She could be back in her apartment by noon, curled up under a cozy blanket and ready to forget all about the outside world where she, more than likely, would be both single *and* unemployed by that time.

Twenty-Five

Everything was happening around her, it seemed. The conversation flowed, the laughs were exchanged, but none of it could pull her from her reverie. Claire was lost deep inside herself, an observer of her own life and her own family. She sat back with a cup of hot chocolate and a smile fixed on her face, putting out the perfect expression of a loving observer, someone who was just glad to be there, a background player with no needs of her own.

Inside, it was a different story. Inside, she was crying to be noticed and seen and cared for...and yet she couldn't bring herself to ask for it or even let on that she needed something like that. This wasn't the place, after all. While on a different day, she might confide in her mom or even her little brother, the last thing she wanted to do was let Alison know that her life wasn't picture perfect. If there was ever a time when she couldn't handle an extra help-ing of scorn and judgment, it was today. As long as she could keep up the facade and not attract any attention to her less-than-ideal emotional state, then no one need be the wiser and she could save the meltdown for whenever she was alone in her apartment—or on a video call with Emma.

It almost worked, too. Or at least it would have gone off like a charm if her dad hadn't put his arm around her shoulders in the kitchen, pulling her in for a quick squeeze and to ask, "You alright, kiddo? You've been quiet today," for only her to hear. Claire's eyes had filled with water as she blinked rapidly and nodded almost as quickly.

"Fine, Dad. Just tired, I think." And she was about to excuse herself for a nap—thank goodness for jet lag and all the easy excuses it opened up for her—when someone linked an arm through hers and she found herself being bodily escorted up the stairs, watching her dad's look of concern be replaced by something warmer, with perhaps just a tinge of hope in it.

Claire looked to her side, expecting the body pressed firmly to her side to belong to her mom, Jeremy, or even Trish, but she tripped over her feet at the realization that it was her sister who was clinging to her so tightly, keeping her upright in that moment as her toes caught on the stairs and nearly took both of them down.

"What are you doing?" she asked Alison, trying to pull away at the top of the flight of stairs but surprised by the unrelenting grip on her arm. "Where are you taking me? And *why* are you so freakishly strong?"

"I lift weights," said Alison, and Claire groaned.

"Is this an intervention to get me to join your workout cult? Because I've got to tell you—"

"It's not." Alison steered Claire into her bedroom and pushed her in the direction of the bed, blocking her exit by standing in front of the door. "I just want to talk with you."

"And you couldn't have just told me that like a normal human? You had to drag me up here?"

Alison shrugged. "Would you have come if I had asked nicely? Or would you have made up an excuse? Refused to make eye contact with me in the first place? Or, I don't know, pretended you suddenly lost the ability to speak English?"

"That was one time!"

Alison's soft chuckle surprised Claire, containing something that resembled affection. "You were the cutest little kid," she said, then tilted her head to the side. "I mean, until Wendy and Amelia came along to claim your title."

"I'm going to tell Jeremy you said that."

"Somehow I don't think he's going to be that upset about it." Alison tentatively stepped towards Claire. "Can I come sit and talk with you, or are you going to bolt for the door?"

Claire let out an exasperated sigh. "Fine, I won't try to escape. Not yet, at least." She moved her hand in a circle through the air. "Can we just...I don't know, get this over with?"

Alison came and sat next to her. The silence between them stretched, but Claire was determined not to be the one to break it. It wasn't as if this little private meeting had been her idea, after all, so the agenda of it was entirely a mystery to her.

When Alison finally spoke, her words came out of left field. "I'm sorry." She took a deep breath, then reached for Claire's hands, looking her in the eyes with a sincerity that nearly forced Claire to look away. "I...I have been the worst big sister to you for a long time, and I just kept letting things get worse and worse between us until...I didn't know how bad it was, Claire. Or...maybe I did? But I was just pretending that it wasn't, that I was imagining it all or something, but then Trish said something about it and I was so ashamed that she could see it, too, and—"

"Wait." Claire was shaking her head. "I am *so* confused. I know things have been...less than great between us for a long time. I don't even know where it began. Do you?"

Alison nodded, her gaze falling back to her lap. "It's so embarrassing, Claire. But I know I owe you honesty. It started..." She shuddered. "It started a long time ago. Remember when I moved to college and suddenly we weren't so close any more?"

Claire's laugh was a humorless bark. "Oh, do I remember when my best friend suddenly became cold and distant and I felt like I had done something wrong to cause it? No, I think I'm going to need you to refresh my memory." She could feel herself closing off to her sister at the mere memory and all the pain it contained. She tried to pull her hands back, but Alison tightened her grip.

"You didn't do anything wrong, Claire."

"No." Claire shook her head. "You just made new friends and were too busy for me and then you were figuring out what you wanted to do with your life and everything I cared about was too small and silly to even matter. That's it, isn't it?"

The look on Alison's face was pained, and Claire felt the faintest glimmer of compassion buried underneath the thick layer of frustration and hurt. "Let me guess," she said, "it was hard for you, too?"

"Of course it was." Alison's tone was incredulous. "How could it not be? I don't know if it's about being the oldest or what, but there was so much pressure to get it all right. I felt like I had to make everything look easy so you and Jeremy wouldn't get scared off, but...I was so alone. So lost. So...confused."

It was Claire's turn to feel confused now. "But you never showed us that. You were just so...busy all the time and then you were gone. And it's not like you couldn't have told us what was going on. We would have understood."

"You would?" Alison raised an eyebrow at Claire. "Because maybe you don't remember what else was happening around that time." When Claire shook her head, she continued. "Your first story idea. National Novel Writing Month, or whatever it's called. I was newly off at college, fumbling my way through life, and every time I talked to you, your eyes were all lit up about this novel you were writing and how the words were flowing and how you had found what you wanted to do in life..." Alison's words trailed off.

Claire remembered it well, of course. It had been the most magical time of her life, the first time something had come easily, and she had immersed herself in the work of the story every day, always fearing that the magic was about to slip away, that she would discover that she couldn't write, after all.

And yet it had continued, and it had changed the course of her life. Or rather, defined the course of a life that up to that point had been lived without any indication of what the future might hold.

Something clicked into place. "You were...trying to find your way, and then you felt jealous because something was coming easily to me?" she hazarded a guess.

Alison's nod was full of shame. "It was never about you. I just couldn't...I couldn't even look at you. It made me realize how lost I was. Every time I talked to you, I was tempted to...be honest, I guess. To tell you that life in college wasn't what I expected, and I hadn't figured out what I wanted to do with my life and I wasn't even that *good* at anything, as it turned out. Being a star high school student doesn't exactly translate into university-level success when you're surrounded by a bunch of other star high school students."

"Why didn't you tell me? I would have understood."

"I couldn't even talk to you, Claire. As lit up as you were about writing, it just made me realize how adrift I was. I tried...but then you sent me the first chapter of the story you were working on, and..."

"What?"

Alison shook her head. "I read it. And it was everything I was afraid it would be. I had told myself that maybe if you weren't any good at this writing thing, then I could start just being a normal sister again."

Claire huffed out a humorless laugh before she could stop herself.

"I know," Alison continued. "That's a terrible thing to think and an even worse thing to say, but at least it's honest."

Claire nodded. "You're right. I appreciate that, even if it's a bit overdue." She paused for a beat, then forged ahead with the question she was both dying to know the answer to and also terrified to ask. "So what happened when you read the chapter?"

"Oh, it made everything worse." Alison looked into Claire's eyes. "It was so good, Claire. I was hooked from the first line and filled with dread at the same time. Because you had found something that was such a natural fit for you and that was the most unrelatable thing you could possibly do."

"It's not like it was *easy* for me." Claire felt herself bristling at the implication. "I didn't start writing because the words were flying and they never stopped. I mean, sure, there was a little bit of that. But my first drafts are just as shitty as anyone else's. And even if you thought that story was so great and I was destined to...I don't know, *become* something, I think you're remembering it all a little inaccurately." She shuddered. "If I had that draft here now to read, I'm guessing the dominant emotion I'd feel would be embarrassment."

"That's not the point, though. Of course you have only continued to get better at what you do, Claire. Because it's so clearly what you are meant to do. You don't know how proud I am of you."

Claire's eyebrows climbed her forehead. "You're right, I don't. I...honestly, I'm shocked. All this time I thought you were, I don't know, embarrassed or ashamed of what I do. Romance novels don't exactly have the most high brow reputation out there. I figured you wouldn't want people to know you're related to me, and if they ever happen to figure it out, you'd change the subject."

Alison's hands were back on Claire's, grasping with a desperation that was shocking. "Never." Her tone was strong, unwavering. "Not once. I have *never* been anything but proud of you. But I have never been able to show that to you the way I needed to because I was always too busy making everything about me."

Claire was silent, trying to let the words sink in. "I...don't know what to say," she finally offered.

"It was never about you, Claire. Not from the first moment when I pulled away, and not any time since then. It's been my baggage creating all this distance between us, and...I'm just sick of it. Ready to move past it."

Claire shook her head. "Where is all this coming from?"

Alison's laugh was watery as she batted at her eyes. "Therapy? Trish? Getting my ass kicked by parenting and watching those two little monsters downstairs reflect the most childish parts of me back to myself? I don't want their relationship to turn out like ours, of course, so I'm always working with them on sharing and communicating and being respectful...and then I realized I was being the world's biggest hypocrite."

"So that's why you're here, humbling yourself before me in my childhood bedroom?"

Alison nodded. "Precisely. So what do you think? Can you forgive me? Can we move forward? Try having a new relationship? A fresh start?"

Claire thought about it for a moment, but she felt herself nodding even as the thoughts were circling in her head. The awareness that the rift between them hadn't been something she had created, hadn't really even been about her, was shaking her to her very foundation. A voice in the back of her head asked what else existed only in her mind, but she ignored it. That was a question for another day.

"Of course we can." Claire pulled her sister in for a hug, warmed by her arms from without at the same time she was warming from within at the most unexpected Christmas gift of a fresh start with her first friend. No matter what else the next days had in store, she would be emerging from this holiday season one sister richer, and with that thought in her mind, she couldn't stop smiling.

When the sisters rejoined the rest of the Davis family, the knowing glances exchanged as they entered the room arm in arm told Claire all she had needed to know. This had been no secret, not nearly as well hidden as she might have thought. And Alison had likely shared her regrets and wishes to reconcile with all the other adults in the room, yet another indicator of just how much effort she had put into "getting it right."

Claire pulled Alison in for a quick hug—the difference in their embraces now, with no one bracing or shielding themselves from the vulnerability of the act, was a stark change from the day before—before joining her mom on the couch, where she was reading to two sleepy kids. She thought she heard Trish whisper "So how did it go?" to Alison and glanced up to smile at the two women.

Claire and Alison had already made a tentative plan to spend some time together, coffee at Claire's apartment in the first week of the new year and the promise of a brunch invitation at Alison and Trish's house soon after that.

The lightness Claire felt at the reconciliation with her sister was almost like the sensation she had experienced walking through the Christmas market with Jack. It was just as surprising, just as magical, just as apt to make her believe in the Christmas spirit again.

At the thought of Jack, she felt a brief pang of anxiety about the following day. Would Jack appear at the Empire State Building and the two of them pick right up where they left off? Or, as her rational mind was more inclined to believe, would she never hear from him again?

She snuggled deeper into the couch, pulling a blanket over her knees and Wendy's and tossing another to her mom. Those were questions she could do nothing to answer right now, and all she could hope, as she looked at her sister, happier and more at ease than she had seen her in years, was that her Christmas miracles would extend for just one more day.

Twenty-Six

When Claire set off the following morning for New York City, it was with only the smallest amount of hope that the day held anything positive in store for her. Over shared cups of coffee in the early morning, her mom and Alison had both reminded her that anything could happen that day. She hadn't told them her fears about Bianca and Velvet Leaf Publishing, of course, unwilling to face the possibility of professional and financial failure, but since they already knew about Jack, it felt safe to direct her concerns towards him.

"It's like one of your stories, Claire, isn't it?" Alison asked, earning her an eyebrow raise in response.

"Why would you say that, Alison? You haven't *read* one of them, have you?" The meeting at the Empire State Building, apart from being a classic scene in *Sleepless in Seattle*, had also figured heavily in *Moonlit Melodies*, but she didn't expect her older sister to know that.

Alison rolled her eyes at Claire. "Of course I have. I've got the whole collection in my office, including all the special edition covers. Why wouldn't I?"

If Claire had been surprised to learn that Jack's sister was a fan of her work, that didn't remotely compare to the shock she experienced upon learning her own sister was. "Really?" she asked, shaking her head. "But I've never—"

"Never seen my office? Never seen me reading one of your books?" Alison pursed her lips and shrugged. "Can't all of these things be explained by us being bad sisters for the last, oh...ten years? But now that part is behind us, so catch up."

Laura's smile stretched wide as she wrapped her hands around her mug, warming them. "You two have no idea how happy it makes me to see the two of you talking and getting along like this. It's what I've wished for for Christmas for a very long time."

Claire leaned her head onto her mom's shoulder as Alison patted her knee. "I'm sorry it took us this long, Mom."

"You raised some stubborn kids," Alison agreed, "but now that we've cleared the air, we can be stubborn about the right things. Not letting each other go. Things like that."

"Alison is even being stubborn about making me keep the faith that Jack is going to show up today," said Claire, immediately wanting to kick herself for bringing the topic back around to him. She was like a teenager with a crush, somehow able to make every topic relate back to the thing—person—she really wanted to talk about.

"He'll be there," said Alison with a confidence that made both Claire and Laura sit up and take notice.

"How do you know?" Claire asked, her voice quiet enough that she was surprised the other women heard it.

"I just do." Alison was nodding. "Now go get ready and get out of here. You can't be late."

Claire had taken the PATH train into the city, not wanting to navigate traffic or parking on the day after Christmas. Thanks to Alison's urging, she had left with plenty of time to enjoy the journey rather than wishing it would go by more quickly and working herself up into an anxious later.

There was a lingering festive mood in the nearly empty train car. Even though the anticipation of Christmas was gone, her fellow travelers hadn't yet taken on the bland gray mood and attire of late January in the city, when the short days and endless cold has taken its toll on the collective psyche. She spied a festive sweater across the car and a pair of bauble earrings on a passenger near the door. They were holding on to the holiday spirit a little longer, extending it at least until the new year.

It was one of the best weeks of the year, one of Claire's favorites when she wasn't carrying the burden of work stress and an uncertain future. Time stretched, expanding and contracting in the days between Christmas and New Year's Eve in a way that made her lose all sense of time. Pajamas for days on end? The perfect attire. Leftover pie for breakfast and gravy on everything? Why not?

It was also one of the rare times in the winter that she was willing to leave the house when it was dark out, something that happened at a shockingly early hour. She would venture out after five o'clock for a holiday party or to meet friends in the city for drinks within view of Christmas lights, carols playing on the sound system. But ask her to a happy hour in January and you could just get ready for any one of Claire Davis's patented excuses.

As Claire surveyed the expressions of her fellow passengers, noting an unusually high proportion of smiles for public transportation—had Santa Claus brought all of these people just what they had wanted, or what?—she let her mind wander to her impending meeting with Jack.

Because, for the first time since their farewell at the Newark airport, she was letting herself believe that he was going to be there. Sure, his lack of communication didn't exactly bode well for what was about to happen. But Claire was willing to entertain the possibility—thanks to a stern reminder from Alison just as she slipped out the door—that not everything was about her. Jack may have been so busy helping his family with Christmas dinner and counseling his sister about her relationship troubles that, truly, all he had had time for was one tap on the screen of his phone.

Claire smiled to herself as the subway pulled into the 33rd Street station. She didn't need to do the mental gymnastics of figuring out where Jack had been and what had been keeping him busy...she would hear it all from him soon enough.

She checked the time on her phone as she walked back up to street level, noting that she was early for her meeting with Jack. She took a deep breath as she stepped away from the stairs and let the energy of the city wash over her. The feel of being back after being away for an extended period of time always took her breath away. New York City was always alive with an energy that no other place she had visited had been able to match.

As much as there was a part of Claire that wanted to retreat to the countryside and live in a gingerbread house—what was she, a witch from a children's fairy tale?—she loved New York too much to imagine leaving. More even than the cozy living room of her parents' house, this felt like home. She couldn't wait to get back to her apartment, to settle in for her winter hibernation surrounded by the lights and sounds of a city that truly never slept.

Or rather, she *could* wait. Because there were a couple of very important meetings between her and unlocking the door of her apartment. She stopped at a Starbucks on the corner to grab a coffee to give her something to do and keep her hands warm while she waited for Jack, and then she made her way to the Empire State Building.

The line was short, and she was waiting for the next elevator well before she had expected to be. A family waiting in front of her brought a smile to her face, noting the tired eyes of the parents who were leaning on each other for support and the two young ones who were playing peek-aboo around their parents' legs. It was the holiday spirit encapsulated in one scene—the energy and newness of childhood and the sheer exhaustion of the adults who had worked to bring it all to life. Claire imagined the afternoon ahead of them, hoping it would contain a nap for all four of them.

When it was her turn to take the elevator up to the observation deck, she tucked herself into the back corner, continuing to observe the young family and the rest of her fellow travelers. It was still too early to be looking around for Jack, but that didn't mean she couldn't enjoy some quality people-watching with her caffeine. The joy and wonder surrounding her—she would guess the crowd visiting the Empire State Building over the holiday season had to be almost entirely tourists, very few locals opting to see the sights from 102 floors up the day after Christmas—were infectious and by the time she got out of the elevator she had a permanent smile fixed to her face.

Claire found a quiet spot with a nice view of Central Park to wait for Jack, just a short walk from the elevator. Should she text him and let him know where she was, or would that spoil the serendipity of it all? She leaned against the glass, sipped her drink, and continued to survey her surroundings. From this high up, she could almost imagine the city was quiet down below, had she not known the truth. But from her current vantage point, she was definitely experiencing the reality check of just how big her problems—or anything else happening at street level—really were.

From the observation deck, people down below were smaller than ants, and as she watched a few of those ants cross streets and enter buildings, it was almost a spiritual experience to imagine seeing herself down there, too small and too far away to discern even one of her features. Her fears and the worries that creased her forehead and turned her stomach didn't translate to the observation deck.

She wished Jack were there already, knowing he would be amused by the thoughts she was having and would surely have an interesting addition to make, or at least a joke that would make her chuckle.

Claire checked the time again as she found a trash can to deposit her empty cup into. Her stomach dropped with disappointment at the awareness that he was late. Sure, it was only two minutes, but the fact that she wasn't a high enough priority for him to be on time threatened to tank her festive mood.

That was before she reminded herself that not everything was about her. Maybe Jack was in line for the elevator right now. Or maybe he was two blocks away, stuck in traffic. A glance out the window at the relatively empty streets told her that the second option was unlikely, but she forced her chin up, regardless. She would have her answer soon. She couldn't wait long, after all, given that she had scheduled a meeting with Bianca just half an hour after she had been supposed to meet Jack.

Claire saw the young family from the lobby making their way back to the bank of elevators, and she felt resignation wash over her, a sort of sad acceptance. If she had been there long enough for the family to see all they wanted to see, she had been there long enough for Jack to make his appearance.

And he hadn't.

It wasn't the truth she wanted to accept, but it was the truth she was confronted by. Jack wasn't here, and there was no indication that he was even on his way. The phone worked both ways after all, and as she checked the screen of hers again to confirm that it was time to leave to meet Bianca, she also confirmed that Jack hadn't called, hadn't texted, hadn't given so much as a sign of life.

He wasn't coming, and she already knew she wouldn't try again to arrange a meeting. She had made the effort this time, and considering how apathetic his response had been, she wouldn't expose herself to that rejection again.

As Claire made one final circuit around the observation deck, taking in the view from all angles one last time, she felt an odd peace wash over her, mingling with her disappointment to create a bittersweet ache that couldn't quite me named.

Her heart was hurting, but she was still proud of herself for opening it up.

A potential love had turned out to be less than she had hoped...and yet she knew these feelings would turn into art. She would alchemize this pain, this loss, maybe not right away—the last thing she felt like doing today was sitting down in front of her keyboard—but someday soon, she would pour them into her next book.

She was richer for having known Jack, both as a woman who had opened herself up to believe in a man's potential and as a writer of love stories who rarely let herself experience them away from the safety of her word processing software. And if she had learned anything from the countless stories she had written, it was that pain always catalyzed growth and ultimately made the main character stronger. Strength and vulnerability weren't polarities that couldn't coexist; one was essential for the other.

Claire pulled her coat tighter against the cold as she approached the bank of elevators, feeling like a main character. Like even if she was in pain now, this pain was going to have a purpose. Because in the end, it wasn't about Jack at all. As much as it disappointed her, he had revealed today that he wasn't a fellow main character whose job was to sweep her off her feet and into the next chapter of life.

He had been a supporting character and nothing more, someone who reveals a truth the main character is missing, who helps her find her way ahead in the story but never reappears.

She had gotten him wrong, as it turned out. Seen main character energy in his smile, in the way he looked at her. But she wanted to believe, *had* to believe, that if Jack hadn't been "the one," then she couldn't even begin to fathom how much more magnetic, more magical the *actual* one would have to be.

Claire sighed as she stepped into the elevator. She wanted so desperately to believe that nice adage she had heard so many times before, that if things didn't work out, it was because something better was on its way. But two things could be true at the same time: she could be hopeful for her future happiness and yet disappointed right down to the core of her being that Jack hadn't shown up today. That the two of them had clearly valued what had happened between them in Munich so differently.

She had thought they were on the same page, that the connection she felt to him was mutual and would survive the flight back to the US unscathed. Even with all the doubts she had experienced in the past days, she hadn't let go of the hope that she was reading it all wrong. That just because he wasn't communicating with her didn't mean he wasn't chomping at the bit to see her again.

With every floor lower that the elevator traveled, Claire felt herself coming back to earth. She was gathering strength, leaving behind the dreamer that had waited in the cold of the observation deck for her own sweet reunion, complete with a soaring soundtrack and slow motion running into an embrace. Disappointment was one of the unfortunate uncertainties of life, and she would get through it. Just because it hurt more than any other recent disappointment didn't mean she couldn't weather it.

As the elevator arrived in the lobby, Claire waited for the crowd—as the sun rose higher in the sky and melted off a little of the chill in the air, the building had become more popular—to clear. She stepped out the door, pulling her scarf a little higher on her neck and lifting her hand to hail a cab.

Before her hand was even high enough, a yellow taxi pulled over in front of the Empire State Building, screeching to a halt. *Wow,* she thought, *are things already looking up or what? Did I just manifest a taxi?*

The back door of the vehicle opened, and a very familiar man rushed out, almost bumping over her in his hurry to get to the building.

"Jack?" she called, one hand still on the door of the taxi while the other pulled her scarf down from her face. "You came?"

Twenty-Seven

J ack wheeled on the spot, his eyes wide and almost manic as they landed on her, his whole visage dropping with
relief at the sight of her.

"Claire." He rushed to her, taking her in his arms and
pulling her in for a hug.

She let herself enjoy his warmth, his solid presence for
just a moment before pulling back and studying him.
"What the hell, Jack? What took you so long? I didn't
think you were coming. I..." She gestured to the taxi. "I
have to go. I have a meeting with my agent and I actually
care about being on time for it."

His face fell. "Claire, I'm so sorry. I—" He gestured
towards the open door of the cab. "Get in. I don't want
you to be late. I...I'll come with you. Wait for you."

Before she could protest, he was pushing her gently
inside and scooting in next to her. Claire stared at him,
incredulous.

He was here. He was really here.

As much as part of her wanted to just lean into his side,
to soak up all the heat he was radiating, to take whatever he

could give her, there was another louder part of her that demanded answers. True, he had shown up. But he had waited until the last minute, suggesting that his ability to be punctual and to communicate both left something to be desired. It wasn't just that, though. It was the fact that not bothering to be there on time *and* not bothering to let her know that he was coming said something she didn't want to hear.

Both of those actions told her she wasn't his priority. That something else, whether it had been a conversation with his sister or a little extra sleep on a cold morning, had been more important than her. And it hurt to think that she had gotten up early, had hauled herself across a state line to be there and he had sauntered in almost half an hour later.

Be fair, brain. He didn't exactly saunter. *You saw the look in his eyes.*

Claire took a deep breath and shook her head at Jack. "So what happened? Where were you?" She needed to give him the benefit of the doubt, not just jump right down his throat with accusations and assumptions, but she also couldn't camouflage the hurt of feeling like she'd been abandoned up there on the observation deck.

"I'm so sorry, Claire. I..." Jack sighed out a long breath and Claire caught a glimpse of something like exhaustion under all the tension and stress she had seen there. "I'll explain it all."

The cab was racing through the streets of Midtown Manhattan and the familiar block containing Velvet Leaf's offices was already almost in sight. It wasn't that Claire couldn't have walked there from the Empire State Building, after all, but that she had stayed until the last possible moment to give Jack a chance not to disappoint her.

And he didn't disappoint you, did he? He did *show up, in the end.* Claire shook her head at the voice in her head. *That's the problem, though, isn't it? He was there, but at the last possible moment. I almost missed him.*

The cab came to a stop in front of Velvet Leaf Publishing, where, much to Claire's surprise, Bianca was waiting on the sidewalk. Claire and Jack got out of the vehicle, and after a solemn promise that he would stay put right where she left him, Claire walked over to Bianca with an entirely new set of butterflies acting up in her stomach.

Bianca tipped her head in Jack's direction as Claire approached. "Hey, who's your friend?"

Claire waved a dismissive hand before pulling Bianca in for a quick hug. "It's a long story. I'll tell you later."

The quizzical look on her agent's face let Claire know she would be holding her to her promise. "Let's go to the cafe, my treat."

There was a small coffee shop on the corner, and with one glance over her shoulder to confirm that Jack was still standing in front of Velvet Leaf, Claire let Bianca steer her inside. The tension in the air between the two women was foreign, and Claire found herself fighting the urge to fidget, to pull out her phone and pretend to send an important message, to do anything to keep from facing Bianca, her friend and agent.

"So," Bianca began as they joined the end of the line, "how have you been? Was it a good trip?"

Claire gulped as she nodded, then shook her head. "Yeah. I mean...no. Sorry. I...I'm just all jumbled up right now, Bee." Before she could stop herself, she blurted the question that had been tormenting her for days. "I have to ask before it kills me. Is something happening to Velvet Leaf?" She lowered her voice at the look in Bianca's eyes, the realization that starting rumors about the publishing company's future less than a block away from their headquarters was probably not the brightest move. "I've just been dying, not knowing what you were going to tell me. I have this sinking feeling that everything is about to change and that I'm going to be jobless very soon."

Bianca's eyes were sympathetic, her expression changing from alarm to concern. She reached for Claire's arm before stopping herself with a small nod. "This is my fault. I should have been more communicative." The smile she gave Claire was small yet confident. "Everything *is* about to change, Claire, but you are definitely not going to be jobless. Don't worry about a thing, okay? I'll explain everything after we get our drinks."

Slightly reassured, Claire moved as if on autopilot towards the front of the line and then down to the end of the counter to wait for their order. She was only partially aware of their order being called—a peppermint latte for her and a decaf one for Bianca—before she was nudged towards an open table tucked away near the kitchen.

"What's going on?" she asked as they sat down. "Sorry for the lack of niceties and small talk. It's just...well, I've had a lot of time to myself to think about all of this, and we haven't exactly been having a ton of conversation these past weeks."

Bianca winced. "It's all my fault, Claire. But I can explain." She took a deep breath, closed her eyes for a beat, and when she opened them again, she blurted her next words. "I'm pregnant."

Claire shook her head as if she had heard wrong, as if the action would improve her hearing. "What?"

Bianca took a deep breath. "That's why I didn't come on the tour with you, because of the morning sickness, and it's why I haven't been as communicative as I would have liked to be." She let out a nervous chuckle. "To be honest, this morning sickness...well, the word 'morning' is totally inaccurate. I've been sick day in and day out. It pretty much kicked my ass for the first trimester." She reached one hand down to her belly, rubbing softly there before replacing it on the table. "I wanted to tell you sooner, but..." Her eyes met Claire's and the smile there was small, tentative. "I didn't want to jinx it. I'm high-risk—*geriatric* was the word the obstetrician used, I believe—and the advice was just to keep it as quiet as possible, at least through the first trimester."

"And that's over now?" Claire felt the corners of her mouth lifting in a smile she couldn't stop if she wanted to. "When are you due?"

"We're into the second trimester now. I'm due in April."

Claire's silence was stunned. "You are going to be such a good mom." She could feel moisture growing in her eyes, but she kept speaking. "And of course I understand why you didn't tell me. I wish I could have supported you through it—or at least not been a source of stress—but I'm just so glad you're both healthy. You *are* both healthy, right?"

Bianca nodded. "We are. And I could have told you why things were different between us, but the morning sickness was a pretty natural boundary setter. Even though I wanted to talk to you a lot more than I did while you were in Europe, if I looked at my phone screen, I'd be hugging the toilet." She smiled. "It's much better now, though. And before you can ask, I'm still going to be working with you."

Claire's cheeks heated, and she gave a dismissive wave. Was she such a baby that she needed to be managed? That Bianca had worried about her feelings at the same time she was worrying about her child's health and wellbeing? "You shouldn't worry about me. I'll be fine. Really."

"Oh, I know." Bianca's eyebrows were climbing high. "And that's why the deal I struck with the agency is that I'm staying on *only* as your agent and the rest of my authors are being handed off to other associates."

"Really?"

"Really." Bianca's nod was confident, decisive. "I know a winning racehorse when I see one, Claire. And your career is only going to get better from here—not that it isn't already my proudest professional achievement signing you."

All the nerves that Claire had felt, every concern about her career...all of it vanished with those words. Her worries and fears about the future of her career now revealed themselves for just how much a waste of time, energy, and life they had been.

But Bianca wasn't done yet. "I'm taking maternity leave, though, and only coming back in a very part-time capacity when I actually come back." She leveled a look at Claire that Claire couldn't quite read. "You know what that means?"

Claire shook her head and shrugged. "You're giving me time to work on the next project on my own before we start working together?"

"The opposite, actually. Your mission, should you choose to accept it—and you *will* accept it, Claire, because you'd be a fool not to—is to take a break. You've been going non-stop, and it's not sustainable. We need to fill the well, too, you know." The shrug and overly nonchalant look on her face spoke volumes. "Look for some romantic inspiration of your own. Speaking of which, if you'd like to tell me about the young man you left outside the office, I'm all ears..."

The meeting with Bianca didn't—*couldn't*—last much longer once Claire shared the story of her meeting in Munich with Jack, the connection they had shared, and their nearly botched meeting at the Empire State Building. At Bianca's insistent prodding, Claire had fled the coffee shop, making a beeline back for the Velvet Leaf building.

She didn't even have a minute to wonder if he would still be there waiting. Almost as soon as she had taken her first step in that direction, there he was, blocking her path and filling her field of view. Claire couldn't help but grin at the sight of him. He was there. He was real. He was *more* than she remembered him being—more handsome, more intense in his focus on her, more intimidating in the realness of his presence. The idea of him had been nice, but the physical presence of him was almost enough to make her feel shy.

Almost.

Before she could stop herself, she called out to him. "So where the heck were you? I thought you weren't coming." Because that's right. She hadn't forgotten that she had nearly been stood up that morning, and she had to stop herself from crossing her arms over her chest and closing herself off to him.

But his sheepish smile, the way his teeth were worrying his lower lip...all of it pulled her in. "I left my phone in the cab."

"Just now?" she asked, frowning. "Come on, then. You can use mine to call the dispatch and get it back."

Jack shook his head. "Not now." He pulled his phone out, wiggling it in front of her before pocketing it again. "On Christmas Eve. I just got it back."

Oh. *Oh.* It all made sense. "That...that's why you weren't communicative, I guess." She shook her head, chuckling at herself. "It wasn't about me at all, then."

"The opposite." He stepped closer, taking her hands in his, his warmth permeating her chilled fingers. "You were the reason I fought so hard to get it back. I didn't even know it was missing until that evening, what with all the holiday shenanigans. But I called the dispatch." He chuckled softly. "It almost ruined Christmas, considering that I was about to spend the day chasing down taxis until Hazel stopped me. Reminded me how holidays and work shifts work and that it was unlikely I'd find the same driver. She made me promise not to do anything until this morning. I've been here since six, alternating between calling dispatches—Hazel gave me her phone—and flagging down random cabs."

"And you finally found it?"

Jack nodded. "I did. The driver who had it told me about the message you had sent and rushed me to meet you. Just barely in time by the look on your face when you were leaving the Empire State Building. I'm so sorry, Claire. I would have been there sooner, would have called you sooner, but—"

She held up a hand to stop him, a genuine smile wrinkling her eyes at the corners as understanding dawned. Jack hadn't been the one to see her message, to "like" it. That had all been the driver, the same man who had gotten him there just in time to meet her. She owed him one.

"But it wasn't about me," she said. "Don't be silly, Jack. You left your phone in a taxi, and then you searched all over the city to get it back just so we could meet. I think I know a grand gesture when I see one."

"Really?" There was hope in his eyes now. "I should have tried harder to get it yesterday, but it was Christmas and Hazel convinced me not to and then spent the day listening to me talk about you instead."

"Oh?" She quirked an eyebrow at him. "I'd love to be a fly on the wall for that conversation."

His cheeks were blooming pink. "Well, I'm glad you weren't. It's nice to have a secret or two. Keep my cards close to the vest."

"I think you've revealed your hand." She gestured around them. "You're here, after all. And if I ever meet your sister, I'm guessing she'll tell me exactly what you said." As soon as the words were out, she wanted to pull them back in. Meet his sister? Was that the natural next step in a relationship like theirs?

"Oh, she definitely will. She's already shopping for plane tickets to go on a little solo adventure of her own, so sure is she that the universe is going to reward her with a love story just like ours."

Claire raised both eyebrows at that. As if Jack had heard her thoughts, that hand of cards he had claimed to want to keep under wraps were laid out on the table now. "A love story like ours? And what exactly does that entail?"

He pulled her closer to him, still leaving enough distance for her to pull away. "A meet cute. A grand gesture. Maybe even a happily ever after, if you're up for it."

"Oh, I'm definitely up for it." She took the final step towards him, her hands coming up to his cheeks to pull his head down towards hers. And just before her lips met his, she spoke softly. "I'm so glad you found me today."

"I wouldn't have given up until I succeeded, one way or another. But I wanted so desperately to give you the observation deck slow motion running into each other's arms."

"Another time."

"Another time." He smiled against her lips and then kissed her. It was a spark in the cold, bringing feeling back to her numb face and flooding her being with hope.

He had come for her. It had all been real. And the future?

The future would be whatever the two of them wanted it to be. For the first time in her life, Claire knew she would be writing the next chapter with someone else.

Author's Note

Thanks so much for reading. I hope you enjoyed spending this time with Claire and Jack as much as I did.

If you're wondering whose book is next in the "Home (Abroad) for the Holidays" series…any guesses?

It's Hazel! Stay tuned for her story coming in fall/winter 2024.

To stay updated on other works in progress or purchase books and bundles directly from me, please visit my website at kcmccormickciftci.com.

If you loved this book, please consider leaving a review, as that is one of the best ways to support indie authors like me. Reviews left on major retail sites (wherever you bought this book is a great start!), Goodreads, and BookBub will help other readers discover this book, too.

About the Author

KC McCormick Çiftçi is an English teacher turned romance writer. She spent the majority of her twenties living and working abroad, collecting the experiences that inform the stories she tells. She enjoys telling multicultural and international love stories through romantic comedy and women's fiction. She lives in Turkey with her husband and a herd of cats.

Prior to diving into the world of romance, KC published two self-help books for intercultural couples, *Loving Across Borders* and *The K-1 Visa Wedding Plan*. Both are available wherever books are sold.

For updates on upcoming releases, behind the scenes news, and all my favorite book recommendations, visit kcmccormickciftci.com (or just point your phone camera at the QR code below).

Books by KC McCormick Çiftçi

Austen in Turkey

Pride, Prejudice, & Turkish Delight

Sense, Sensibility, & the Mediterranean Sea

Home (Abroad) for the Holidays

Christmas on Inishmore

Christmas at Terminal One

Intoxicated by You

Intoxicated by You

Cats of Istanbul

The Vet Upstairs

Intercultural Relationship Self Help

Loving Across Borders

The K-1 Visa Wedding Plan